To Dovile

Well done on your Good...... ....

The Watchers

Russell Turney

This book is a work of fiction. Names, characters, places, and incidents either are products of the author's imagination or are used fictitiously. Any resemblance to actual events or locales or persons, living or dead, is entirely coincidental.

This book is Self Published by Rule of Three Press.
www.ruleofthreepress.com

The author can be contacted at russell@russellturney.com

ISBN 978-0-9836622-4-2
ISBN 098366224X

In memory of

Stephanie Ann Joy Fox.

15/09/1993 – 30/12/2011

Taken too soon.

Preface

The Watchers started as nothing more than a one line note scribbled in a workbook. No plot, no characters, not much of anything except a simple premise, that déjà vu is the product of external influences, outsiders correcting anomalies on the earth plane.

It sat quietly, waiting its turn. The big day came in November 2011. I needed something to write for NaNoWriMo, National November Writers Month. The idea is ... you sit down and bang out a short book in a month. Forget editing, forget fine detail, and in some cases, forget sleep. 50,000 words in a month doesn't sound like a lot ... until you start to fall behind the daily word count.

I wanted a new idea, not a book I'd already started, or an idea I'd studied from every angle for months. Fresh meat for the grinder. How would the story work? What direction should I point it in? Well, that's half the point of NaNoWriMo. I discovered I didn't need to know any of that. Just start writing and see what the grinder spits out. First hurdle, a name for the heroine and a quick, eye-catching opening. What now?

The character guides me in an interesting direction. An antagonist and a love interest appear. A book begins to form.

It actually took longer than a month, but, I did go on to 74,500 words. The Watchers took six weeks to reach first draft and was then put aside as I started the next book. When I finally came back to the book another six weeks later, the editing brain was functioning. The book offered here is the final result.

I hope you enjoy reading this story as much as I enjoyed writing it.

Acknowledgements

The finished book may never have happened without the help of the people listed below.

My first, and primary thanks, go to Robynn and Cynthia who critiqued the early drafts and pointed out the flaws, and gaps that needed filling, to Jackie for a thorough proof edit and Carolyn, Monica, Robynn and Kahui for beta reading the finished book and catching a few more errors.

A final thanks to the creatives of crowdspring.com who offered dozens of different covers, making the task of selection almost impossible.

Thank you one and all.

The first principles of the universe are atoms and empty space. Everything else is merely thought to exist. The worlds are unlimited. They come into being and perish. Nothing can come into being from that which is not, nor pass away into that which is not. Further, the atoms are unlimited in size and number, and they are borne along in the whole universe in a vortex, and thereby generate all composite things—fire, water, air, earth. For even these are conglomerations of given atoms. And it is because of their solidarity that these atoms are impassive and unalterable. The sun and the moon have been composed of such smooth and spherical masses [i.e. atoms], and so also the soul, which is identical with reason.

- Democritus

CHAPTER ONE

Gaia's gaze flicked from left to right behind mirror-lensed designer glasses, taking in the rush of the mid-morning masses. Her target would be here soon. The designated time approached, drawing with it the possibility of failure. She grinned, her head swiveling to the left. She'd never failed. This assignment would be as easily completed as those before it. She eased up onto the balls of her feet, stretching, preparing. There would be only a tiny window of opportunity. If she missed that, there was no second chance.

Gaia glanced left again as she stepped into the busy pedestrian traffic on New York's 47th Street. Ahead, the gigantic ticker display announced dismal stock news to the scurrying ants that were the people of New York City. She stared at the small device in her hand and nodded. *Three minutes, eighteen seconds.* The early-morning sun filtered through gaps between the towering structures around her, leaving an alternating play of shadow and light on the pavement, reminding her of a piano keyboard.

She crossed the road, darting between yellow cabs, smiling and waving good-naturedly at the blaring horns and shouted abuse. Gaia grinned. *New Yorkers.* This was only her second visit here, her second assignment to this crazy city, but she loved the melting pot of people and cultures here. Full on, in your face, no fear. Now all she had to do was find one person out of the multitude. *How many? Seven? Eight million?* Easy with her skill set. A walk in the park.

She could feel it now: the tingling that came when the target was close and the moment of truth a millisecond behind. Her hands clenched and stretched, muscles loosening. No second chances. *No mistakes.* She dodged round one of the many food vendors. The aroma of polish hot dogs, sauerkraut, and something she couldn't immediately identify assailed her nostrils. *Hmmm. Maybe afterwards.* Before she sped to her next assignment.

She turned right and jostled her way along the crowded sidewalk, her muscles warming, her senses alert. *Any minute. He'll be here. He always comes this way. He'll come this way today.* She smirked. It was predestined. The intersection where she would perform the deed was two blocks ahead. *Plenty of time.* The smile faded. *Don't be cocky. You can't afford to make a mistake. Concentrate.*

Gaia ignored the muttered apology of the young man who bumped into her. His searching hands found nothing in her coat pocket. No purse or identification to steal. If she'd had time, she might have bent his fingers back until one cracked, but he was lucky today.

There. Her heartbeat jumped a notch. Her target was half a block away, heading in her direction, on the shaded side of the street. She crossed over nimbly, ignoring yelled comments and gestures of frustration. Gaia wished she could remove her sunglasses, but she couldn't afford to reveal her eyes. It was the one downside of this vessel, this body: the bright yellow irises. Once seen, never forgotten. She swung her shoulders and hips as she eased into a slow jog. Loosening. Stretching.

Her target was a mere fifty yards away now, almost at the crosswalk. Crowds swarmed in front of her, blocking her sight. The throng dissipated. Panic flared. *He's gone!* Ahead and to her right, his shining dome popped above the crowd standing at the curb. Breath she didn't know she held escaped pursed lips.

A flashing red hand across the intersection commanded her target to stop. He pushed the button and waited, edging closer to the street. He turned and smiled at her as she pressed right up behind him. Gaia returned the smile, then glanced away and inhaled deeply. The tingling was stronger now. Small hairs on the back of her neck stood up. A roar of raw energy roiled and turned in her occipital lobe, waves of hormones pouring through her body.

Four seconds.

Where is it? Panic flashed its chemical message through her body. *There!* A small vortex opened at the man's feet, unseen to all but Gaia. It swirled and tugged, drawing her target forward. She glanced left. The merciless, uncaring, steel and glass front of a city bus barreled down the lane closest to the walkway. Her hand snaked out toward his shoulder. *Now.* She grabbed his collar and pulled backward. The airwave from the passing bus first pushed, then dragged them. She released her grip.

He turned and grinned. "That was close. Those damn buses should slow down." The crosswalk sign flashed white and buzzed.

"Yeah. Someone could get killed," she said, smiling as she stepped off the pavement behind him.

Another mission successfully completed.

Next assignment: Vancouver, Canada. In twelve minutes. Then off to Australia, twenty-three minutes later. A big grin split her face. Plenty of time. *Maybe even enough for that hot dog.*

***

Gaia drifted between time and space, her awareness, her soul, riding waves of energy, neither awake nor asleep. The collective consciousness of the Watchers ebbed and flowed, a spinning, rolling kaleidoscope of colour and sound. It pulsed around and through her, part of her. Pure energy, the potential of all that was, had been, and was yet to be. Energy, colour, and sound, none of them within the range of human comprehension. But no sensation. Sensation was the reason she liked the chance to take human form and cross through the veil. The ability, albeit brief, to feel, to smell. To taste.

No one here ... She stopped and considered. By mutual agreement, they called themselves the Watchers and their home Sanctum, or The Source. A decision made eons, or was that seconds, ago. When didn't matter. Time had no meaning here.

To take human form and operate within the laws of physics and universal laws on the earthly plane had been a challenge. Gaia called herself feminine, but every entity in Sanctum contained the potential to be whatever they wished. Male, female, and many variations in between. But always human when they crossed. Any other form was too shocking, too sensational for the human psyche.

She'd lost count of the number of interventions her form had made over the centuries. The number was increasing at an alarming rate. Vortexes were appearing everywhere, dozens of times a day, altering the course of human direction. For the previous hundreds, no, thousands of human years, there had been only a few a week, or year. Something was changing. Something or someone's presence or activity was generating these changes.

She wondered for a moment if it was the ever-swelling number of humans or their massive technological advances. Other Watchers answered, sharing their ideas and replies. Was it the violence that pervaded their modern society? The wave flowed over her. "No," was the consensus. Violence had existed for millennia.

Gaia sensed a subtle vibration across the ether and tuned in. She couldn't help thinking it was akin to the human's radio, leaving one channel to find another. She searched her personal knowledge of these things. Surfing. The humans called it channel surfing.

"Gaia." The masculine nature of elder Medus Banam found her.

"Medus. Salutations."

"We have another assignment for you." Elder Savanha Lingus' essence merged with that of Medus. "There is a problem with the stability of the earth plane."

"I know. I've been busy lately." She sensed a shared concept between the two, something kept from her awareness. "I don't mind. It is ..." she searched for the appropriate word. "...fun."

"What is this fun you speak of?" Curiosity flowed from the two elders.

Gaia's energy flashed a purple hue as she considered. Any Watcher who had not made the crossing would not understand. Sure, she shared the details of every encounter on her return, but neophytes, the uninitiated, did not experience feelings or emotions. Only those in the earth plane. There was no equivalent here. She searched her consciousness for words.

"My apologies, Medus. Savanha. It is a human term. A state of pleasing excitation is the best way I can think to summarize it."

"Hmmm. Perhaps we ask too much of you, Gaia. Others are available. Would you like a break, a rest from the humans?"

Gaia felt nothing. She visualized her solid human form and imagined the sensations it would now be feeling. Panic. Fear. Worry. Jealousy that others may take her place. "No. I exist to serve. I wish to return." She locked the personal space of her thoughts. *Odd. Why do I hide from them? I want to return. Has human contact corrupted me? Should I take a break?* Her other half resisted. *No. Go.*

4

"Very well. We believe we have discovered the source of the increase in activity. Your task is to find a device an earth male has built - a vortex generator. This machine is the work of one Bartholomew Cooksley. Find it. Destroy it and any documentation that would enable another to be built."

"What of this Bartholomew Cooksley? Surely he has memory enough to build another."

A flash of red pulsed from the two elders. "You must erase it from his mind, confound his memory."

"That is contrary to the principal directive." Gaia's energy surged. "We do not interfere with human free will." Her form flashed a myriad of colours, her shape bending, pulsating, resisting the instructions given. She realized that this was what humans called anger, although she felt no actual sensation.

"It must be done. This device, this vortex generator of Bartholomew Cooksley's, is but a tiny step from a time-space manipulator. In the wrong hands, stupid hands, it could rend the very fabric of space and time apart. In cunning hands, the entire history of the universe - past, present, and future - is at risk. Or even destruction. Our vow to protect the souls of humankind demands aggressive action. Bartholomew Cooksley and his machine must be stopped," the two elders echoed, as if in stereo.

"Very well. I will leave immediately. Are there any other instructions?"

"He is in the city of Wellington, New Zealand. A professor at Victoria University, an edifice of higher learning. Travel safely, Gaia. This mission is unlike any you have undertaken before. You will need to mingle and communicate with the earthforms for an extended period."

She sensed something odd. "Is there something you wish not to tell me?"

The elders were silent, but Gaia registered a strange impulse. Medus communicated first. "Another seeks the device."

"Another? Who?" Caught halfway between her energy and human form, she registered anxiety. Fear.

"Yes. One called Terra," Medus confessed. "She covets the device for her own ends. Dangerous ends."

"Terra?" Gaia felt human anger colour her thoughts. "Why? Who is she? This Terra."

"We cannot say. Only that if you encounter her, she must be captured or destroyed. Once you cross, we are sealing the veil until you return. No one can cross to assist you, nor can you draw energy. You will need the device in order to reenter here. Be careful. Protect yourself at all times, in all ways."

"Why do you seal Sanctum?"

"We do not yet know Terra's intent. We cannot risk her coming here."

"She has that ability?" Gaia felt troubled.

"She does. We cannot allow her entry. Her … history could corrupt all here. We must seal the veil, even at the risk of leaving anomalies unattended."

"I will do as you ask. Bartholomew Cooksley and this Terra will be no match for me." Gaia flashed bright white and vanished from the Watchers' realm. She hung in her natural form, invisible to human eyes, in a quiet spot near the university campus.

Savanha's final words reached her, a deep solemn voice in her mind. "Cooksley is not your problem. Beware of Terra. She is unlike any you have ever encountered."

***

The swirling kaleidoscope of colour and energy that represented Medus and Savanha observed the flash of white light as Gaia crossed through the veil once again. Their shared thoughts were experienced as one, as a conversation with oneself.

"Should we have told her?"

"How could we? We are not sure ourselves. Terra may simply be … confused. There is no precedent for what we are thinking."

"No. Nonetheless, I sense the disturbance. Terra is operating outside her domain."

"I agree. I hope we are wrong. Gaia will find her. It's a difficult task we have set her. Never before has she spent more than a few hours in earthly form. The body will need fuel and repair."

"And hopefully, she is not seduced by earthly sensations, or worse."

"Worse?"

"Love. The most powerful of the human emotions. Should she be exposed …"

"It is a risk we must take. This device of Bartholomew Cooksley's is too dangerous to exist. It must be destroyed."

"I still think we should have left the veil open, sent as many as were needed to find Terra."

"You know that is not wise. We tried that once, and look what happened. Every Watcher who crosses increases the risk of an incident."

"Yes. I sometimes forget the reasoning behind that decision. Hopefully Gaia, of all of us, will be immune."

What we call matter is only a complex of energies which we find together in the same place.

— Carl Wilhelm Wolfgang Ostwald

CHAPTER TWO

Gaia hovered in ethereal form, seeking a suitable place to materialize without attracting attention. The university hallways bustled with the crush of students scurrying toward their next lecture, workshop, or social engagement. Gaia floated through several floors of Kauri hardwood that made up the supporting beams and flooring of the century-old building. She gravitated toward a darkened room that caught her attention. Even in the dim light, she recognized the layout as being that of a small theatre, numerous seats curving around to face a large silver screen.

Still in her natural state, she alighted on the small stage. She made one quick mental sweep of the room and took shape. The first surge of sensation, of hormones, as she took form never failed to amaze and stir her. She ran tingling fingertips over her face, the mound of her breasts, and the curve of her hips and sighed. *So complex, so fragile.* She liked this body. It had taken her many trips to get used to its intricate workings and abilities.

The first journey, eons ago, had been the most difficult. Finding herself suddenly in the physical realm, her first task had been a huge gulp of air. She had fallen to her knees on the soft, grass-covered ground, gasping at this strange weight in her chest, the pull of gravity on her newly-formed body.

Her form, as she called it, came preprogrammed. It knew how to walk, talk, and do all the things humans took for granted. The abilities they took a lifetime to master, Gaia learned in minutes. But unlike humans, she reveled in the sensations. The faintest smell, the way the hairs pricked on her skin, the cool rush of the breeze against her face. She envied humankind, an emotion foreign to her until that moment.

Moreover, she understood the mechanism of changing from pure energy into matter. Humans were only beginning to understand the process. She laughed. There was no process. Energy and matter were one and the same. Everything, living and inert, was comprised of energy. Broken down into its tiniest state, all matter was atoms, pure energy. Pull enough different atoms together, vibrating at the right frequency, and you had the building blocks of all matter. So easy to manipulate and change. But once she selected a form, it was easier to stick with it. She could vaporize and move great distances in a short time, something she called 'flashing', but it was tiring and used up energy. In the past, she simply returned to Sanctum, recharged in milliseconds, and flashed back to the earth realm.

This time, with the veil sealed, she could not. For the first time in her existence, her energy was finite. She was completely, utterly human. Well, almost. She could still vaporize and move, she could vibrate her molecules to appear invisible, and she could still make small items or objects materialize. Anything organic. Never a weapon. And she was still stuck with the yellow irises of her eyes, the one peculiar trait the Watchers couldn't seem to change when they crossed over.

Gaia stretched her arms above her head, then bent over, legs held straight, until her palms were flat on the floor in front of her. *Yes. This body functions perfectly, as it always has.* She wondered for a moment if she should have made it younger for this assignment. *No.* Her current twenty-eight-year-old appearance would easily pass as an adult student. She liked the distinct hourglass shape her mature figure had over the younger, more athletic version she had briefly considered.

Gaia grinned broadly, feeling the small lines that pulled at the outside edges of her almond-shaped eyes. She reached into the rear pocket of her Levi's and extracted the required mirror-lensed sunglasses. Leaping off the stage with a graceful, easy movement, she took long steps, stretching her leg muscles as she moved toward the exit. She hesitated at the door, casting an appraising eye over her ensemble. She frowned, instinctively scratching her forehead. Something was missing.

The clothes seemed appropriate for the mid-summer weather. *Shorts maybe? No. Stick with the hipster jeans. Remember you're twenty-eight, not eighteen.* A form-fitting, button-front top snuggled tight around her abdomen and breasts. She concentrated on changing the brassiere and snorted, her lips pressed tight together in humour, as her breasts changed shape and position with the new choice. Her hand was on the worn brass handle of the exit before she realized what she needed. *A bag. I should be carrying a bag, or wearing it over my shoulder. A bag with books.*

She considered her options, then chuckled. Quantum Physics. *Something on quarks and matter versus energy.* The sort of thing Bartholomew Cooksley would doubtless be lecturing on. She visualized the neat leather satchel, and it appeared on her shoulder. The books she would find in the library, along with the details of lectures, Cooksley's class times, locations, and reading requirements. She tugged the handle down and pushed the door open enough to check the hallway. Satisfied she would not attract attention, she exited and made her way in the direction of the library she'd spotted while still in her natural state. Up two floors and across the walkway to the next building.

The hallways buzzed with the quiet hum of people in muted conversations. Rubber- and leather-soled feet glided over carpeted and wooden floors, while malleable brains soaked up information, much of it spewed by rote from the mouths of bored, underpaid academics. She alone could feel the history, the energy of all who had passed before, the wordy, sometimes worldly, professors of a hundred years previous, and the combined learning of all the hopefuls. The awe-inspiring energy of it sent shivers up her spine and goose bumps over her body. Men flashed smiles at her as she moved steadily toward her first objective. *Do they know? Have I been discovered?* A feeling of self-consciousness settled over her.

Gaia shrugged the feeling off with a laugh. The cold shivers she experienced had caused more than just goose bumps. Men were discreetly ogling her erect nipples. Well, they thought they were being discreet. She wasn't sure whether to be flattered or outraged. This had never happened to her before. Her awareness of the situation seemed to help. Her skin relaxed and returned to normal. Still, she enjoyed the attention and the cover it provided.

It was one of the reasons she always chose the female form, an attractive one at that. Men invariably came to her assistance, offered advice, and were generally helpful. A great asset, one that appeared available only to the good looking. *Humans. Weird. Easily manipulated.* Gaia was intrigued as she noticed that even a few women stared at her.

Ahead, she saw the huge, native Rimu wood double doors of the library, with their stained-glass surrounds and inserts. The Latin script above the doors proudly proclaimed 'Sapientia magis auro desideranda'. "Wisdom is more to be desired than gold." Gaia shook her head. That had not been her experience with many humans.

Sun streamed in from the full-height windows on either side of the walkway. After passing through the hallowed portal, she stopped and swung round to enjoy the shafts of light cascading through the Victorian-era glass panels. The play of colours and design made her think of home. She breathed in the atmosphere. The smell of books wafted out of lofty shelves set around the outside of the voluminous room. Many more sat in dark, polished wood towers that ran in long, serried rows. *Ah, history.* She could smell it, feel it, taste it. In some cases, she'd been present on the earth plane to experience these events as they happened.

Gaia spun on her toes, tilting her head to one side as she took in the room. Heavy mahogany desks separated a phalanx of librarians from the common masses. To one side, stood the library's old card system. To the other, there were three rows of computers for those who preferred their information electronically. *Cards. How quaint.* She selected an empty seat at one of the available computer terminals. Eyes closed, she ran her hands over the keyboard, sensing how to operate the unit. She scanned for information on the devices and how they worked, then visualized the data she required. The screen flashed up with a logon sequence. A tingle on the back of her neck alerted her to watching eyes. *Bother. I'll have to do this the hard way.*

She glanced round the room, her gaze drawn to the erratic energy of one of the librarians, an awkward young man who looked away as soon as she peered in his direction. She concentrated on the alternating colours and patterns, noticing the large chunks of grey and black pulsing in his aura. *He's hiding something.* Gaia stood up, placed her leather satchel on the chair, and drifted in a circular pattern toward the youth. He continued his furtive glances as she edged toward him.

"Hi…" She glanced down at his name badge. "Nigel." She decided to try a direct approach on the gangly young man, who appeared to be no more than eighteen. "Are you watching me?"

"What!" He nearly slipped from his seat, standing up quickly instead.

Gaia didn't require her abilities to see his shaking hands clenching and unclenching nervously.

"I … I … you're not wearing a student identification tag." Having found a fault with her, he straightened, confident in his ability to deal with this unauthorized person.

Gaia forced back the laughter that threatened to break loose as his energy patterns told her what he was feeling. A combination of intimidation and lust. The intimidated portion pulled back from her, while the desire reached out, trying to wrap itself around her, to pull her closer. She put her hands on her hips in defiance. His energy retreated farther. *Enough*. She slowly unbuttoned the two top buttons of her tight top and leaned forward over the counter, allowing Nigel a view of her cleavage.

"Don't change the subject, Nigel. I know you're lying to me. Why are you watching me?"

A line of red moved rapidly up Nigel's neck to his hairline as his gaze darted from Gaia's bosom to her face. His mouth opened and closed several times.

Gaia realized the effect she was having on the poor boy and ground her teeth together to avoid grinning.

"It's … well … I … you're the only person wearing sunglasses in the library."

"Is that so unusual?" She leaned farther forward. Her sunglasses slipped down her nose, revealing her yellow irises.

A pattern of color flashed through him at the speed of light. Fear.

The words came out as a hoarse whisper. "You … your eyes. You're one of them. Please, don't hurt me. I haven't done anything." His lust vanished behind a wall of terror. Nigel tried to pull away from her.

Terra's been here. Gaia reached across and grabbed hold of his shirt, drawing him nearer. Her gaze darted left to right, making sure no one else had noticed the exchange. A bullish-looking female four seats away watched through squinted eyes.

Gaia released Nigel and brushed a hand over the front of his shirt, smoothing the fabric. "Sorry, Nigel. I didn't mean to frighten you." She leaned in and whispered in his ear, at the same time wrapping a blanket of calming energy around him. "What did you mean, 'one of them'?"

"Another lady, like you. The same eyes. She …" His voiced trailed off as his gaze darted around the room. "She threatened to hurt me if I didn't help her. You're not going to hurt me, are you? I'm supposed to keep a watch out for you."

"For me?" *How would she know what to look for?* Gaia tried to comprehend Nigel's statement. *How would she even know I was coming?*

"Not you, really. Someone like you. In sunglasses. It's rather rare in here, you see." At her puzzled look, he added, "For people to wear sunglasses. It's so dark. You stood out like …" He stopped himself on the verge of reciting what she guessed might have been one of the colourful colloquialisms she'd heard over the years of service.

"And then what? If you see someone?" She ran a hand down his arm, feeling the goose bumps her touch caused.

"I'm supposed to phone her."

"Phone?"

"Yes. Phone her."

He held up a small electronic device.

She smiled, pretending to understand the use of this simple-looking gadget.

"Will you? Phone her?" She flashed her warmest smile at him, her fingers caressing the elbow of one arm.

He glanced around again, uncertain of his reply. "No," he stated, his confidence massaged by Gaia's stroking fingers.

She leaned over the counter and kissed him on the cheek. The line of red rushed up his face again.

"You're … you're much nicer than the other girl. What is your name, by the way?"

"Gaia. Gaia Hassani."

"Gaia. Hmmm. The earth goddess. That's odd."

"Odd? How so, Nigel?"

"The other girl's name was Terra. Terra also refers to the earth in ancient mythology, like your name."

"Oh." Gaia's eyebrows arched upward. "How do you know all this?"

He shrugged his shoulders. "History major. Ancient civilizations. I'm hoping to become an archeologist. I work in here part-time to help pay my tuition. Your last name is unusual, too." His manner grew bolder as he delved into a subject well known to him. "Hassani. It's a derivation of Hassan, ancient assassins. The word eventually became assassin in modern language." He stopped, his eyes wide as he realized the possible implications of Gaia's name. Gaia felt the panic rising in him.

"Nigel, it's not what you think. I'm here to help, not hurt. Have I harmed you in any way? Threatened you?" She grimaced as she remembered. "I mean, apart from grabbing your shirt. Sorry about that." She gritted her teeth and tried to smile at the same time. She pulled her eyebrows together as she'd seen others do, trying to look innocent.

"Not like Terra. She hurt me. Bent my arm 'til I thought she might break it." He trembled as he recalled the other woman's cruelty. "She was searching for someone, one of the professors. She made me help her." Again, the ripple of fear.

"I know nothing of her, Nigel. She shouldn't behave in this fashion toward you, or any human. As for our eyes, it's a rare genetic disorder." She was surprised to find the lies rolled easily off her tongue.

"I wondered what it was, the eyes. Never seen the like of them before. Just a moment." He quickly dealt with an enquiry from another student before returning to Gaia. "Do you want her phone number?" Gaia's obvious blank expression spurred him to add, "in case you want to call her."

"Number? I've never used a phone before, but I'm a quick study. How do they work?"

"Now you're yanking my chain, aren't you?" He shook his head. "Bloody hell. Where do you come from? Outer space?"

Gaia felt panic rising. A quick scan of Nigel's energy field told her he was teasing. She relaxed. "I was brought up Amish. In Pennsylvania, America. We didn't have phones."

At nearly six feet tall, Nigel towered over Gaia's five-foot-two-inch frame. His blue eyes sparkled as he leaned over the library counter. "It's simple, really. Each one of these has its own number." He held up the device. "You simply dial the number of the one you want to connect to."

Gaia laughed, for Nigel's benefit. "Hmmm. Yes, I see now. How silly of me."

"So. What brings you here, Gaia?"

"Here?"

"To my library."

"I just wanted to look up some courses."

"Let me guess. Quantum Physics, with Professor Cooksley." He grinned at her. Gaia couldn't help feeling he was holding something back. But it went against her ethics to scan his thoughts, at this time.

"Yes. How did you know?"

"It was easy, really. Terra wanted to know the same things. She just wasn't as pleasant about it." He handed her a small card. "This will give you a temporary logon to the system. Once you have the information you want, you can go down to enrollments on the first floor and sign up for Professor Cooksley's classes. If there's any space left. He may be a little flaky, but his classes are very popular."

"Thank you, Nigel." Gaia leaned across the counter and planted a kiss on his cheek. The boy beamed. Still, there was something odd about him she couldn't put her finger on.

Gaia settled back into a chair and logged into the computer terminal. She swiveled her head to give him one last smile. He was on the phone and failed to notice.

CHAPTER THREE

"**Security. Officer Norman.** How can I help?"

"This is Nigel Quinn in the library. I have another person here asking after Professor Cooksley. I've had a short chat with them. They, I mean she, is not a student, and some of the things she said made me wonder if she was another of the nutters who've been threatening the professor."

Officer Harold Norman bolted upright in his chair, the hand not holding the phone tapping a second officer on the arm. "Is she still there, Mr. Quinn? Can you identify her?"

"Yes. She's still at one of the computer terminals. You might be able to see her on the security camera. She's on computer B7."

Norman cupped his hand over the mouthpiece. "Kyle. Check the library cameras, computer terminal B7." As Kyle busied himself with the CTVs, he keyed a microphone. "Security central. Anyone near the library?"

Static popped from the overhead speaker, then a voice. "Bill here, Norm. I'm one floor away. Moving there now. What's up?"

"We have a suspicious woman in the library, asking after Bart Cooksley. You're aware of the threats his research has drawn?" Norm glanced over at the screen the second officer had pulled up. "I'll get back to you in a few seconds, Bill." He returned his attention to the phone. "Mr. Quinn, we have the cameras online. Is she the long-haired blonde?"

"No, ya ... wrong terminal." The caller sounded exasperated. "Two terminals along, shortish-length red hair, leather satchel hanging over the chair."

"Ah. Yeah, we got her. Stay on the line, please, Mr. Quinn. An officer is on the way."

"Just one? What if she is the real McCoy? She might be dangerous. The previous woman threatened me."

Norm rolled his eyes. *Damn amateur policemen. Bill should be plenty big enough to handle one small woman.* He keyed the mic again. "Bill, you're looking for a redhead, medium-length hair. She looks small. Ya want to wait for backup? Just in case. It's procedure …"

A long sigh crackled over the speaker. "I see her. I'll approach cautiously, but send a backup. Keep the boss happy."

Norm laughed. "Yeah, I hear ya. Anyone else close?" he asked of the wider security force.

"Grant here, Norm. I'll be there in about ninety seconds. Can't have Bill getting beat up by a little girl." A series of unidentified chuckles echoed from the speaker.

"Good job, guys. Now be polite. This is probably just an over-anxious librarian. The lady might be perfectly legit. We don't want any bad publicity or court cases. You getting this, Bill?"

"Yeah, I hear ya. Be kind to the redhead. She looks cute, guys. Closing on her now."

"Right behind ya, Bill," sounded Grant's voice.

***

It had taken Gaia a scant three minutes to find Bartholomew Cooksley's class schedule, the locations of the rooms, and most importantly, she thought, the location of his office and workroom. A quick check of the phone records on the internet had not revealed any home number or address. She committed the information to memory and logged out of the computer.

Gaia stared vacantly at the rows of books as she considered her luck. Professor Cooksley had not been in class since the previous Friday. Therefore, she surmised, he'd probably not been at the University. Terra, despite her head start, had possibly not been able to track him down yet. This was good. Very good. It was beginning to look like Terra, whoever or whatever she was, had gone rogue. She shook her head, a deep frown across her brow. *How is this possible?* It was unprecedented in the history of the

Watchers. Deeply consumed with this problem, she might have missed the warning.

It washed against her like a tsunami, causing her to sway in the chair. The energy was coming from two directions. She swiveled her head. Nigel was on the phone, but his furtive glance spoke volumes. She followed his gaze. It intersected with the second energy burst, the tidal wave that had alerted her. A tank of a man in a blue security uniform was bearing down on her. He smiled broadly, but his energy revealed an entirely different motive. He approached from the opposite end of the library, summoned there to question and possibly detain her. Gaia estimated she had maybe ten seconds.

She stood slowly, her arm curling under her satchel. Swiveling on her toes, she turned toward the nearest exit. *Take your eyes off me guys, just for a second.* She pulsed a signal out to the numerous surveillance cameras she'd noticed on the ceiling and walls, turning the security office screens to a blur of white noise. Nigel appeared panicked as she began to move, his stare sliding from her to the uniformed man. She glanced over her shoulder to the 'tank'. The man was hurrying now, talking into a small microphone pinned to his shoulder. His gaze darted right as he moved left, avoiding another student.

Flash.

Both the Watchers and physicists alike called it quantum locking. Gaia recalled a classic earthly experiment, known to most as Schrödinger's cat, which sought to explain the theory. Any object, while observed, cannot change. Once unobserved, for even a millisecond, it can change or move in infinite variations. In this case, Gaia had moved thirty feet to the exit, the farthest clear line of sight she had. She could only do this so many times, before it would begin to drain her energy resources.

Gaia heard Tank's voice call out as she turned left and ran down the hallway. The air thickened around Gaia. It was like butting up against a wall of water. A warning. Someone else interested in her presence was coming from this direction. The energy to her left was softer, so she took that fork, the going easier, quicker.

She passed the cafeteria on her right. Gaia had experienced the rich aroma of coffee before, but the plethora of sweet, savoury, and spicy aromas were new, distinctly kiwi. The scents threatened to overwhelm her. Her eyelids fluttered behind the sunglasses, her knees weak for a second. In that instant, she began to understand what might have happened to Terra, why she'd turned dangerous. She'd been seduced by sensations. Sins of the flesh and gluttony. *But are these really sins, or just the failings of humans?*

Another wave of warning energy pulsed across her. The man from the library, and others, were still in pursuit. She pushed through a large double door on her right and proceeded down two flights of stairs, emerging on the second floor of the building. She stopped for a moment by the door, her senses alert. *Nothing.* Her chest swelled with deep, cool breaths as she calmed herself, pushing down the panic that had overtaken her. She scanned the numbers of the lecture rooms on either side of the deserted corridor.

Gaia chuckled at the realization her instincts had led her directly to the area where Professor Bartholomew Cooksley was lecturing. She counted off the room numbers as she jogged along the hallway, coming to rest outside 219. She placed her hand against the door, feeling the vibrations and energy in the room.

Terra. Terra is here.

Gaia took another deep breath. She leaned her weight against the door, pushing it slowly inward.

She stood on the threshold, gaze sweeping the space. Half a dozen rows of approximately twenty chairs curved around a flat stage, each arc of chairs elevated higher than the one in front. A tall man with short, dark, curly hair stood at a small lectern to one side of the stage, his arms waving as he made a point. Behind him was a wall taken up with two whiteboards. One was covered with nearly indecipherable equations; the other displayed images projected from an overhead device.

Professor Cooksley seemed to weave a spell across the assembled masses. So rapt were the students in the impassioned delivery of their tutor, no one had noticed her entry into the room. Almost no one. One head, the person seated near the front right of the room, swiveled to appraise her.

Terra.

A smile played across Terra's face as, even through dark sunglasses, the women locked eyes.

Gaia fought the twitch that appeared in her left eye. She slipped into an empty seat and turned her attention to the young professor, mulling over information she possessed. Professor Cooksley was thirty-five years of age, a widower, and a prodigy in his field. His ground-breaking research polarized other academics and religious organizations. As a result, he was either hailed or reviled. Many people didn't like his theories on energy and matter and the way they questioned creationist philosophy. His secret work had led him to develop a device that he hoped, once the bugs were worked out, would convert pure energy into matter. This was the device Gaia sought.

Terra sought it too.

Gaia ran her eyes over the complicated equation on the board. She wasn't sure whether to smile or panic. The man was almost there. A couple of small errors were all that stood between him and success or total annihilation. From the Watchers' point of view, it led to a path that risked tearing time, space, and matter apart. Mankind was avaricious and power hungry. They must not be allowed to possess knowledge that would give them almost godlike powers. History had proved them incapable of using this type of know-how wisely.

She appraised the professor from her high spot. He was tall and broad shouldered, his torso tapering to the waist. *He works out. Some balance to the man. Not totally lost inside his own head.* His voice had a deep hypnotic timbre, enhanced by a glowing charisma that held all present in its thrall. Gaia had expected some nerdy, fact-filled academic.

The man's chin lifted, his piercing blue eyes flashing in her direction, as if he sensed she was examining him. She shivered at his glance. A sensation new to her fluttered in her stomach. She found herself mentally stripping his shirt off to see his muscled chest.

The professor's mouth twitched, as if he'd heard something funny. He strode across the stage, waving his arms like an evangelical preacher. In some respects, he was, preaching a new way, a new idea to his congregation.

"…and that, people, is how you convert energy to matter. What you're really doing is combining the correct atoms and altering their vibration. Well, that's the theory." A wide, toothy grin split his suntanned face, revealing a dimple in the wide, solid chin. The class applauded and stood. He raised his hands palms down, urging them back into their seats. "So. Before the next class, think on Einstein's quote: 'Concerning matter, we have been all wrong. What we have called matter is energy, whose vibration has been so lowered as to be perceptible to the senses. There is no matter.' Have a good week, everyone." He waved a hand to acknowledge the student applause as he made his way back to the lectern.

Gaia found herself torn between the need to deal with Terra and the importance of recovering the professor's device. Keeping a wary eye on the motionless Terra, Gaia worked her way down the steps, weaving between exiting students. Putting herself between Terra and the professor, Gaia hung back from a couple of other students who'd lingered, asking questions. She turned in time to see the fire-exit door closing behind a departing Terra.

As she swung back toward the professor, the main door burst open, admitting Tank and a second security guard.

"Miss." Gaia felt the guard's voice directed at her. Trying to put her normally placid, controlled thoughts in order, she ignored the man and edged toward the fire exit. "Miss." The guard's voice was more insistent. "Please wait there." The second guard made his way down the steps as Tank swept round the edge, trying to cut off Gaia's exit.

"Is there a problem here?" Bartholomew Cooksley's previously calm voice blasted out, freezing both guards and Gaia on their spots. His gaze darted from the guard to Gaia. "Well? What is this ruckus in my lecture hall?" His glare remained fixed on Gaia.

"No problem, Professor. We were asked to check the credentials of the young lady there." A finger pointed accusingly in Gaia's direction. "Someone reported she didn't have a pass for the building."

"Is that true, miss? Have you committed the heinous crime of trespassing?" A smile crept up one corner of his mouth.

"Professor, you're making this harder than it should be. We have instructions …"

"Piff paff. When did we start banning potential students from taking a quick look around before they enroll?" The professor tapped a bunch of papers on the lectern, leveling the ends neatly. "Well?"

"Professor, sir. In light of the threats you've received, we were …"

"Does she look dangerous? She's been here for nearly five minutes. You think she needs more time to attack me?" He leveled his piercing blue eyes on Gaia. "Are you dangerous, miss?"

Gaia's mouth dropped open. *Five minutes. He said I've been here five minutes. He noticed me come in.* Her whole body trembled, a delicious, yet uncomfortable numbness welling up inside her. Gaia found herself at a loss to understand why.

Tank was edging ever so slowly toward the exit door she herself sought to escape through. "No, Professor. I merely wanted to listen in on one of your lectures before I decided to enroll." *Where did that come from?*

Tank called out. "Regardless of that, miss, we still need you to accompany us to the security office so we can verify your identity. It's just a formality."

"NO!" The word rolled over the roof of her mouth, resonating in her skull before exploding out of her gaping maw and across the open space, knocking the two guards off their feet. She gave the professor one last weak smile, spun on her heel and dashed through the door. The last thing she remembered was the look on the professor's face. Two chairs sat against the wall just outside the room. She slid them both in front of the door and ran down the final two floors and out into the asphalted, open-air parking area.

Even with the sunglasses, the transition to bright sunlight shocked her. Ahead loomed a wide green area edged with huge ancient pohutakawas. Gaia dodged between the parked cars of academics and lost herself from sight in the dark shade of the trees. She stopped behind one particularly large specimen, putting her hands on her knees as she leaned forward to catch her breath and order her thoughts. She tilted to one side, enabling a view of the building she'd just left. The two guards were standing among the cars, heads rotating from side to side. Tank was on the radio, and she noticed two more uniforms converging from either end of the area. Try as she might, she couldn't make out what they were saying.

Their heads turned in her direction, scanning the surrounding green and brown landscape. Gaia dodged back behind the tree. One of the men walked toward her but pulled up short when a white and blue car, with coloured lights on the roof, screeched into the parking lot. She scanned her memory for the meaning of the letters plastered on the side. *Police?* She sucked a deep breath in as the significance became apparent. This was the peace- and law-keeping group of the country. *Bailiffs.* Endowed with the power to detain and question her. This she could not allow.

She eased deeper into the shadowy safety of the stand of trees, keeping a wary eye on the animated exchange taking place between the bulky security guards and the two fit-looking police officers. These officers appeared to pose a much greater threat than the university's internal security. As her rapid breathing and heart rate returned to normal, she could hear their conversation. One of the police was writing into a small notebook as the other wandered in and out between the cars, searching for her, she presumed.

"Red hair, about 5'2", 25-35 years of age, you say. Any distinctive clothing?"

"Nothing out of the ordinary, Constable. Dress jeans and a skin-tight, button-front top. She was carrying a leather satchel over her shoulder."

"That's not a lot of help, really. Take a look around. Apart from the red hair, you just described half the women in sight." The constable shook his head. Another security guard joined the huddle, offering the officer a piece of paper. "So this is our suspect?"

Bother. They have a likeness of me. She concentrated on the group and blew a small stream of air toward them. The paper, a photograph she thought they called it, whipped out of the constable's hand, twisting and turning its way across the car park on the wave of the sudden breeze. Two guards started after it but pulled up short at a call from Tank.

"Don't bother. Kyle, be a good lad and run upstairs for another copy. Better make it two. In case our police colleagues here lose it again."

The officer gave the security guard a cold stare.

Oh well, it was worth a try. Gaia's gaze followed the running security guard.

"So. Mr. …" the constable consulted his notebook and looked at Tank. "Mr. Jackson. You say the girl hasn't actually committed any real offence, apart from a possible trespass. Does the university wish to pursue the matter?" He closed his notebook, seeming to indicate he'd already made up his mind. "Hardly seems worth all the hassle. No damage done, no one hurt. No actual threats made."

"Um. Well. I guess not. We just wanted to make sure she was no risk to the professor. If you do find her, perhaps just a warning, a trespass notice or something."

"Hmmm. Indeed. We'll keep on eye out for her, as you say. I'll call it in while we wait for the photograph."

"Thanks, Constable. Sorry to be a pain. We've had a few threats from radical religious groups over some of Professor Cooksley's research and ideas. Just a bit jumpy."

"No problem, sir. Don't want any assassinations on the campus, do we?"

"Definitely not." Tank grinned, casting one last look around the car park before he turned and waved the other guards back into the building. Gaia waited. It seemed she'd gotten away. A few moments later, a red-faced Kyle trotted out of the building with the copied photographs.

"Here ya go, mate." Kyle's head bobbed up and down in time with his panted breathing.

"Thanks. We'll pass them on."

"No worries, Constable. Hope it's all a false alarm." He stood, hands on hips, as the two police swung their car around and departed the lot.

Gaia waited still. What to do next? She had to get to Professor Cooksley before Terra. *Where did she go, anyway?* The easiest option was to change form and assume a new shape and identity. But that would require all the temporal, quantum energy she still held within her aura. Cut off from The Source, she could not recharge herself at a rate that would prove sufficient for such a change.

Free from the risk of detainment, Gaia picked her way among the soothing darkness cast by the trees, moving closer to and in a better position to overlook the car park. Bartholomew Cooksley would have to leave sometime. *Maybe he has a car here.* She settled down on the ground, her back to a twisted, gnarled old tree. She and the tree sighed together, sharing energy. Gaia smiled. A warm summer breeze wheedled its way among the rough trunks, bent branches, and red flowers. Gaia's head dropped onto her chest, her make-shift body taking the needed recharge.

The smell of damp earth, crisp, fresh-cut grass, and a nearby flower bed saturated Gaia's nasal passages, soothing her. Small birds darted among the ancient trees, their bell-like song clear and resonant.

Gaia set her thoughts on Terra as she drifted off. It appeared Terra would prove a worthy adversary. Terra's expectation that a Watcher might appear at the library, even before Gaia materialized to pursue her, spoke of a cunning, scheming mind.

Or a plan long in the making.

CHAPTER FOUR

Bartholomew Cooksley sipped cold, bitter coffee dregs from a large chipped mug. His part-time assistant kept threatening to throw the mug out, but Bart persisted. It was a memento, one of the few things left from his time with Rebecca. The last gift she had given him.

The fingers of one hand traced the scar running along his left jaw line. Bart closed his eyes, fighting the tears that still welled up when he recalled that night. The Toyota Landcruiser had drifted across the center line and all but ripped the right side of their car off. Bart had been drinking, so it was Rebecca's turn to drive. In the passenger's seat, he'd been a mute witness to the split second of carnage before his airbag cushioned him, the car spinning in a circle, glass and plastic raining down. One cut was all he received. The wound to his heart was the deeper, more traumatic. Survivor guilt. He'd held Rebecca's feeble hand, listened to her cries of pain diminish and quiet as her life essence left her. Soothing, helpless words had drifted from his mouth, tears running down his cheek to mingle with the blood on his face.

A drunk driver.

It had been over two years ago now, time for the wounds to heal. The physical ones at least. *Why her? It should have been me.*

"Professor, did you want another cup of coffee?" The cheery voice of his assistant wafted fresh air over his brooding thoughts.

"How many times do I have to tell you to call me Bart, Elizabeth?" In lieu of better candidates, the tall, rake-thin, black-haired, black-clothed Elizabeth had got the job as Bart's assistant four months earlier. The Goth

27

girl intimidated many, but she'd proved an excellent assistant and a brilliant foil to Bart's relaxed, she'll-be-right attitude.

"Humph. You can talk. I'm Liz, remember? Did you want another coffee, Bart?"

He grinned and swung his feet off the ancient mahogany desk. "Righty oh, Liz. No thanks. I'm heading out in a minute." The equally prehistoric leather-covered chair creaked in protest as he swung round in a circle. "I've got a couple of documents I need typed up. They should be in your inbox."

"Can't see them, Bart." She over pronounced his name.

Bart dropped his feet to the floor and shook his head to clear the spinning. *Ooops.* He hit the send button on the email client. "Must be. Check again." He smirked as he imagined Liz rolling her eyes.

"Yeah, I see them now. Must have missed them the first time, eh, Bart?"

He chuckled, their war of words one of the small constants in his office. *Gotta have fun in life.* His mind flicked back to the incident in the lecture room. *Odd.* He'd noticed the redhead as soon as she walked in the room. There was something about her, something … attractive. He'd almost lost his train of thought. It hadn't been easy to put her out of his mind. She was the first woman since Rebecca who'd impacted him that way. *And now she's gone again. Dag nabit.*

He looked at the photograph campus security had furnished him. Just in case the dangerous fugitive shows up again, he'd told the bulky guard. *I'll post it on the wall to alert the students to the dire peril she poses. Ha.*

Liar, liar, pants on fire. Rebecca's voice echoed in his consciousness.

Rebecca was right. The redhead was cute. He pondered the weirdness that accompanied her, though. Security chasing her about the building, thinking she was a threat. *Hmmm. No. The threat was more likely the other woman, the brunette sitting by the exit door.* There was something odd about her.

He'd sensed it straight away. As pretty as the young brunette had been, she'd exuded a strange, almost sinister presence. *Thank god she bugged out the same time security showed up. Hmmm.* Bart absentmindedly twisted a Rubik's cube, all the while staring at the redhead's photograph pinned to the wall. *A strange day indeed. Especially the thing she did when she said "No!" to the guards. What was that about? Amazing voice projection. Stunned them both off their feet. Red. I'll just call her*

Red, for now. He tossed the cube through a small hoop hanging on the wall. *Yes.* Nothing but net.

Bart leaned forward in his chair, one hand cupping his chin, trying to read the mind of the petite redhead in the grainy black-and-white surveillance photo. *Hmmm. What are you doing to me, Red? Will I ever see you again?* He sighed, planting his feet firmly on the floor. He slid a number of student papers into his case and looped the strap through a wide brass catch. *Time to go.*

"Professor." He heard the sigh of exasperation. "Bart."

He smiled. *I'm winning. She's calling me Bart.* He replied in kind. "Yes, Liz."

"A parcel just arrived by courier. From some tech company. I can't pronounce the name. It looks Japanese or something."

He bolted through the door, excitement coursing through every fiber of his being. *My parts. Please let it be my circuit parts.*

Liz sat back in her chair, an expression of surprise on her face at his abrupt appearance. "Whoa. Didn't know it was that urgent, Bart. I'd have brought it straight through."

"Gimme. Gimme. Gimme." He bounced on the spot like a kid waiting for his presents on Christmas day.

"All right, all right. Here." Liz handed across the small FedEx Express carton.

"Yes!" he exclaimed, reading the senders label. Takamuchi Technology. His custom-made parts had arrived. He dashed back into the office, closing the door before ripping the top of the box open. There, carefully encased in anti-static pads and sealed, transparent boxes were the parts he'd waited so long for. It took him months to pay off the credit card he'd charged them to. Custom designed, handmade electronics. For his project - version two.

He ran a hand lovingly over the sealed containers, almost reverent in his appreciation of their potential, the possibilities they allowed. Bart's long-suffering chair groaned its displeasure as he plopped back down. His mind flitted from the parts, to Rebecca, and then to Red. He shook his head and bit his bottom lip. *Decisions, decisions.*

The new parts would allow him to complete, possibly even that night, the second prototype of his new toy, his brainwave modifier. He pondered the implications of the modifier actually working, the second version being many times more powerful than the first. The world of quantum physics and man's understanding of energy and matter were balanced on the edge of an advance way beyond the likes of Einstein's $E=MC^2$. And therein lay Bart's problem. The potential to change matter and energy, and beyond that, to bend it and move between time and dimensions, weighed heavily on him. Just because he could, didn't mean he should.

His initial postulations that energy and matter were one and the same had won him critical acclaim from some. But other scientists were jealous. Certain religious groups threatened, worried his teachings contradicted religious dogma and accepted science. And what if, one day, he could prove them all wrong? The overreaction of the security people that day spoke to the paranoia of some in the university administration.

He had not mentioned to anyone, anywhere, what he was working on at home. Others had tried similar experiments. That was well known. Bart worked at the problem from a new angle and developed his prototype for a mere few thousand dollars in his garage at home. Unlike the multi-million-dollar laboratories and their overpowered, under-delivering engineering. Their approach was to generate colossal amounts of power to bend matter and energy. Working from the scientifically-acknowledged idea that energy and matter were one and the same, Bart used a solar-powered battery and his own brainwaves.

Instead of throwing multi-gigawatts of power at the problem, he had designed a simple brainwave interface. He did admit the device could benefit from more power, but in the big scheme of things, twelve volts hardly counted. The first few experiments were stunning successes. While not actually manipulating energy and matter, he'd bent it a little, giving him the ability, albeit briefly, to look, but not travel, back in time.

Unable to stop himself, he'd gone to the scene of the car crash. It had been like standing there as a tortured observer, powerless to affect the outcome. There was nothing he could physically do. And even if he could... should he? The scientist in him realized the possible earth-altering paradoxes that could result.

Regardless, he had ordered the parts to build a more powerful device. And now they were here. Yet, other thoughts tempered his excitement.

Something about Red's arrival this afternoon had thrust his awareness in a different direction. Away from a course of action that might damn his soul to eternal hell. *Maybe Rebecca's reaching out beyond the veil, telling me to stop. Before it's too late.*

***

Terra stamped her feet in a tantrum. *Damn you all.* The elders had sent Gaia, one of the most experienced Watchers, to retrieve the device. *And to take care of me, no doubt.*

Gaia was smart, but Terra had one major advantage. She'd spent three whole days on the physical earth plane, without using any of her special abilities. Those days had taught her plenty, hopefully enough to deal with the threat Gaia posed. Terra scoffed. Her own nineteen-year-old form was much bigger, stronger, and fitter than the older, petite, less-athletic body Gaia had chosen.

It had been an unfortunate coincidence that Bart Cooksley had been untraceable for that time. *And when I finally find him, Gaia turns up.* She shook her head. *Coincidence? Not likely.* She splashed water on her face and stared at herself in the mirror. *How did it come to this?* Hiding in the clinical, stainless-steel-lined walls of the ladies toilets. *Uck.* Terra pushed some of the water back through her medium-length brunette hair, plastering it down. *The things you have to do to get things done.*

There'd been that wimp at the library. *Nigel?* She'd had to put up with him ogling her breasts just so she could get some information. Then he had clammed up. She had been forced to get rough with him. Terra had been surprised the boy didn't wet himself. And even when she probed his mind, she couldn't find a location for Bart Cooksley outside of the school. She shuddered as she recalled the incident. Going through a few of his thoughts, she stumbled onto the one where he wanted to do … *Whatever it was, it appeared frantic and messy and … ick. Are all young boys like this?*

When Terra left him there, he was white and shaking. There was no way he would do anything to stop her. The seed she planted in his mind would see to that. Laughing, she paper-toweled the excess water from her face. She sensed Bart Cooksley was still in the building. He would probably use one of those four-wheeled contraptions to depart, so it made sense to stake out the pavement area where these devices gathered. She pulled her shoulders back and effected a smile before exiting the stark, steel-lined room.

31

Gaia would be lurking nearby. Terra could feel her presence. Gaia would doubtless go after Bart Cooksley and the device first. *Without that device, I'll be stranded here. She knows that.* She glanced out the tall, dust-specked windows as she strode down the long hallway. *I'll wait for that overconfident cow to make her move on Cooksley. Follow them. Ambush the two of them together, once Gaia has done the hard work of finding the device.* Terra sniggered. It would be touch and go. She couldn't afford to let Gaia actually get her hands on Cooksley's device. She just needed her to find it. *Then I'll take it from her. From both of them.*

***

Bart strode toward the stairwell, the skip in his stride occasioned by the precious parcel jammed under his arm. A blissful sense of purpose propelled him down the steps three at a time. Tomorrow, maybe even tonight, he would be ready to test the second prototype. *It needs a name.* Mindwave frequency manipulator? *No, too long winded. MFM for short. Worse. Sounds like some internet advertisement for group sex. How about … subliminal time distillation? Oh my god! STD.*

Bart rolled his eyes. Since the appearance of Red, sex was raising its not-so-ugly head. He tried to push her from his mind. What were the chances of ever seeing her again? *Unless … she enrolls in my class. Shit. That would make her a student, and there are rules about those sorts of things. Or were they merely guidelines? Stop it, you prat.* He burst out the stairwell doors on the ground floor, crashing into a student.

"Professor Cooksley. So sorry."

"No. No. Fault's all mine. Nigel, isn't it? From the library?"

"Yes, Professor. Did security stop by?"

"Security? How did you know about that, Nigel?" He stressed the boy's name, the question carrying the weight of a demand.

"There was a woman asking questions about you. I let security know."

"So you're the one responsible for that ridiculous farce." He shook his head, turned on his heel, and headed toward the exit door.

"I thought it was the best thing to do, Professor, after the first woman threatened me."

Bart stopped in his tracks. "First woman? What are you talking about?" He swung back to face Nigel, who had followed him.

"Yes. Two women. The first - called herself Terra - asked about you a few days ago. She was scary. Then …"

"This first woman. Did you report her?"

"No, I didn't, Professor."

"Why not?"

"I … um … I don't actually know. She did threaten me, but …"

Nigel appeared decidedly confused, standing there scratching his head and rocking from foot to foot.

"All right. So you didn't report her. What did she look like? Do you remember that?"

"Oh, yes. Attractive girl. About eighteen to twenty, I guess; tall for a girl. Close to my height: 5'10". Longish brunette hair, nice … well developed up top."

Bart frowned. She sounded a lot like the girl in his lecture hall, the creepy one sitting by the exit. *What the hell is going on here?* "All right. What do you know about the second girl, the redhead, if anything?"

"Gaia. She said her name was Gaia Hassani. Red hair, short, about 5'2". Late twenties maybe. I'm never sure about ages. She …"

"Gaia. Did you say Gaia?" Bart felt a surge of energy pulse through him. *A name.*

"Yes. Gaia. The earth goddess from …"

"I know what her name means, Nigel. What else do you remember?"

Nigel took what Bart thought was a somewhat snooty posture and attitude. "Do you know what her last name means? Huh?"

Bart hadn't given it a second thought. He considered for a moment, searching his memory for a reference so he didn't have to admit to this snotty little shit he didn't know. "Hassani. A derivation of Hassan. Later evolved to …" He felt a shiver, "… assassin."

"See, that's the thing that made me wonder. An odd coincidence, don't you think, Professor? Still. She was much nicer than Terra. Oh. I meant to say - the similarities between their names, Terra and Gaia. That was the other thing that made me suspicious."

Bart had to admit, Nigel had a point. Both of them earth goddesses from another, simpler age. An odd coincidence. And Bart didn't believe in coincidences. He remembered the quote that coincidences were God at work.

Or from his point of view, a universal life force manipulating energy and matter. "Hmmm. You probably did the right thing, Nigel. Gaia Hassani. It has an exotic ring to it." He rolled the name over his tongue. "I'll be sure to keep an eye out for her." He smirked as he turned back toward the exit. *Shit.* Bill Jackson from security stood in his way. "Now what?" he demanded.

"Now, now, Professor. I know it's been a trying day, but the Dean insisted we escort you to your car. We don't know where that girl got to."

"Okay then." Bart huffed loudly. "Thanks for the information, Nigel," he called over his shoulder. Nigel was almost in his face, following.

"That's okay, Professor. Anytime. Have a good weekend."

"Yes, thank you. You, too. C'mon Bill, let's do this." He followed the burly man through the door, down a small access way, and into the car park, Nigel right behind. Bart turned left, and Nigel peeled off to the right. As a library assistant, the University allowed him access to one of the unallocated parks, first-come, first-served.

Bart shivered. The sensation was one of a cold hand brushing over his body. His father always used to say, "Someone just walked over my grave." Except, his father hadn't been dead at the time.

For a reason he couldn't place, Terra's face flashed through his mind.

CHAPTER FIVE

Gaia awoke with a start. *How long have I been asleep?* The steadfast tree she rested against had caressed her matrix, recharging some of the energy she'd expended. She felt better, empowered. "Thank you, tree." She put a hand against rough bark, feeling a warm response. She stretched her arms above her head and swiveled her hips as she turned in a circle. The third round, she saw him. *Professor Cooksley.* And Tank. *That explains why I woke so abruptly.*

The sun angled through gaps in the building, fingers of sunlight stabbing into the shade and the cover it offered her. Gaia skirted around the huge trunks, careful not to trip on the haphazard network of roots snaking across the ground. At the edge of her protective barrier of shadows, she stopped, analyzing the possibilities. Cooksley was at his car, watched over by the security guard. "Curse that man." She held her hand to her mouth and recanted. "We should not curse each other." She detected a scurrying movement out the corner of her left eye. "Nigel, you tattle tale."

The part-time librarian had a box of books balanced in one arm as he tried to open the door of his car. She smiled, amused. He could still be of some use.

Flash.

She made it to within eight feet of Nigel's back. At that point, she crossed into someone's field of vision. The moment she became visible to someone, she quantum locked again. *Still, close enough.*

"Hello again. Nigel, wasn't it?" She caught the box that tumbled out of the shocked young man's arms.

He turned to thank Gaia for her help, then realized it was her. The colour faded from his cheeks.

Odd. Last time I saw him, his face went red. Strange creatures, these humans. I can't understand half the signals they send.

"Ms. Hassani. I ... I didn't know you were still here." His gaze darted over her shoulder, pleading for the distant security guard to take notice, she thought.

"No need to be so formal, Nigel. Call me Gaia. Seeing as we're going to be such good friends."

"Friends? I don't understand." He fumbled with the keys, finally managing to insert the correct one and unlock the door. Gaia handed him the box.

"Well, it's like this, Nigel. I know you sent the security people after me." She held up a hand to stop the protest forming on his lips. "I'm not mad at you. You did what you thought was right. But it is imperative I speak to Professor Cooksley before ..." She stopped to consider how much to reveal. "... Before Terra gets to him. She's the one you should be worried about. Now, hand me the keys and get in. No, no. This side. I want the keys to make sure you don't try to lock me out before I can join you." She flashed a wide smile at him, all the while touching his arm. The boy's body language changed as he melted to the soothing energy she emitted.

Seconds later, she dropped into the passenger's seat of Nigel's two-door Honda. She glanced around the leather interior of the worn but tidy car. It still held a little of the scent of the leather in the soft seats. "Nice, Nigel. You buy it?"

"Um, no. My parents got it for me when I came to Wellington for my courses." What do you want with me, Ms ... Gaia?"

"I want you to follow that silver Range Rover." She pointed to the vehicle as it emerged from the far end of the parking area.

"Professor Cooksley's car?" Nigel's natural timidity overcame the cerebral sedative Gaia had administered.

She sighed. *Why did it have to be so hard?* She laid a hand on Nigel's thigh, noticing the change in his energy field. *Hmmm.* He seemed somehow calmer, yet more excited at the same time. *Weird.* She glanced away from the Range Rover to award Nigel another of her stellar grins. A force, like a pressure wave, washed over her. Her head wrenched back toward the tall silver car. *Terra. That was her. Where? Where is she?*

"Go, Nigel. Go! Now." She squeezed his thigh, eliciting a hormonal response she didn't understand. The young man accelerated out of his parking space, the tires squealing as the small car hopped, then steadied itself. She shrunk down into the seat as they passed within fifteen feet of a scowling Tank. The man waved a finger at Nigel. For the squealing tires, Gaia presumed. Then they were out of the car park, turning left, heading up a hill.

"Good boy, Nigel. I knew we'd get along." She ran her hand up the inside of his thigh, squeezing gently again. If nothing else, whatever she was doing seemed to be distracting Nigel. Gaia pushed herself back up in the seat, using Nigel's thigh for a leverage. The boy gulped, the colour returning to his face. *I just don't understand human boys.*

"Um, Gaia. Put your seat belt on, please."

She glanced around, trying to determine what he meant. She knew what a car was, just not the fine detail of how it functioned. "This." He gestured to the strap running across his chest and lap. She swung her head left to right and nodded. Releasing her grip on Nigel, she retrieved the indicated belt and swung it across her torso, clipping it in place. Gaia noticed that Nigel's emotions seemed to waver between relief and disappointment when she removed her hand. She put her hand back on his knee and swept her fingers up his inner thigh, coming to rest a few inches from the juncture.

Nigel squirmed in his seat.

"Right. Go right, please." Gaia pointed with her free hand to make sure he understood.

Nigel pulled the steering wheel down on the right, the car tracking round the corner. "Not too close. Don't let him know we're here. Good boy." She made her point by tapping her fingers on his thigh. *Hmmm. He likes that.* If the signals she was reading were correct, his whole body chemistry changed. *Such complex organisms, these bodies.* She realized how little she really knew about her own.

The trip settled into a rhythm of its own. The silver Range Rover would turn in one direction, Nigel would follow at a discreet distance, each time rewarded with a flutter of finger tips. Only once did Gaia need to manipulate a set of traffic lights that threatened to halt them. Other motorists shook their heads and blew horns at the odd behaviour of signals. Gaia smiled. A sign indicated they were entering the suburb of Karori.

The professor's car slowed on a tree-lined street that boasted a number of large, gracious-looking mansions, before turning into a private driveway. Nigel pulled the Honda to a stop under the cool shade of another ancient pohutakawa. Behind the tinted windows of the Honda, it felt like a safe, private cave.

Gaia focused her attention on Nigel. Although the young man still appeared wary of her, he didn't seem to want her to go, either. Her touch had his aura glowing bright orange. She detected a veritable battle raging in his system, chemical messages surging through his body. The source was the area next to where her hand lay, then from there to the brain and out to other parts of the body. His respiration had increased, heart rate also, pupils dilated, and the appendage near her hand seemed to be increasing in size.

Gaia probed Nigel's mind deeper, not something she normally allowed herself to do. *Hmmm. Some sort of male mating decoration? Is this how the male attracts the female? Interesting.* A number of images flashed through his mind and hers. *A penis. That's its name. Hmmm. Other names as well.* It was a source of pleasure for the male, engorging with blood in response to the female.

They sat there, an odd silence between them. Gaia pushed a bit farther. She sensed that Nigel had been the butt of many a cruel jest by other women, girls. It was an object of personal shame not to have attention lavished upon you by a woman, forced to keep the appendage in good order yourself, the act called masturbation. But others had different, derogatory terms for it. *Ohhh, poor boy.* No female has ever stroked it for him. This conjoining was almost a rite of passage for boys; the lack of it was a matter of some embarrassment. Any approach needed delicate handling. Gaia rubbed her hand up and down the inside of Nigel's thigh. *Yes.* The want was there. She suppressed a laugh. His thoughts told her he would perform this ritual regardless when she was gone.

"Thank you, Nigel. You've been a great help. It is very important I talk to the professor before Terra gets to him. I wish there was something I could do to thank you." With her free hand, she slipped her sunglasses off, holding his nervous gaze with hers as she smiled, top teeth biting her bottom lip.

"I … I …" His whole body trembled. The lump in his throat bounced up and down. " I …"

"Yes?"

"I ... I'm just happy to help, Gaia. It's been ... lovely. To spend time so close to such a hot-looking lady. And you've been really sweet. I'm sorry I called security on you." His gaze darted away, his shoulders slumping. There was something she could do, he just didn't have the nerve to say it.

Gaia leaned over and kissed him on the cheek, then whispered in his ear. When she'd finished what she wanted to say, she pulled back and looked him in the eyes. "If you can't say anything, just nod your head."

Nigel's face turned the darkest shade of red Gaia had seen thus far. He was shaking so hard, Gaia could feel it transmitted to the car. His head nodded ever so slightly.

"You've never had that done before, have you? Not by a girl, anyway. Can I be the first? I've never seen one before." She ran her fingers over the fabric separating Nigel's penis from what he thought of as heaven. "May I?" The organ beneath, this penis, twitched as she stroked it.

"You've never seen one?" Nigel's voice squeaked, the sounds choked off. "I find that hard to believe. You don't talk like any girl I've met before." He stopped, eyebrows pulled together for a second. "Are ... are you really Amish? I thought you just made that up. It would certainly explain a few things."

Gaia watched as his shaking hands tried to undo the buttons. The fingers wouldn't work. "Here, let me help." With deft fingers, she popped the several buttons on his jeans, unclipped the belt, and helped him slide the trousers down as he lifted in the seat. Another thin garment held Nigel's penis imprisoned, bulging as it tried to escape. Gaia squeezed it through the fabric, giggling as Nigel squirmed and let a sound out. "Go on. Take them off too."

Gaia could feel an odd sensation in her stomach. Nigel's excitement and nervous energy was rubbing off on her. He hooked his thumbs under the waistband, then looked at Gaia.

"You sure?"

She could tell he wanted to but needed that one last piece of encouragement. He was expecting her to say no, to be another of the mean girls. "Yes, go on. Off. I want to see."

Nigel glanced around and pulled the garment down.

"Oooo. It's beautiful." At that small comment, it appeared to grow in size. Gaia was astounded that such a large object could be hidden away so well. "Is it always this big?" she asked, her fingers encircling the main shaft. At her touch, it swelled further. "Did I do that?" She giggled at Nigel's husky reply.

"It's not usually that size; you made it like that. And it's not that big." He shuddered as she caressed him.

"Are you kidding? It's huge." She began sliding the encircling fingers up and down it's length. "Is this how I do it?"

"What?" He jerked in the seat as she ran her finger tips over the plum-shaped head. "Uhhh. Yes. That's it. Just keep on like that." He reached down the side of the seat and grabbed a box containing sheets of soft paper.

"What are those for?"

"You really don't know, do you?" Nigel grunted and placed the box on the dashboard. "You'll find out in a minute. Maybe sooner. Oooo."

"It's so hot. I can feel it pulsating in my hand. Oooo. This is fun. Does it feel good?"

"Gaia, you have no idea how good it feels….oh … god."

"I can feel your pleasure, really. I can. It … it's not like anything I've ever felt before." Twisting in the seat to get more comfortable, she reached over with the other hand and tickled the fuzzy sack at the base. "Ohhh, sorry. Don't you like that?"

Nigel's knee banged the steering wheel as his hand pushed against the roof. "No. I mean, yes." He sounded like there was something tight around his throat. "It's great. You caught me by … oooo … oh my god … yes … oh shit."

Gaia felt the shaft twitch rhythmically in her hand, a viscous white fluid ejecting from the end. Her mouth dropped open. Nigel's eyes rolled back in their sockets, his body convulsing as further twitches sent more of the fluid onto the dashboard and over Gaia's hand. She sensed the right thing to do at this time was to just keep going. It wasn't so easy to keep a rhythm.

Gaia swooned, awash in the overwhelming feeling of bliss emanating from Nigel, transferred to her through her touch. Her own head felt light, dizzy. *Wow. Now I understand why boys perform this ritual. It's amazing.* She slowed her stroking as Nigel jerked and twisted in his seat, the sensations winding down. A feeling of giddy peace overcame her.

Nigel reached out his hand to stop her. "Enough. Please."

She saw him twitch each time she reached the tip of the shaft. *Too much.* It was too sensitive now. She laughed, and he joined her.

"Oh. My. God. That was absolutely incredible, Gaia. It's never been like that when I do it. I never thought a woman's touch would be so … pleasurable. Especially one as attractive as you. Wow." He sucked in large gulps of air, bringing his breathing under some sort of control. He started laughing again.

"I'm happy I was able to provide some small gift for your help. I see why you wanted the soft paper now." She chuckled and plucked a few of them from the box, wiping most of the fluid off Nigel's shrinking penis. She stopped, looking closely at what was on her hand. Her head tilted sideways as she tuned in to it. "Oh my." *It's alive. This is the actual seed of the male. He must need to eject it frequently to keep it fresh.* She wiped the last off her hand and handed the box to Nigel. "Does it always shrink back like that?"

Nigel regarded her, slack jawed, his eyes seeming unfocused. "For a short period. It is usually able to become erect again in a short time. I'm not sure about this time, though. That was intense. Phew. Thank you so much. The boys at uni will never …" He cut the sentence short.

"Never what?" Gaia saw the new twinkle of confidence in the boy's eyes. "The boys will never what?"

"I … I wouldn't. Tell, I mean. It was a figure of speech. No one would believe me anyway." He squirmed his way back into this jeans.

"Telling? Is that part of the ritual? You tell others when you have a woman touch you. Is that normal?"

"Well, no. It's not. I was just so surprised at what happened. I never dreamed a hot woman would, well, do what you just did. I'm sorry. I didn't mean to upset you."

"I'm not upset, Nigel. I was just trying to understand this complex mating ritual you engage in."

"Mating ritual." He almost choked, then snorted. "Mating ritual. You really don't know, do you? Man, are you in for a surprise." He looked thoughtful for a moment. "You should save that for someone special. Don't do what you just did to me to too many other people. It is special."

"Oh. Was I wrong to do this for you?"

"Well, no. It was wonderful. Just don't do it for every guy. Men think poorly of girls who share that sort of thing too freely."

Gaia shook her head. "Such complex rituals. I don't think I'll ever understand. I won't forget what you told me or our time together. I should go." She smiled at Nigel.

"And I'll remember this time for the rest of my life." A broad grin nearly split his face in half.

"Now, you're not going to call the police or something like that, are you?"

"No, no. Not now. That would be churlish of me, my lady. I think I trust you now. There's something innocent about you. I don't think you're a danger to the professor."

"Thank you, Nigel." Gaia leaned across and kissed Nigel's cheek. "For everything. That was … spectacular. I experienced what you felt. It was … educational. My, I'm still a little giddy." They both laughed as she fanned her face with her hands.

"Will I see you around, Gaia?"

"Probably not. Once I complete this assignment, I have to return home."

"Where is that? Really?" His eyes pleaded to her.

"Humph. Like your friends, you wouldn't believe me if I told you. Goodbye, Nigel." She pushed one leg out the door, turning to give him another smile.

"Go get 'em, tiger. Watch out for Terra." He blew her a kiss.

She waved as he swung the car in a tight circle and drove slowly back down the quiet street. Standing alone under the branches, Gaia felt a shudder. The small deed she'd just performed somehow made her feel closer to Nigel. He'd been a bit of an annoyance at times, but now that he was gone, she missed him. *Odd.* She scratched her head, trying to understand the workings of the human body and it's multitude of interacting systems.

With a sigh, she turned toward the professor's driveway. Time to get on with her mission. With the cloying sexual energy of Nigel gone, she noticed a new sensation.

Terra was close by. Too close.

Gaia needed to work fast.

CHAPTER SIX

Bart dropped the packaging from his frozen pizza in the trash bin and pulled on a cold bottle of Corona. He propped the bottle on the coffee table, watching cold droplets meander down the sides as he waited the last few minutes for the oven to produce yet another instant meal. His precious parts shipment sat near the front door, along with a few still-to-be-opened bills and advertising pamphlets. He yawned and stretched out on the old leather couch, the smell of processed cheese and tomato paste wending its way to his less-than-discerning nose. Save for a few bird calls reaching through partly-open windows from the world outside, the house was silent.

The silence bothered him tonight, weighed on his peace of mind. Thoughts of Rebecca intruded. And Gaia. *Hmmm.* Such a crazy notion to pursue. A woman he'd seen once and may never see again. Still. She had rattled his cage, shocked him out of the waking dream his life had become since Rebecca's death. A life of frozen dinners and half-lived promises. And now he truly questioned the sanity of his experiments. *What if I get it to work? Someone, somewhere will try to weaponize it. Or commercialize it. Shit.*

Bart gulped down the cold ale and rolled off the couch, fingers searching for the remote for the sound system. *What will it be tonight?* Some old classic rock, some Tchaikovsky, perhaps. He selected some thirties jazz and blues, the soothing tones of Duke Ellington floating through the house as he wandered back into the kitchen for another beer. The bottle opened with a tiss, and the first drops slid down an eager gullet. *Tomorrow. I'll work on it tomorrow.* Time for a night off. Still, he couldn't take his mind completely off the device.

He retrieved the prototype from a cabinet in the garage, returned to the living room, and sat there staring down at his invention. The two retracted antennae of the silver disc stared back. Bart chuckled, recalling how badly he'd done as a teenager, assembling models manufactured by others. Yet he could build this from scratch. The first prototype was not much bigger than a small cake tin, with a tiny solar panel built in to trickle-charge the experimental storage cells. The two antennae always made him think of "My Favorite Martian," a TV program from his childhood. Version two would be little larger than a portable CD player, but more powerful. Again, he worried. The risks still seemed to outweigh the gains. *If I even once caused a paradox …* He sipped on the bottle and plonked it back on the coffee table. He sat there with his chin resting on his hands.

Ding. The oven signaled dinner time. *Finally.* Using a tea towel, Bart scooped the tray out of the oven and onto the dark granite bench top. He paused long enough to cram a piece into his cavernous chops. "Ow." The hot cheese burnt the hard palate. *Bugger.* He grabbed for his beer, splashing some around his mouth to cool the burn. *Damn. I hate it when that happens.* Half of the remaining pizza went onto a plate, a generous portion of extra tomato sauce spread lavishly over top. Now he was ready. He walked the plate and beer back to the couch and squatted to sit.

A loud knocking dragged his attention to the door. *Bloody typical. This better not be a blasted Bible basher come to annoy me.* Bart stormed to the door, flinging it open with vigorous intent.

The petite redhead who'd troubled his thoughts all afternoon stood in the doorway. He opened his mouth to say more, then froze. *How did she find me? I'm unlisted. Why has she come here? Shit. Maybe she is some sort of crazy. Calm. Don't be a tosser, Bart.* He glanced at the three martial arts certificates on the wall. *All right. Be calm.* He found his voice now. "Gaia?"

She took half a step back. "How do you know my name?"

"It's a long story involving security guards and a librarian with an overactive imagination. You haven't come to attack me, have you?" Despite the friendly banter, he positioned himself to repel a sudden attack. He tried to tell himself that if she were dangerous, surely she wouldn't stop and chat in the doorway. Still, these days, who knew what went on in people's heads.

"You mean Nigel?" Gaia smiled pensively.

"Yes. How did you know?" Bart's senses went into overdrive, his first instinct to slam the door and call the police. She'd been making enquiries about him.

"He … I mean, I got him to follow you. From the university. I need to speak to you. Urgently." He noticed Gaia fidgeting.

"Why didn't you just come and see me at the university? And … why are your hands wet?"

"Oh. I had an uncontrollable urge to wash them, so I used the faucet down there." She pointed toward the side of the garage. "I tried to see you at the university, but those men in uniforms kept trying to stop me, to detain me. I couldn't let them do that."

Bart had one hand on the door and had already closed it halfway, but he was unable to finish the move. To close the door on this cute woman seemed unthinkable to him. Once closed, it might never open to Gaia again. She'd made no threatening moves toward him, in fact, she'd stepped back a little. He couldn't detect any sort of danger from her. And she was so small. He should be able to handle her if she did go off.

"Come in. Have you had dinner? I was just about to eat." He stepped to one side to let her enter and closed the door. "Did you want to dry your hands?" He smiled as her head bobbed. He pointed to a door across the room. "Second on the right. You'll find a towel in the cupboard." His eyes followed the sway of her tight Levi's as she glided across the room and vanished through the door. *Yes.* He punched the air silently. *This your doing, isn't it Rebecca?*

He glanced around the room. *Shit.* In a flurry of activity he swept debris and dishes off the counter top and found a plate for Gaia's portion of pizza. As he slid the pizza onto the plate, he saw his hands were shaking. *Ya big wuss. It's just a girl.* He leaned out over the counter top to see if she was back yet. *Yeah. One very cute girl. Behave yourself. Be a gentleman.* The voices of his conscience raged on, one laughing like a giddy school boy, the other stern and proper. A melodic humming preceded Gaia's return from the bathroom.

"Lovely home. I adore all the wood paneling and posts." The smile she flashed sent a tingle up his spine, completely disarming Bart.

"You might want to take off those sunglasses in here." He grinned. *Has she forgotten?*

"Oh. All right. But I need to warn you, I have unusual eyes. It's why I wear the glasses. It stops people from constantly asking questions." She tilted her head forward, slipped the glasses off, and dropped them on the counter top. Gaia's head came back up, her gaze holding Bart's.

Oh, wow. They are unusual. He found himself drawn into them, as if falling into a pool of liquid honey. The yellow of her irises held him captive, a possum in the headlights. He found himself unable to move, until she glanced away. *Wow. This tiny redhead is sex on wheels. A bright red Ferrari, at that.*

"See? People see my eyes and think I'm weird. I see it in their reactions."

He coughed to clear his constricted throat. "No, no! Not weird. Hypnotic. Alluring." He hesitated. "Sexy."

"Sexy?" Gaia's gaze swept around the room, coming to rest on the cake-tin-sized device. She tensed.

"So, Gaia. I've got some spare pizza, if you'd like to join me. And we can talk about whatever it was you came to see me about." He passed the plate across. "C'mon. I don't bite."

"You won't? Is that something people do? Bite?"

Bart was having trouble reading this woman. Her face had taken on a thoughtful look when he mentioned not biting her. As if she considered that was a possibility. *What a strange woman.* There was something innocent, pure about her. He watched as she sniffed at the pizza, then prodded it with a finger. A frown formed as she pushed the melted cheese, then put her finger in her mouth to taste it. *Has she never eaten pizza before?*

"Okay. I guess I can stop for a few minutes. But please be aware, Bartholomew Cooksley. You are in danger. Another woman may try to contact you, harm you."

Bart snorted beer out his nose. He coughed and spluttered, trying to gather himself. "Bartholomew Cooksley? Only my mother calls me that. Please call me Bart. And this other woman you speak of. Her name wouldn't be Terra, would it?" He coughed again, then turned away from Gaia laughing. "Bartholomew Cooksley." He snorted again.

"Are you making fun of me, Bart Cooksley?" Gaia looked annoyed now, hands on hips, mouth pulled tight.

"Please. Bart, just Bart." He tried to pull the twitching facial muscles tight, to look serious for her. He failed, the failure highlighted by another snort. *Heck. This girl is funny.*

"Bart, stop it. I'm serious. Terra is dangerous." Her look stripped all the humour out of the situation.

Bart put his hand over his mouth and coughed. "Okay. Sorry, Gaia. Why so serious? It's a look that doesn't suit your beauty." *Oh god, that was corny.*

"Terra is after your time device. She will do anything to get her hands on it."

Bart felt an icy chill crawl to every corner of his body. He dropped the beer bottle to the bench top and stood back from Gaia. All traces of humour were gone, buried. "How do you know about my prototype? I've told no one about it. You're one of those religious nutters, aren't you?" He ground his teeth together. "You need to leave."

The warm feeling that had simmered since he first laid eyes on Gaia vanished, swept away by a deluge of suspicion and doubt. He moved to place his hand in the small of her back, to help her out the house. Bart glanced at the front door. When he looked back to where she'd been, she was gone. He swung his head around, finding she now stood where he had a second before.

He spun quickly, balanced on the balls of his feet, ready for an attack. "How did you get there so fast?"

"I'm trying to warn you, Bart. Your device is dangerous. Terra wants it. I need to take and destroy it."

"No. You don't know what you're talking about. Get out of my house." He reached out to grab her arm. She moved out of his reach. *Damn this.* He didn't want to use his years of Jeet Kune Do kung fu training on Gaia, but she didn't seem to be leaving him any option. His hand flashed out to grasp her, but she twisted aside, deflecting him. *Wow. She's quick.*

Now he held nothing back, using all his considerable skills to grasp and lock her arms. Every reach, twist, and grasp left him empty-handed. It was like trying to fight water, like fighting himself. Nothing he did worked. He grinned. He was actually beginning to enjoy this odd encounter.

He started to laugh. The reason he liked Jeet Kune Do was its similarity to the laws of physics. The equal and opposite moves. Not actually resisting, but deflecting, going with the flow of energy. Gaia appeared to be a master of the art of either Jeet Kune Do or physics. Beads of sweat began to drip from his brow. Something about the blinding speed of their engagement puzzled him. She wasn't attacking. And she showed not a hint of exertion. No raised breathing, no sweat. *What is going on here?*

He blinked. She was gone. A finger tapped him on the shoulder. He spun around to find her behind him. "How the hell?" As if to answer, she hit him. Not hard. But enough to get his attention. Five fingers bounced off his chest, knocking him back a foot. He never saw it coming. *Damn her. She's been holding back. I was never going to get a hand on her. What gives?*

"Bart, please stop. Listen to me."

The voice she'd demonstrated so effectively in his lecture room hammered against him, pushing him back three feet. Now he understood. The guards didn't trip, she knocked them over. Yet, oddly, he wasn't afraid of her. He was intrigued. He put his hands up, indicating enough. "All right. All right. You got my attention. What is going on?"

"I have to recover your time device and destroy it before Terra gets it."

Bart laughed. "Well first off, it's not actually a time device."

"Yes it is, Bart. You just don't know it. Yet."

"How on earth do you even know about my prototype?" He shook his head, feeling the familiar burn in his hard-worked muscles.

"The 'how' is not important. Where is it?" Gaia's voice brooked no argument.

"Why should I tell you?" Before he could stop himself, his gaze darted to the box.

Gaia's followed. "That's it, isn't it?" She took a step toward it.

Bart hung his head. "Yes, that's it. I still don't ..."

Bart's ears popped as the heavy wooden front door exploded into small fragments, peppering the wall across from them with fragments of timber and glass. The tsunami wave of energy blew them both off their feet. Gaia tumbled over the counter top as Bart slammed into the leather couch, upending it.

Terra flashed into the room. "I'll have that, thank you." She stopped several feet short of the silver box as Bart staggered to his feet. "You gonna try and stop me, little man?" She sneered, taking a boxing stance.

Gaia groaned from behind the counter.

"Yeah. Bring it, bitch." Bart advanced on Terra, his balance carefully poised.

"Oooo. Such a hero." Terra's eyes widened mockingly.

Bart shook off the first blow and settled back into the rhythm he'd found sparring with Gaia. Terra was bigger, stronger, and younger, but she lacked Gaia's finesse. *Good thing I had that warm-up match with Gaia.* Something pushed inside Bart's head, as if a second mind had joined with his.

Gaia?

Terra frowned as Bart went from defense to attack. The heel kick caught her square in the sternum, driving her back almost to the door. She fell hard, knocking over two chairs, then came to rest against the old worn china cabinet. Glasses and plates toppled off, smashing on the floor around her.

"You fucker. That hurt!" she screamed, lifting off the floor as if attached to ceiling wires. She charged at Bart, crashing into the far wall as he swiveled and directed her away. The next scream of anger rocked Bart back on his feet, its primal energy tearing at the very fabric of his consciousness. Terra's yellow eyes turned red. She glared at him and clapped her palms together, pushing toward him at the same time.

The energy hammered into his chest, driving the air from him. He lifted off his feet and sailed almost the full length of the room. A large leather chair cushioned him from more serious injuries, even as it smashed into the wall. He gasped for breath and tried to rise. He blinked, and she was on him. Three punches rocked his jaw and cheek. White stars danced before his eyes, and he fell back into the chair, panting.

"Move again, and I'll kill ya."

His vision swam. He could make out Terra behind the counter. The action of her body indicated she was kicking something. *Gaia.* Helplessness washed over him.

"Stay there, you cow. Or I'll have to …" she grunted as she lashed out again "…keep this up until that pretty face is mince meat. Supposed to be the best, eh? And now you can't even go back to your precious Sanctum. Poor Gaia." Cruel laughter reverberated off the walls. "That's a nasty cut you got on your face."

Bart tried to push out of the chair again. He got halfway up before his knees gave way. From the floor, he watched as Terra strolled, whistling, to the prototype device. *At least she won't know how to work it. No instruction manual.* He tried to chuckle, but it hurt.

He rolled onto his back, beginning to recover his breath. From the corner of his eye, he saw Terra place a hand on top of the silver box. She swayed and laughed again.

"So simple. Thank you, Professor. Gaia." She extended the two antennae, adjusted a small dial, and waved as she touched the only button. The look of triumph on her face sent a wave of nausea through him. He thought he saw a swirl appear in midair, akin to a distant heat shimmer. Terra picked up the box and stepped forward.

"Bye."

The swirl opened and snapped shut with a blinding flash. Bart gasped in horror.

Terra was gone.

CHAPTER SEVEN

Gaia winced and tried to pull away as Bart dabbed antiseptic on the gash across her cheek.

"Sorry. It'll help. Let me finish. Please."

He squeezed excess hot water out of the washcloth and wiped blood off Gaia's neck, out of her hair. She hadn't spoken since Terra's sudden, vicious attack. The bruises forming on her face made Bart suspect she was either in shock or mildly concussed. The slightest move caused Gaia to flinch. She put her hand to her side.

Bart clenched his jaw. "You hurt there, too? Let me see."

Rather than lift the side of her top, Gaia stripped her upper torso naked without a moment's hesitation, discarding the clothing on the couch.

She's … exquisite. Bart could have looked at her soft, creamy-coloured skin, her firm, well-formed breasts with their small puffy nipples, or her small freckles forever. *B cup, I'm guessing. Nice, very nice.* He swallowed and handed her bra back to her. "You can leave that on, Gaia."

She regarded him with a tilt of her head and small frown, then complied.

For the briefest of moments, he wondered if her injuries extended further. God. *What would she do if I asked to see that injury?* A small shiver ran through him. There was definitely something different about this woman.

Bart forced himself to focus, gently prodding the bruised ribs.

She exhaled loudly as he touched the affected area.

"Sorry." Bart turned to the chest of supplies Rebecca always kept for emergencies. He rummaged through it until he found what he sought. Arnica. "Here. This will help with the bruising. May I?"

She examined his face intently, then nodded.

He was aware of her probing gaze. Her cool, soothing fingers touched his own bruises, leeching away some of the ache.

"I'm sorry, Bart. I brought her here." The words were so quiet he almost missed them.

He finished applying the arnica to her ribs and handed her top back.

She slid it on, a tightness to her mouth as she stretched.

Tough little thing. She's hurting more than she will admit. He wiped the last blood from her face and applied some arnica to the bruises, avoiding the cut Terra's shoe had opened. Gaia's closeness, her touch on his face, held him spellbound. He wanted to lean in and kiss her.

He couldn't explain what happened next. It was as if she read his thoughts. He felt her hand in his hair, the fingers combing through the curls. An electric charge shot down his spine, terminating at his groin. He looked in her yellow, gold-flecked eyes. The irises moved and changed, pulling him in. Her eyes moved to each of his in turn, to his nose, the bruises, and finally his lips. She eased his head forward, his neck muscles responding to her touch, heedless of his ability to control them.

She stopped, lips poised so close he could feel the warmth of her breath, smell her natural scent. *Odd. No perfume, toothpaste, shampoo. Nothing. Just her.* His stomach fluttered. He flashed back to his first kiss. Shirley Kirk, at thirteen years old. That memory faded at the sensation of Gaia's lips brushing his, the touch so soft, so tender. He trembled. He let her lead, each touch intoxicating, like no kiss he'd ever experienced. Every nerve fiber in his body seemed to be involved, wide awake, alert. He heard a small whimper escape her.

My god. This woman. She'll enslave me. He sighed, his kiss firmer, more assertive. He felt her flinch, then pull away. *Shit, her bruises. I forgot. What a total oaf.*

"You're not an oaf, Bart." Her voice reached inside him, caressing his soul.

"How did … I mean … oh heck." He started to stand, to give himself some thinking space, then realized he had a partial erection. He turned his back to her quickly. *Concentrate. You need to find out what's going on.* He took a deep, controlling breath. *Okay. All good.* He faced Gaia once again.

"What's 'all good'?" She smiled pensively.

"How do you do that? It's not fair." He felt a flash of exasperation, of anger, that cooled as he looked into her eyes. "Sorry. But how do you do that?"

"If I concentrate, I can look into someone's energy field, see the pulses, waves, and colours, and read what they are thinking. I'm sorry. I know I shouldn't. I wanted to know if you were angry with me." She looked at the floor.

Bart stroked her jaw with his fingertips and lifted her chin toward him again. "I'm not angry with you, Gaia. I ... like you. I'm just confused. What's going on? Who or what are you?" He ran his hand from her jaw to the nape of her neck, one arm sliding round her shoulders as he sat next to her on the now upright couch.

Gaia sucked in several deep breaths and began. "I'm a Watcher, Bart."

"A Watcher?" He grinned. "Round here, that has a number of meanings. You better explain."

"I will, if you don't interrupt." The rebuke was sharp but delivered with a smile. "You, of all people, may be able to comprehend what I'm about to tell you. I'm trapped here now. With your device gone, I can't return. The path is blocked. I'm stuck in human form."

"Stuck in human form?" *Yeah. Right.* Bart crossed his arms and legs and fitted a suitably stern look to his face, in an attempt to avoid laughing at the preposterous statement. People barging in the front door and vanishing was one thing, magicians did it all the time, but stuck in human form? *This I gotta hear.* "Go on," he encouraged.

"We exist in another dimension, one of pure energy. We neither feel, taste, nor experience all the sensations you take for granted. We just are. In that state, we can see everything, from everywhere, at every time. Some of us are asked, invited, to enter the earth realm to fix anomalies."

Bart found himself excited, if somewhat skeptical. "What sort of anomalies?" This was his field of study. Most peoples' eyes glazed over if he began to speak of such things, of his postulations on energy and matter. For once he had a willing, if captive, audience.

"Time warps, vortexes, worm holes," she continued. "Any number of things that affect life on Earth but are not of Earth. Our fixes are experienced by humans as déjà vu."

"I've often wondered about random energy aberrations somehow being fixed by some outside interference," Bart exclaimed. "But déjà vu. Wow. It kinda makes sense." He looked at the now-silent Gaia. "Sorry. It's exciting. Go on."

"As you well know, energy and matter are one and the same. You've seen small demonstrations of it. The jump, or flash, where we move from one spot to another when not quantum locked. The observation of your thoughts by reading the energy stream. And ..." She glanced at the gaping hole where Bart's front door once stood. "... projected energy bursts."

"I understand all this. But ..." Bart rubbed his brow. "It's another thing to actually see it proven. And how am I involved? Why is that silly prototype so important?"

"That silly prototype, as you call it, is capable of time and spatial travel. But because of its flawed design, every time you activate it, hundreds of vortexes, invisible gateways, open. Anyone near one of those gateways is drawn toward it. Normally that is not a problem. But, for example, say you are standing next to the roadway, and a vortex pulls you in front of a bus. That's serious. It disturbs the time-space continuum, causing paradoxes. Those are the events we cross the veil to prevent."

"My device does this? Are you sure?" Bart jumped to his feet and began pacing the room. "That can't be right. So far, it only allows me to look back in time, not physically travel."

"All right then, how do you explain where Terra went? Can you? No. What you need to understand is that your device needs work. Your equation is incorrect. I saw that in your lecture room. It's close but has two flaws."

"How is it that you can use the device to travel, and I can't?"

"Oh, but you can. You just don't remember how."

Bart stopped pacing and faced her again. "What do you mean?"

"You've been in human form for millions of years. The spark that drives you, that energy essence you call your soul, has forgotten how to use many of the gifts you once had."

Bart shook his head. "Are you saying that humans are, in essence, pure energy manifested as matter? I understand that, but you're also suggesting a separation of body and mind."

"Yes. You've been in that physical dimension for so long, and developed such intellect, that the skills you once possessed as energy beings are now vague memories. Your intelligence overrides your instincts. Surely you see that."

"Well, yes. Energy and matter are the building blocks of what I work with. But it's one thing to theorize. It's blowing my mind to actually see it in practice, to know that all the cranks who criticize my ideas are wrong."

"It's bigger than just you being right, Bart. Back to your device, though. My mission was to retrieve it, in any way necessary, destroy it, and ..." Her voice trailed off.

"And what? Tell me. What else were you supposed to do?" The chill Bart felt penetrated to the marrow.

Gaia's shoulders slumped. "I was instructed to 'confound your memory' of the device."

"Confound? You mean wipe my mind, don't you?" Bart noticed he was clenching his fists.

"Yes. I'm sorry, but it's too important. We used to deal with a few anomalies a year. Since you activated your device, there have been instances of hundreds a day."

"So you have this power to change human existence for the better. Why don't you stop the wars and world hunger?"

"We never interfere with human free will, the right to choose, to determine their own lives."

"Well, how high-minded of you all." Bart felt his temperature rising, a wave of anger. "You won't stop, for example, Adolf Hitler wiping out tens of millions of people, but you'll come into my life and take away my free will, my choices."

"I hear what you're saying, but it's different."

"How so? My first prototype is gone now. Doesn't that fix it all?"

"No. Terra is rogue. With her power and the ability to jump around time, she could alter the course of history. But it's worse than that. The device you built opens unstable vortexes. We've managed to track them all, so far. But the risk is ..." Gaia pulled her mouth tight and wrung her hands. "... there's a risk one of those vortexes could tear a hole in time and space."

Bart stood with his mouth open. "You don't mean ...?"

"Yes. The total destruction of time, space, and even energy. A reverse of what you call the big bang. Everything would cease. A total void. Now do you understand why we had to act? I didn't want to hurt you, or manipulate your mind, but there is simply too much at stake."

"Jesus H. Christ." Bart shouted and stormed out.

"Bart." Gaia called after him. "We need to find a solution to the problem. One option …"

Bart walked back into the room dragging a whiteboard behind him. "Yes. You said there was an option. Go on." He positioned the board for Gaia to see. Bart's flawed equation flowed across it in blue pen.

"Oh," Gaia said, reading the board in a glance. "How did you know that was one possible, at least partial answer?"

"Sorry. I don't understand." Bart glanced at his equation, years of work, feelings of pride evaporating as Gaia stood there shaking her head.

"Well. It's simple, really. Part of the problem is the faulty equation."

"How so? It's just an equation. It doesn't factor into the physical devices."

"Oh, but it does. You're missing the bigger picture." She flashed that smile.

"But it's just an equation. It's not …" He froze, not one part of his body moving. The realization of what Gaia meant was like ice water on his head. "Oh my god. I see it. Let me think for a minute." He walked into the kitchen and rattled about there for a few minutes. The smell of fresh coffee drifted across the room. "Are you hungry? I'm afraid the pizza's had it. Unless you like wood splinters." The ideas buzzing around in his head were both exhilarating and sobering. He recognized the feeling, that creative release he lived for. Athletes pushed for the endorphin, dopamine high. For Bart, it was the flow of creativity.

"Yes. I guess." Gaia's voice sounded hesitant. "I've never actually eaten before."

"Say what?" Bart reappeared in front of her. "You've never eaten? How is that possible?"

"I've never been in human form long enough to require fuel. I usually have unlimited access to Sanctum, The Source. Pure energy is food to me."

"Holy shit. And I was gonna give you pre-frozen, oven-heated pizza. Some host I am." He vanished back into the kitchen area. Gaia swiveled in the couch to watch him. "By the way, Gaia. FYI. Oh, sorry. That means 'for your information'. It's not normal protocol or behaviour for the female to disrobe in front of a man so readily. Like you did before. Pleasant, but not normally done." He felt his grin reaching both ears.

"Oh. I didn't know that." Gaia's face coloured slightly. "In that case, can I ask you something?" She leaned an arm over the couch.

"Yeah. Fire away." Bart's voice was muffled, his head buried in the refrigerator.

"On the way over here…" Gaia explained the ritual she had shared with Nigel.

A loud snort echoed from behind the counter top. "You did what?" The snort turned to laughter. Bart found himself on his knees.

"Are you okay? Are you laughing?" Gaia's voice called to him.

Bart thought he might choke. He hauled himself off the floor and leaned on the counter top. "You don't know, do you? Gaia. You have a lot to learn. That boy will remember you for the rest of his life. You made his day." He gulped down a glass of water, trying to calm his laughter.

"What?" Gaia's voice sounded annoyed. "You're laughing at me. Why?"

As much as he found himself attracted to her, he just couldn't find it in him to be jealous of what had taken place. "I'm sorry, Gaia." He wiped the tears from his eyes. "Ah. That explains the sudden need to wash your hands outside." He started laughing again.

"Stop it. What did I do? Tell me. You're starting to anger me."

Bart could tell she was about to lose her temper. He cleared his throat. "I'm sorry. Really, I am. Let me get something to munch on, and I'll explain. Okay?"

"I guess." Gaia folded her arms and gave Bart a cold stare.

Maybe there is more human in her than she realizes. She's got that womanly trait down pat. He suppressed the laugh that threatened to break loose with that observation. *Not now. Don't piss off the cute woman. If she's stuck here on Earth … hmmm.* He peeked above the top of the fridge door, watching the back of her red-covered head. *Nice. Yes. Very nice.* He ducked back down again as she swiveled to face him. *Gotta watch that. She reads minds, sometimes. That could be a problem.*

"What could?" Her voice carried a hint of suspicion.

"No mayo. There's no mayo for my creation. And it's considered rude to intrude into other peoples thoughts." He risked the rebuke.

"I know. I'm sorry. I won't do it again." Her response was quiet, subdued.

Bart felt a weight lift from him, the release of a subtle pressure around his head. *Ah-ha. Of course. If she's tapping energy, there'll be a feedback of some sort. If I'm alert, I can tell if she's reading me. Excellent.*

He plated his food offering and walked it and two cups of coffee into the living room. "Hope you like milk in your coffee." He placed the tray in front of Gaia. "Oh great and bountiful goddess of Earth, please accept this humble offering."

He thought she might actually laugh. She held it back, watching him through half-closed eyes as he arranged the offering.

"And about time too, puny earthman." Now she laughed, the sound rolling out of her like a bellbird's call.

"So you do have a sense of humour. Good. Eat, Barbarella."

"Who?"

Bart laughed out loud. "Maybe I shouldn't tell you." He watched Gaia's eyes narrow. "All right, all right. Barbarella was my fantasy girl when I was a boy. A character in a movie. You understand what a movie is?"

Gaia nodded. "A series of images projected at a frequency that makes them appear to move." She looked pleased with herself.

"Correct. I've forgotten most of the movie now, but there are some parallels to you. And Nigel." He snickered, then pulled a serious face. "Suffice to say, Barbarella was this amazingly-hot space chick, with no understanding of human sexual rites or behaviour." *Man. That is so on the money. Barbarella. Hmmm.* Bart wondered if a childhood fantasy might yet come to pass. *Just not with Jane Fonda.*

A small smile twitched across Gaia's lips. "Are you saying I'm a hot space chick?"

"Oh yes. Way hot." He felt the heat flash in his face and dissipate.

"That's good, right?

He smiled.

"Thank you, Bartholomew Cooksley." She clutched the front of his shirt and pulled him down for a kiss.

He felt hormones begin to stir again, before she released him.

"That was for saying kind things," she said. "Is that an appropriate response?"

"Well. Yes, I suppose." He scratched his head. "Not for every man or every occasion, but I'd say it's okay between us." He sighed. "And it's lovely."

"What? Kissing?"

"Kissing you. It makes me feel all … funny." Bart sat down next to Gaia on the couch.

"Kissing me makes you want to laugh? Why is that?" Gaia had her head tilted to one side, watching him closely.

"No. That's not what I meant. It gives me an odd sensation inside. A pleasant feeling. Man. There is so much I need to tell you. But first, let's eat." He pointed to the lopsided stack on the plate.

Gaia scooted in closer to Bart and leaned over the plate. "What is this?" She sniffed, then went to prod the food.

"No." Bart slapped her hand gently. "First rule: don't prod at your food, at least not around other people. I call this a Bart Burger. It's not really a burger, more like a mega sandwich, but 'Bart Sandwich' doesn't sound as good. If I'd known you were coming, I'd have prepared something more … sumptuous. Here. I'll show you how to eat one." He picked the thick tower of food up with both hands and took a bite. "It'f goodth." Muffled words escaped between pieces of food. He put his hand over his mouth. "Sorry. Another rule: you shouldn't talk with your mouth full."

Gaia took a tentative bite of her sandwich, then looked at Bart. "Good. It's good." She attacked it with gusto. "What's in it?"

"I start with fresh multi-grain bread, then add - and not necessarily in this order -butter, mayo, mustard, ham, tomato, salt and pepper, lettuce, beetroot, cheese, and whatever else I can find in the fridge that needs using up."

"It's superb." She took another bite, wiping a dab of mustard off the edge of her mouth. "I thought you said you were out of mayo?"

"Ah. Yes. I found some more." Bart lied without losing the smile on his face.

"This yellow stuff is hot."

"That's the mustard. Like it?"

"It's good. Which bit is which? I especially like the purple thing."

"The beetroot? You want to make sure you don't get the juice on your clothes." Bart opened his half-eaten sandwich and pointed out the various components. "If you hang around long enough, I'll cook you a proper meal."

Gaia's eyes smiled while her mouth continued to work like a conveyor belt.

"Whoa, slow down. Chew slowly. If you've never eaten before, you should take your time." Another thought flashed through his head. As Gaia washed down her dinner with some fresh orange juice, Bart twisted his body on the couch to face her. She let one arm fall over his leg, her hand resting on his knee.

"Before we go any further, there's a few things I need to tell you, Gaia. About men and women. About sex." He put on his best serious face. *God. I never thought I'd be having this conversation. Thought I'd escaped that one. And certainly not with an attractive woman. Shit.*

"Okay, I'm listening. This sounds like it might be fun."

Lady, you have no idea. The picture of a topless Gaia flashed through his head, an image etched into his brain for eternity. *Concentrate, man.* "Okay. First off …"

It took Bart the better part of an hour to deliver his impromptu birds and bees lecture, stopping for questions and doing his best to impart some of the moral judgments considered normal in New Zealand. He refrained from laughing as the colour slowly deepened in her face. She covered her mouth in horror as the incident with Nigel made itself known in this new context. He held nothing back, trying his best to describe the physical differences, the actions performed for mating and potential conception. At one point, she looked down between her legs and frowned.

He stopped for a few minutes to allow Gaia to visit the bathroom, to make a quick examination of herself. He wished he had a camera handy. The look on her face when she returned was priceless. He hid most of a guilty grin as he explained her bare-breasted display, to which she sat back with her arms wrapped around her self. Overall, she took it well, he thought. Apart from a few pointed questions, she said not a word. At the end of his presentation, she sat there staring at the floor, a hand resting on his knee.

"Sorry. I'm not supposed to do that, am I?" Gaia withdrew the hand. "There's so much to learn. I never knew how complex it was."

"Well, it's all right sometimes. Between us, just relaxing as we are, it's probably fine." The hand returned, much to Bart's pleasure.

She shook her head. "What must Nigel think of me? And you. I stripped off and exposed myself to you. I'm a … what's the term … slut?"

"No. NO. Nothing of the sort. What you did, you did in absolute innocence. No blame or titles can be ascribed to such actions. And you are gorgeous, Gaia. I haven't seen better … toplessness. It was natural. And beautiful. You have nothing to be ashamed of."

"That's kind of you to say, Bart Cooksley, but it appears I have a lot to learn."

God. I hope I'm the one to teach you. Bart's nostrils flared as he considered the prospect.

"Nothing exists except atoms and empty space;
everything else is opinion"

– Democritus

CHAPTER EIGHT

"Okay, Gaia. The equation. I think I worked out what you mean."

Her mouth twitched, her eyes probing, questioning. "You have? Let's hear it."

"Righto. I kept saying it was just an equation, it can't affect anything. But … the fact that I have it written down or even in thought form in my head makes it real, physical. Yes?"

"There is hope for you, Bart Cooksley." She squeezed his knee and grinned.

"So, because it exists in a flawed form, it affects the universal energy flow, ergo, my first prototype. Yes?"

"Very good. You're quite clever. For a human."

"But where is the equation wrong? I've looked at it again since you said it was flawed, but I can't see any error. So, miss smarty pants. Show me."

"Smarty pants? No. I'm sure these are Levi's. It's what most of the girls are wearing. Did I pick the wrong ones?" She swiveled around, trying to read the label on the back pocket.

Bart snorted, covering his mouth with a hand to stop laughing. "No. Levi's are correct. Smarty pants is an offhand phrase we use when addressing someone who appears overly clever. A compliment."

Gaia fixed him with a steely gaze. She pulled one side of her mouth tight and shook her head. "I'm not sure I completely believe you." She stood, her hip brushing against Bart as she stepped around the coffee table to the whiteboard. He wanted to reach out and grab her, pull her into his lap. Instead, he tried to focus on his first love, Science.

Gaia stood looking at the board, her hand tracing the lines of Bart's equation. She stopped three quarters of the way through and moved to the side. "Here. This is the first error." She erased $^2A_a = -u_oJ_a$ and replaced it with $^{D3}A_a = -u_o{}^2J_a{}^{D4}$.

"Whoa. You can't do that! It … hang on … let me think about what you've done."

"You didn't allow for dimensionality, Professor. You need to think beyond the third dimension." She grinned, then continued tracing, her lips moving as she worked through it.

"There's more? Bloody hell. I'm not sure I've got the first bit yet."

"Of course there's more. That mistake was fundamental. It flows through to … here." She rubbed out the second to last set of figures.

Bart jumped to his feet. "Wait just a minute!" he said. "It took me years to come up with that."

Bart's $\Sigma\ m_iv_i$ became $\frac{1}{4}\ \Sigma\ m_iv_i{}^2$. Gaia stood back and smiled. "Does it make sense?"

"No. I don't see it." He frowned, frustrated at his inability to grasp what Gaia had written.

"Come on, Professor. It's basic continuum mechanics. Think. Deep down, you know this. Look."

"All right, all right. Give me a minute." Bart's brain felt like someone had injected him with a memory-loss drug. Numbers and figures tumbled in his head, colliding and veering off in random directions. He blinked his eyes. Had Terra's blows rattled his brain? "Look, Gaia. I need some time with this. Maybe a good night's sleep. By the way. If we get this right, won't it help Terra?"

"In some ways. It will stabilize a lot of the vortexes, but not all of them. Terra can only go back in the past or move spatially with this equation. And in the past, there is no correct formula. It's effectively hard-wired into the device at this point. Even so, the damage she could do is incalculable." Gaia stopped. "I never expected her to make such a sudden, brutal attack. I knew she'd gone rogue, but I didn't realize … "

Bart put comforting arms around her. "We can go after her. She can't get far. The first prototype is underpowered. And there's a bug in the solar power circuit."

"How? She took it …" Gaia seemed to stare right through him. "You said *first* prototype! You've got another? You wonderful, brilliant man." She threw her arms around his neck and kissed him. Not the soft, hesitant kiss of earlier, but a full-blooded, passionate kiss. Bart couldn't stop himself. He returned it, with interest. He forgot who she was, what she was, forgot about chasing inter-dimensional terrorists through time. For those few moments, she was his, one with him. The heat of her petite body filled him. But he knew it wouldn't last, couldn't last.

She let go and glanced away, unable to look him in the eyes. He caressed her face.

"It's all right, Gaia. That was a natural human response to the situation. You feel comfortable with me, and I like you. You're a wonderful kisser, by the way."

"Thank you, Professor." The whispered response nearly failed to reach his ears.

Damn. She won't say my name. She's reverted to the professional hunter. The fixer.

"Professor. Bart. Is the second device ready? Can I, can we, chase her?"

"No. I need to finish assembling it. The parts arrived today." He sighed. "What happens after you find her?"

"I take her and the devices back to Sanctum, to The Source."

"Will I ever see you again?" Bart took her hands. They entwined fingers. Hope swarmed out of him, washing unseen over Gaia. Unseen by Bart.

"No. I have to return. I cannot stay. It would be … contrary to normal procedure."

Silence filled the space between them.

"What about visits? Would you be able to visit me?"

"No, I can't. I shouldn't. Bart, please."

"I like you, Gaia Hassani. I want to see you again."

"No, it's not possible; I'm not human."

"You're more human than most humans I know, Gaia."

"No. That's an end to it. No." She pulled from his grasp, walking a short distance away.

"Well, can I at least help you?"

"No. It's too dangerous. You've seen what she can do. And there's the risk of paradox."

"Then I won't assemble the device for you." Bart folded his arms across his chest and pushed out his chin.

"I could just build it myself, using your thought energy." She pursed her lips, her eyes glowing orange.

"But you won't, will you? We talked about this. You bluster and push me, but you won't. You have too much honor."

She glared at him, her eyes darkening to red. Then they cooled, returning to the natural yellow. "No, I won't. You're right. You win, for now. You can help, but I lead. All right?" The eyes flashed.

"Okay, space lady. I have to get to work. This will take me most of the night. You can crash on my bed if you want."

"Crash?"

"Crash. Fall asleep. Rest."

"All right. But I'll crash on the couch. The bedroom is for … well … you said …anyway, the couch will be fine."

"If you insist, Gaia. It's normal for a gentleman to let a lady sleep in his bed while he sleeps on the couch. Except, I won't be doing much sleeping." He strode to the kitchen and reloaded the coffee machine. "I'm gonna need lots of caffeine. You get some sleep. Recharge those batteries of yours. Regenerate, heal, eh?" Gaia followed him to the kitchen. He ran his fingers over her purple bruises. "Phew. That Terra doesn't like you, does she?"

"No. It was a painful surprise. We are somehow connected, yet separate. There is a memory of her buried beyond my reach."

"I wish you had time to tell me all about it, but I need to work." He hung his head and sighed. "I'll see you in the morning."

He went to pull her to him one more time, but she twisted away. "Please. Don't."

He hid the small surge of anger. "Right. Whatever." It cooled quickly. As the coffee brewed, he retrieved a blanket from the bedroom and tossed it to her. "Sleep well." He poured a cup of coffee, grabbed the box of components from near the front entrance, and closed the door behind him as he headed for the workshop. *Damn women.*

***

Gaia blinked her eyes open. Bart's house echoed silence, broken only by the rhythmic ticking of a clock. Moonlight beamed through the lounge windows, augmented by the pale glow of distant street lights. She rolled over on the couch and stretched. The first thing that caught her eye was the makeshift front door. Bart had secreted a piece of ply board over the shattered door, secured in place by the china cabinet. How he'd managed that without waking her puzzled Gaia. She attributed it to the extended time spent in human form.

She sat up, a small groan escaping her lips as she felt the bruised ribs. A narrow band of light shone under a door at the other end of the room. She smiled. *Bart must still be hard at work.* She tiptoed to the door and eased it open. Bart was leaning forward on his work bench, one cheek on the surface. Gaia snuck up to surprise him. He snorted and moved, head still on the bench. She placed a hand close to him. *Asleep.* Her eyes fell on a shiny disc-like object lying between his head and hand.

Reaching over him, she picked up the object. A quick scan, and she knew. *Bart's new device. Excellent.* She scanned the device, smiling as she confirmed its status. She took a deep breath and placed a hand on either side of Bart's head. Time to expunge his memory. *How much data should I take? All his memories of me? I'm sorry, Bart. I had fun with you. I liked you. Maybe …* She hesitated. Her eyes softened as she looked down at him. Then she shook her head. *Get on with it, Gaia.* Clenching her fists, she tried again. *Curses, Bart Cooksley.*

Gaia swung on her heel and slipped from the room. A small notepad hung next to the phone. She scribbled a note, then poured herself a cold coffee. She looked at the bittersweet concoction and took a large sip. *I'm going to miss all this. Coffee, Bart's sandwiches, Bart.* She felt a pain in her chest. *I have to do this. He'll be mad, but it's safer this way. And I'll come back one more time. Say goodbye.*

Gaia placed her hand on the silver disc, taking a good twenty minutes to understand its workings, its needs. It was ready. Bart had completed it and fallen asleep. Her fingers manipulated the buttons of the disc, information and coordinates filling her head.

"There you are." Gaia laughed, then put her hand over her mouth. Terra was stuck, for now. The first device was slow to recharge. Terra seemed trapped on an island at the entrance to the Mediterranean. *Wow. She's gone back a fair way. 1,500 BC, give or take.* Gaia detected anger. *So, Terra, the device didn't take you where you wanted to go. In your hurry to escape, you popped out the wrong vortex. You didn't spend enough time getting to know your new toy. Ha. Youthful exuberance.*

Gaia shook her head to relax her neck muscles and focused her concentration on Terra. With Terra as an anchor, Gaia figured her own journey would be more accurate. Images whirled around her, destinations from dozens of vortexes. She picked out the one she wanted, waiting for the spinning to stop. The wavering space floated in front of her. Five seconds. *Goodbye Bart.*

Gaia tucked Bart's silver disc into the jacket she'd borrowed from his wardrobe and put her hand into the vortex. She felt stretched. Her feet left the ground. In a flash of light, 2011 vanished behind her. Her last thought made no sense to her.

Kansas just went bye bye, Toto.

CHAPTER NINE

Gaia tucked and rolled as the vortex coughed her out. Gaining her feet, she glanced around at the tall, columned buildings and carved obelisks. Ducking into a narrow alley, she worked her way east, toward a sparkling-blue harbour visible between the marble and granite buildings.

She emerged into a wide avenue that wound its way down the hillside. A panoramic view of clear water opened up before her. Two isthmuses reached out, curving inward at the ends, to form a pincer encircling the spacious, calm harbour. Small and large sailboats of many designs tacked their way to and from the entrance. By their various configurations, Gaia guessed them to be trade vessels and those bearing the ocean's bounty.

Bright Mediterranean sunshine beat down on the bustling port with its myriad of traders. Gaia smiled. She looked forward to being here long enough to marvel at the ancient city's night lights. The beauty and luminance of the advanced crystal radiance was but one of the wonders of Atlantis.

Gaia sighed. *Ah, Atlantis.* She'd been here thrice before, on various assignments. During one of those visits, she made the acquaintance of a high-government official. Now that she knew where she was, assuming the time frame was lineal, she would call on that official for some assistance in her quest.

She swung in a full circle, confirming her bearings. The city was as she remembered, apart from one structure that had been under construction previously. Setting off in a northwesterly direction, she headed for the centre of the city, ignoring the stares at her odd attire from passing citizens in their magnificent, loose-fitting silk robes.

Atlantis had access to the finest trade goods on the planet. Fabric, spices, foodstuffs, and rare gems and metals. All flowed past or through Atlantis. The major port at the gateway of the Mediterranean to the east and the Atlantic ocean to the west, Atlantis provided a safe meeting point for traders from all countries and its own modern naval fleet. No pirate dared sail within two hundred nautical miles of Atlantis. Summary execution awaited those caught. After her first exposure to food at Bart's, the thought of sampling the legendary local seafood set her mouth watering.

"Justice, altay." Gaia signaled a passing peace officer to stop. The man was dressed as most Atlantians, apart from braided epaulets, with the real secret to Atlantis' power and influence hanging on his hip. The portable this man carried was a scaled-down version of the same device fitted on their warships.

Using similar technology as the night lighting, the cannonoda stored energy in a bank of crystals, then released it as required. By fine tuning, the discharge could be set to cause unconsciousness, or blow a hole through a six-foot-thick marble wall. The hull of a pirate's ship could be turned to kindling at three hundred yards.

"Ave, m'lady. Please to state ye name?" The officer cast a suspicious look at Gaia, his eyes taking her in. "From whence do you hail? Your garb is not of a pattern or cloth I have espied. Please identify yourself."

"I am Gaia. I have travelled far to stand in the avenues of your grand city. I need audience with Senator Kalona Juliard, on a matter of some urgency."

At the mention of the senator's name, the guard lost his slightly arrogant stance and waved to Gaia to follow him. "You have not been here for a while, m'lady. It is now Minister Juliard. Thees way. I but take ye to entrance of parliament. I have nay authority, once there." The man stopped at a niche in a public wall and indicated Gaia join him in the recess. Gaia watched, intrigued, as he rearranged a set of crystals into several receptacles. "This odd may feel." He pushed in the last crystal.

A series of lights flashed. Gaia felt a rush similar to falling. Mere seconds later, they stepped out of a similar wall niche in a wide, busy square. "This is also new. How far did we travel, Justice?"

"About six leagues." He pointed to a towering structure across a wide square. "We go there." Gaia stepped out long to match the man's robust pace.

"Who do I advise the minister helped me, Justice?"

"I am Constable Eronius, m'lady. It is but a small thing I do."

"Nonetheless, you have brought me here quickly, and my matter is urgent. "

"I thank thee." They passed through massive columns and into a broad, cool entrance hall. Four guards in ceremonial uniform and a small bald-headed man barred their way. Her escort bowed. "I leave ye here. The minister expects you."

Gaia frowned and turned to him. "How does the minister know of my arrival?"

The officer grinned and tapped a wide bracelet on his wrist. "I messaged his secretary as we walked. He cleared you to pass immediately." His eyes swept over her again. "You must be someone of importance, m'lady, to get audience so quick."

"Not so important to be of note, Constable. This wrist device. This is also new since I last visited. May I?" The officer held up his bracelet for her to inspect. "Hmmm. Interesting. There have been many advances."

"Many, indeed. Our scientists work on a form of propulsion for ships and carts. We live in interesting times. Ave." He saluted and left Gaia with the stone-faced guards. The small bald man cleared his throat. He had the air of someone small in stature but large in importance, at least in his own mind.

Gaia identified herself.

He shrank when he realized she was cleared to meet the minister. He snapped his fingers, and one of the guards stepped forward. "Show this lady to Minister Juliard. Wait there until she is finished, then escort her back." He swept his gaze over Gaia, his disapproval evident in his dour expression. His head dropped back to his parchments, dismissing her.

"What is the minister responsible for, sir?" She stood quietly, glancing about the overly-large room. The man seemed to ignore her at first, continuing to scrawl on a parchment.

The guards suppressed grins as the small man snorted his annoyance. "I thought you said you knew the minister." He huffed. "Minister Juliard is in charge of Scientific Development. Do you have any other questions? I'm a busy man." The curt glare he gave dared Gaia to make any further queries.

"No. Thank you." She shook her head and followed the straight-backed guard as he marched down a labyrinth of wide hallways. He stopped and opened a door for her, placing his fist to his chest in salute. Gaia nodded as he spun on his heel and stood rigid at one side of the door. A stern-looking woman opened a door to the inner room.

"Gaia, Gaia. Come in." The tall, angular-faced Kalona Juliard moved to meet her, arms outstretched. They met in a hug at the centre of the austere rectangular room. "What brings the Watchers to Atlantis this time, my dear?" His twinkling blue eyes matched the azure waters visible through the double doors behind him. The view made up for the lack of decorations in the room. "Nothing too serious, I hope. Please tell me you can stay for dinner this time. You did promise." He smiled as he glided to a nearby chair. "Sit, please. Something to drink?" His thick eyebrows pulled together.

"Water, please," she answered, sitting. "Thank you, Kalona. May I still call you that, Minister?"

Kalona laughed. "Of course. My title has changed, but I'm still the same man." He rang a small bell, summoning the generously-proportioned woman who'd ushered her in. "Water, please, Ms. Faris. And some spritzer." He winked at Gaia. "So tell me, what brings you here?"

Gaia fixed Kalona with a firm stare. "I'm sorry to say I'm here pursuing a dangerous criminal."

"Oh." He circled a large statue, stopping with his arm draped over the shoulder. He scratched his chin thoughtfully with his free hand. "That's unusual for you. What has he done?"

"She. Her name is Terra. She ..." Gaia considered what to tell her friend. "She's another Watcher. The elders consider her extremely dangerous." Gaia decided this small lie would convey the urgency of her mission without exposing her to difficult questions.

"A Watcher." Kalona scratched his ear. "Dangerous is hardly a strong enough word, Gaia. Your kind have remarkable abilities." He nodded as his assistant placed glass jugs dripping with condensation on the small table between them. A jar with an ornate silver spout sat to one side.

"Spritzer. Have you ever had any?" He poured them both a glass of chilled water and depressed the top of the spout into each. "Go on, try it." Kalona beamed like a kid with a new toy.

Gaia took a sip and laughed. "Soda. They call this soda in …" She trailed off, remembering the caveats about speaking of the future. "I'm sure yours tastes better, though."

"Thank you. I find it quite delightful. A refreshing, effervescent interlude." He tossed his glass back and sighed. "So. To your criminal. Can I help? We owe you a debt."

"No debt that I recall, Kalona." Gaia tilted her head.

He chuckled. "Of course. You wouldn't know. You recall the crack you opened to let water escape? Once the water finished draining, we sent men to investigate and found a new crystal. It's the source of all the new devices you have seen. An amazing resource that has advanced us a thousand years." His eyes took on a gleam of triumph.

Gaia frowned. She wondered at how the discovery might have shifted an already-biased balance of power in the region. *I hope I did the right thing. Still, there's nothing I can do about it now.* She shrugged and returned to the matter at hand. "I need to capture Terra and the device she carries. This device must come to me, Kalona. It is too dangerous for any earth dweller to possess."

"Yes, yes. I understand. Do you have a picture of this Terra?"

"I can draw you one. We only have twenty-four hours." Gaia put her empty glass on the table.

"I'll get some drawing supplies to you." Kalona rang for his assistant and instructed her to gather the necessary equipment, plus an artist. "Why twenty-four hours?"

"The device Terra has will recharge by then, and she can leave again. I can pursue her, but it will be easier to catch her here, with your help."

"Then I will issue the alert immediately. We can send out a picture when it's ready. I assume this Terra is possibly of pale skin and attired similar to you.

Yes, to both assumptions." Even inside the thick marble of the parliament building, the summer heat was oppressive. Gaia poured herself another drink. "The hand weapons your justices carry?"

"Yes. What of them?"

"Terra can not be approached as a normal person might. I suggest your men shoot on sight. To stun, of course. Once she is unconscious, they can restrain her. They must keep their eyes on her at all times."

"Yes, of course. I'll instruct them so. Anything else?" Kalona held his assistant back from issuing the orders.

"I can't stress enough how important it is that she be restrained and watched. Four men should be enough. Maybe. At least one must have her in sight at all times. You understand what I'm saying?"

"Yes. Watch her at all times." He turned to the door. "Make it so, Ms. Faris. And ask Magister Trombe to pay a visit. If I'm still busy, ask him to wait."

"It is done, Minister." The woman left at a speed that surprised Gaia.

"So. You'll have your drawing supplies in a few moments. I'll find you a room to work in. I have other work to attend to, but I'd consider it a privilege to dine with you later. Hopefully we may have news of the hunt." Kalona flipped through some parchments on his desk. "Tell Ms. Faris to find you a suitable spot. I'll send along all you need." He saluted. "Ave."

"Ave, my friend. Many thanks for your assistance in this delicate matter." Gaia rose and moved to the door. "Oh. There's a serious-looking guard waiting for me outside."

Kalona smiled and followed Gaia out of the office. He issued new instructions for the guard. "He'll guide you to your work room, then return to the entrance. You are free to come and go as you please. Freshen up and meet me at Quiante' on the bay, at the normal dining time. You do remember where it is?" He flashed another of his infectious smiles.

"I do, thank you, Kalona. I'll be there."

Gaia followed her personal guard through more corridors to a comfortable room. A nervous young man with a raft of art supplies awaited her. She made a quick circuit of the room, determining it was fully equipped with everything she might need. She introduced herself to the young man as a tray of water and refreshments arrived.

"Hello, I'm Gaia. Whom do I have the pleasure of addressing?" Her gracious introduction seemed to relax the jittery young man.

"I am Diagrus, m'lady. I hope my renderings will meet with your satisfaction."

"So formal, Diagrus. Relax." She patted a chair next to her. The young man sat, organizing his instruments in front of him. He declined the glass of water she offered.

"We should begin. The Minister would not want me to waste your time."

"It is my time to waste, not his." Gaia smiled, pleased to see the artist smile back.

***

Kalona Juliard stood with his hands linked behind his back, staring out the double doors of his office. A cool breeze had sprung up. With it, flowed the scent of spices and fruit from the harbour. Years past, he might have been out on the clear water of the harbour himself, but there was always so much to do these days.

Life had been good to Kalona the last few years, ever since his team found the new crystal deposit. Within six months, he and a partner had unlocked the secrets of the new asset. It had been a speedy promotion from there. Each new use of the deposit bolstered his standing, his power among the elite of Atlantis.

And now, greater discoveries, greater power sat within reach. He turned to a knock at his door.

"Enter." A tall man of skeletal proportions limped into the room. The cold eyes and somber face of Magister Victor Trombe cast a sinister shadow about the airy space.

"Ave, Minister. You summoned me. I obey."

"Ave, Victor. I have a task that requires your skills and discretion. Are you my man in this?" Kalona fixed the Head of Intelligens with a frosty stare.

"As always, Minister. I am sworn to you."

"Excellent. Knowing you as I do, I'm sure you're already aware of the capture notice out for a foreigner."

A sly grin bent the magister's face. "You are correct in this, Minister. What do you wish done with the woman, this Terra?"

"Nothing other than the instructions already issued." Kalona hid a smile at Victor's bemused look. "She carries a device of some sort with her. It must come to my hands."

"And you wish the other woman, this Gaia, to be kept in the dark about this?"

"Yes. Further, Victor, have her followed. I doubt she will find Terra before we do, but if she does, you may use whatever means you wish to neutralize her. Do we understand each other in this?"

"Yes. It will be as if she never existed. And Terra?"

"Alive, for now. We may need her to show us what this device does." He raised his hand as Victor began to speak. "Yes, I know. It is a risk, all for something I don't even know the use of. But if Gaia warns of its danger to man, then I must possess it. It may prove to be of much use to us."

"It will be as you wish, Minister." Victor turned to leave.

"Victor. Don't underestimate either of these women. They are not what they appear. If mishandled, allowed to escape, they could rend the very earth beneath our feet. Be careful. Oh, and . . . " He handed across a chain necklace with a small crystal attached. "Best you wear this around these women. Just in case. It stops them from reading your aura, your mind. Blocks their ability to tell if you're lying. Ave, Victor."

"Ave, Minister."

Kalona returned his gaze to the harbour. "I'm sorry, Gaia. But opportunities like this don't come to a man twice in a lifetime. Minister of Science is a good position of power."

Absolute ruler of Atlantis and its trade would be far better.

***

It took Diagrus forty-five minutes to complete what Gaia thought was an excellent likeness of Terra. The young man scuttled away to deliver the image to Kalona for distribution. Gaia felt pleased. The Atlantian justice force would surely apprehend Terra within hours. As with Gaia, a woman of Terra's coloring and dress would stand out among the dark-skinned, silk-robed locals.

Gaia availed herself of the free-flowing water that soothed her hot skin and washed away sweat the summer heat had raised. *Such a cultured civilization.* Putting her trust in Kalona, she took a nap on the comfortable couch, positioned next to the double doors leading to a small balcony. The cool sea breeze relaxed her. Thoughts of Bart Cooksley pushed out those of Terra as she dozed.

***

Victor Trombe hastened from the transport pad to join the small group of constables concealed in doorways on Avenue Dulee. A *'psst'* from the shadows halted him mid-street.

A short, squat man disengaged from a dark doorway. "Ave, Magister. We have located the woman. We await your orders."

"Where, Constable?" Victor's watery eyes darted about furtively.

"She browses wares in Alley Truole. Both ends of the passageway are watched."

"Well done, Constable. Hand me your weapon." Spindly fingers reached for the man's side arm.

"Magister?" The constable stood with his hand resting on the weapon.

"I will approach her alone so as not to startle her. Is the weapon set to stun? Hand it across. Now!"

The man reluctantly relinquished the device. "I have it on the lowest setting. You may need to fire more than once if she is strong. What of our men?"

"Have them stand by. If she does try to run, they are to stun her on-sight. No warnings. Be cautious. She is said to be dangerous beyond normal standards."

"Ave, Magister. We obey."

"Once she is unconscious, shackle her with these." He pulled gleaming manacles from a bag he carried.

"These are not our normal ware, Magister." The officer held them up for inspection. "So light."

"Our target is not a normal person. These are made from the space rock we recovered many years ago. A special alloy, of immense strength. A precaution." He bared his teeth in a smile.

"As you wish, Magister. There. She shows herself." The constable pointed out a tall, pale-skinned woman handling brightly-coloured silk fabrics at one of the stalls. The trader gesticulated widely, obviously engaged in serious haggling.

"Excellent. Stay out of sight." Victor tucked the pistol-bearing hand inside his robes and maneuvered through the traders and customers of the small outdoor market. Victor took deep, even breaths to calm his heart as he approached the potentially dangerous foreigner. He stopped on Terra's right-hand side, pointing the compact weapon at her from under his clothing. Terra continued to haggle with the exasperated trader.

"Terra?"

Her head jerked up. She fixed him with strange yellow eyes that sent a chill to the very marrow of his bones. The eyes narrowed, the irises warning of danger as they flashed red. His nerve threatened to abandon him as her gaze tore away his meager valor. Somehow, trembling fingers triggered the pistol.

Terra reeled back, colliding with several traders. Words he did not understand issued from her. Curses, he surmised. She spun and staggered away from her attacker, amidst screams of terror at the sound of the discharging weapon. The trader, robbed of a possible sale, cursed Victor in a tongue he did recognize.

Victor fired again, sending Terra headlong into a fruit cart. She fell to her knees on the cobbled ground, then struggled to stand. Victor fired twice more. Terra toppled forward, her right cheek lying against the cobblestoned street, vacant eyes still exuding menace as they stared in Victor's direction.

The screams of alarm abated, replaced by cautious speculation. Curious onlookers watched as several constables rushed in to secure the still-twitching form of a strange, pale-skinned foreigner. One officer produced the special manacles and locked the woman's hands behind her. Two of the strongest constables hauled the semiconscious Terra to her feet, dragging her to the nearest transport portal.

Victor picked up the bag that had fallen from her shoulder. He released the securing clasp and peered inside. An odd metallic box sat there. *This must be what the minister seeks.* He hastened to the portal. "Altay. Search her."

Expert hands moved over Terra's body, finding only trinkets from the local markets.

"Take her to Intelligens headquarters. Four armed men are to stay with her at all times. Do not remove the shackles unless I personally say so. Understood?"

"Aye, Magister. By your command."

The small cluster of constables vanished through the transport portal with their groggy prisoner. Another three officers quickly followed. Victor looked into the bag again, tapping the metal box. He smiled. The capture had been as simple as any he had performed. Now to inform the minister and then convince this Terra to show them what this device did. By any means necessary.

This was the part of his job he enjoyed the most. He hoped the woman would resist. He smirked. As soon as the minister finished dinner with the other woman, this Gaia, he would take her too. She would be as easy as Terra. Maybe she too carried one of the devices, whatever they were. She would vanish from existence. But only after he'd had his fun with her.

CHAPTER TEN

Bart blinked in the glaring sunlight. A quick glance at his watch told him it was still morning. His neck clicked as he tried to straighten from his position, face down on the hard bench. He yawned, blinked again, and leaned forward to peer into his coffee mug. *Yes.* Cold or not, he felt the need for something to push back the furry sensation in his mouth. *It feels like someone's cat slept in my mouth. Bleh.* He downed the cold dregs.

Bart stood slowly, letting the cricks ease out of his muscles. First order of business: more coffee. Mug in hand, he turned to make his way to the kitchen. Then it struck him. *My god. Gaia's here.* Excitement bumped his heartbeat up a notch. Halfway to the door, he remembered why she was there and grinned. He looked forward to displaying the second device, seeing the look of approval. He felt like a small boy seeking kudos from his mother.

He strode back to the bench and reached for the object of his desire. *What? It was here when I fell asleep.* He shook his head and skirted around the free-standing bench, searching every surface and shelf. *Where the hell... No.* His eyes popped, anger flaring. "She better not have ..."

He ran to the living room and checked the couch. "Damn you, Gaia."

For something claiming not to be human, she had the whole 'use you and toss you aside' thing down pat. "I trusted you, you ... you ..." He couldn't finish the sentence. It wasn't anger that raged unchecked through him, so much as disappointment. "I could have loved you, Gaia Hassani." He threw his mug at the ply wood covering the door. "Damn you." It bounced off and rolled along the floor, intact. "Christ. I can't even do that properly." He stormed into the kitchen, busying himself with a fresh batch of coffee.

He stared at the empty cup next to the equally-empty machine. "You couldn't even leave me some cold coffee. Or a note." He clenched his fists and banged them on the cool, unyielding granite. *I need to do something.* As the coffee maker gurgled, he dragged his neglected wooden kung fu dummy out of a corner and set it up. "Coffee first. Then I'm gonna beat the shit out of you, my wooden friend."

The previous evening's encounter, first with Gaia, then the more serious one with Terra, had been an unpleasant reminder that he'd been neglecting his training. Bart dusted a few cobwebs off the oak dummy, talking to it. "Yes. I've been spending far too many hours on the time machines. Ah, time machines. There. I said it." His attention diverted to the smell of fresh java. "Back shortly, Mr. Wood." He swung his arms over his head to loosen the muscles as he went in search of the promised caffeine fix. "Oh, damn it." He eyed the temporary plywood door. "Job number two: phone the builder, after a workout. Phew. What a weird twenty-four hours. No one will ever believe any of this."

Fueled with strong, fresh coffee, Bart punched, blocked, chopped, and kicked his long-suffering dummy for a full fifty minutes. He used the first few blows on the dummy to work out his frustration with Gaia. Bart stopped and shook his head. He spent the rest of the time imagining the stroppy nineteen-year-old who'd smashed in his front door. It felt good to give Terra a whipping. By the time he finished, he had the added training benefit of refining his footwork, a pool of slippery sweat having pooled on the floor at his feet. He blew the droplets off his upper lip.

Gaia wouldn't leave his head.

Bart mopped up the sweat and moped his way to the shower. He blasted himself with cool water before setting the temperature higher for a thorough lather. By the time he dressed and arrived back in the kitchen, his stomach was growling. "Send me some rations," it demanded. The sandwiches from the previous night were long gone. Two Bart Specials later, he pushed the last crumb down with another cup of coffee. He ducked into the toilet for a quick pee, then grabbed the phone off the wall. It was time to get the door fixed. *Whoa.* After Gaia's info dump, the sudden flash of déjà vu worried him.

As he dialed the number of his builder friend, he glanced over at the carnage Terra had caused. The blood froze in his veins. Goosebumps stood up on his skin. The door was back the way it had been the previous day. Every stick of furniture was back in its place. The damage was gone. It was as if someone had rewound the tape to the day before.

The phone dropped from nerveless fingers. "Oh, shit." *A Paradox. Something in the time continuum has changed. Gaia's failed.* Whatever Terra was doing was beginning to show up, already. The phone started beeping. Bart placed it back in the cradle to silence it. His heart leapt into his throat as he spied the notepad. *Gaia. She did leave a message.* In script worthy of a calligrapher. *You idiot. Oh course she left you a note.*

Guilt washed over him at the thought of his earlier notions. He took the pad down from the wall and laid it delicately on the counter, time paradoxes forgotten for the moment.

Dearest Bart. I'm sorry I had to take the time device and leave without you. It's safer for all concerned. Part of my mission was to wipe your memory of these events, of me, and especially of the device. I tried, but I couldn't do it. The little time I've spent in your company has been enlightening. And fun. I'll try and make one more visit before I return to Sanctum. Live a long and happy life, Bart Cooksley. FYI. You are a wonderful kisser. Gaia.

Bart choked back the emotion that rose in him. The image of her face flashed in his mind, the way her eyes changed colour as she argued with him. *Those eyes. That red hair.* Bart's guts churned. He wanted her back here, in his arms. The other image, of her topless, lingered in the background, pushed aside by the totality of the woman. Even his late wife Rebecca had not had this effect on him. With a sigh, his chin fell to his chest. "Rebecca. I loved you. But you're gone."

"And now Gaia's gone as well." His head came up with a start at the realization of unfolding events. *Gaia's in danger. She's failed to stop Terra. Which means ... oh god. Has Terra hurt or killed her? Can I do anything?* He dragged his feet across to the whiteboard. Gaia's changes remained written there in her neat script. She hadn't tried to erase her presence or his memory. *What can I do?*

Bart looked again at the equation that had so confounded him the night before. *Holy shit. I see it. Oh my god. How did I miss this? But what's the point? I can't do anything with it. Even if I built another device, I can't go back. I don't know how.*

"Yes you do, Bart Cooksley. You've always known. A million years in human form has made you forget. But you know. Search deep inside yourself."

Some of the words were Gaia's from the previous evening. The others sprang from some unknown wellhead inside him. A thread, a weak connection to Gaia. "She must still be alive."

Bart ran from the room, ramming the workshop door open so hard the hinges protested. Lecture notes and plans flew over his shoulder as he rummaged through several cabinets. "Yes. There you are. You little beauty." Picking a few delicate components off the bench for further use, he swept the rest onto the floor and spread his original design plans out. "I can do this. No time for new solar parts. A motorcycle battery will have to do. Should be enough for …" He punched numbers into a calculator. "Four trips. Maybe. Shit, I need parts."

Bart glanced at the Timex Expedition wristwatch Rebecca had bought for his thirty-first birthday. No time to order top-of-the-line electronics. The local Dick Smith Electronics store was open until 6:00pm. *Plenty of time. Buy extras in case. Damn it. I'll have to construct a circuit board from scratch.* He added that to the growing list of parts. He shook his head. This device was going to be way larger than any of the earlier ones. He added a shock-proof case and backpack to his shopping list.

***

Bart started awake. His eyes ached from hours of peering at circuit boards through a magnifying glass. Four hours into the assembly, he'd hit a major snag. Three phone calls later, an ancient 486 computer lay in pieces on the workshop floor. The antique had yielded the ROM chip he needed. Another two hours had gone into reprogramming the chip, which now sat resplendent amongst components ranging in price from two cents to eight hundred dollars. The Saturday sun had set hours before. Running on coffee alone, Bart had fallen asleep at the bench again.

It was time to eat, but he was begrudging of the time required for even this simple task. Gaia needed help. Another phone call solved the problem. Bart reviewed the work so far between mouthfuls of home-delivered takeaway Thai chicken curry and rice. He ran his hand over the rough stubble on his chin. That could wait, too. It was time for a pre-test of the circuits. Pushing the rice carton to one side, he hooked up the motorcycle battery purchased that afternoon and flipped the switch. Bart swore. The acrid smell of electric smoke filled the garage.

A capacitor had blown, taking three diodes with it. "Damn, fuck, and blast." He unsoldered the components and swore again. He'd wired one of the diodes the wrong way and soldered the voltage regulator to the wrong terminal. "Not surprising, Bart," he said to himself. "You bloody wally. Concentrate. Just as well you bought spares." At 2:14am Sunday morning, he tested the circuit again, fingers crossed behind his back. It passed. No wisps of nasty-smelling smoke, no horrid popping sounds as components blew apart. A buzzing from a heat-sinked transistor pack worried him, more so after a quick hit to it silenced the unit. He stripped it off and reassembled the set again. This time, it ran silent.

The only thing that still bothered him was the timer. Based on a quartz clock, by the time he got to that section of the assembly, he realized it was the weak link. The worst kind of Taiwanese component. Any shop remotely capable of supplying a better part was closed for another eight hours. He checked every clock in the house to no avail. The timer would have to stand for now, to be replaced at the first opportunity.

Gaia had been wrong about the first two units. In some respects, the incorrect equation *was* hard-wired into them. The board's ROM chip contained an instruction set based on the equation. If he ever recovered them, the prototypes would have to be reflashed. *Prototypes. I need some sort of name, other than time machine.* He decided 'vortex generator' had a less emotive ring to it.

Bart sat, permanent marker poised over the clear plastic shock-proof case, intent on inscribing VG³. It didn't feel right. He scratched his head. *Ah. If I follow Gaia's thinking, I should name it …yes. Of course.* The pen moved in a precise, structured pattern. Bart stood back and admired his handiwork. He laughed, then twisted and stretched his neck. VG^4 was a good name. *Dimensionally correct. Heck. If Microsoft can jump numbers, why can't I?*

He placed the completed VG^4 and battery into the backpack, sliding closed-density foam under and around the unit, eliminating all movement. "Snug as a bug." Three wires, covered in heat shrink plastic, snaked over the left shoulder strap, terminating in a small hand set. Bart shrugged his aching shoulders into the straps and secured the pack around his waist. *Hmmm. Not bad.* He jogged and jumped on the spot for a moment, then went through a series of kung fu exercises, testing the limits of his body, encumbered as it was with the pack. Bart felt happy with his work. "Good to go. Now what?"

He slipped out of the pack and wandered through the kitchen. A quick check of the room revealed no further changes. Yet. He emptied and reset the coffee machine and spent fifteen minutes under a hot shower, letting the water wash some of the stiffness from his muscles down the drain.

Now all he had to do was make the device work, the way Gaia said it could. The way she used it.

How hard can it be?

CHAPTER ELEVEN

Gaia laughed at another of Minister Juliard's jokes. She could understand why he had risen to power as quickly as he had. The man had an easy, affable manner about him, combined with a quick wit and an astute political nose. He was surely respected, even feared, by his adversaries in the government. Waiters and acquaintances buzzed around him like bees serving the hive's queen.

Gaia stole a moment to survey her sumptuous surroundings. Quiante' had an enviable reputation throughout most of the known world. She and the minister sat on ample cushions at a low table in a raised section of the bustling restaurant. Gaia was sure that anyone but the minister would not have gotten a table here on such short notice. On the way to their table, they passed a queue of at least fifty people waiting for a possible opening.

Gold silk and salmon-colored linen drapes softened the harsh lines of the angular white-washed interior. Once a fish warehouse, the wooden floor and beams had been retained, the floor lime-washed to lighten the colour. Each dining area had it's own cascading hangings at the corners, resembling a four-poster bed Gaia had seen on one of her assignments. Fine silverware, laid with military precision, sat awaiting inspection on polished marble tabletops. Gaia inspected a piece of tableware fired from an extraordinary mix of crushed abalone and oyster shells. She chuckled. The Atlantians had made opulence an art form.

A large lobster, selected moments earlier from that day's catch, arrived steaming to their table. Minister Juliard showed her how to break open the bright orange carapace and scoop out the white flesh. She dipped her fingers in the warm water of a cleansing bowl and picked up another piece, savouring the delicate flavour and texture. Chewing was redundant, the sweet, white flesh yielding to the lightest pressure of her tongue, releasing a delicious salty juice into her mouth. Gaia tittered. She felt like a squirrel with a cheek full of nuts.

She smiled at Kalona self-consciously as she wiped a runaway drip of the butter off her chin. The myriad aromas permeating the broad open space, combined with the subtle assault on her taste buds, threatened to overwhelm Gaia's senses. She sipped on some cold water to clear her mouth a little.

"I see you find our lobster to your liking, Gaia. We have some of the best seafood available in the entire Mediterranean. Tonight we have, for your personal gratification, a wide assortment of local delicacies, both raw and cooked." On cue, a waiter placed two dishes on the table in front of them. "Here we have raw oysters, scallops, mussels, and fish." He scooped an oyster out of its partly-open shell with an odd-shaped spoon and shoveled it into his mouth. "Try the oysters. They are to die for."

"On the other plate, we have cooked seafood, with the same selection as before, plus some shrimp and crumbed cod and oysters cooked in hot olive oil. Personally, I think it's barbaric to coat and cook oysters, but each to their own." He took a sip of golden wine from a fluted crystal glass and let out a satisfied sigh.

Between mouthfuls of oyster and cod, Gaia managed to comment. "Indeed, Kalona. The food is marvelous. I'm sorry I never made time to sample your hospitality on previous visits." She tried the raw oysters first, sliding the first one down whole as she'd seen Kalona do. Then she chewed one gently, savouring the soft texture and salty taste. Finally she tried a cooked one. The crispy coating crunched loudly in her ears. She placed her hand over her mouth to disguise the sound she thought must be audible to every other diner. "I'm sorry to say, I think I prefer the cooked oysters."

Kalona Juliard shook his head. "Oh well. Such is life. I did tell you you'd enjoy dining here. Hopefully your duties will bring you here again in the future." He raised an eyebrow. "Or past."

Gaia ignored the good-natured attempt to get her to talk about her assignments. She knew that, sometime in the future, Atlantis would vanish from existence. It was a secret best kept from prying politicians.

She sniffed the wine, then took a cautious sip. It filled her mouth with a complex of flavours. The warmness as it went down her throat warned of intoxication. She'd seen the effects on others many times and chose to be wary, at least on this occasion. Every time a passing friend or colleague distracted Kalona, she took an even larger drink of water. Even in the minister's gracious company, something told her to keep her wits about her. "What are these flavours I'm tasting?"

"Ah, this is a classic local wine, with hints of apple, citrus, and tropical fruit."

Gaia smiled. Kalona had confirmed what her nose had already told her. All scents she'd encountered over the years, they surprised her in the subtle blend she now tasted.

An odd sensation crept up Gaia's neck. She glanced from her plate to Kalona. He seemed to be watching something over her shoulder. An unsavory-looking man with a cadaverous appearance reflected in the minister's eyes. When the stranger nodded, a slight smile touched Kalona's lips. Picking up his wine glass, he turned his attention back to her.

Gaia felt the other man slip away as quietly as he arrived. She wiped her hands and sat back against the comfortable cushion. "So, Kalona. Any news of Terra?" Kalona's face did not move, but Gaia detected deception in his eyes. Oddly, his aura remained unchanged.

"Nothing yet. We expect to detain her within a few hours. Now that dark is falling, she will seek a place to stay the night, which will be reported to us. Or she'll be even more obvious moving about. Don't you worry, my friend. She and her device will be within our clutches soon." He swiveled his head to respond to a messenger.

An involuntary shiver passed through Gaia at the use of the word *clutches*. It confirmed her suspicions.

Kalona read the short parchment the man carried with him. "This can wait until tomorrow. Be gone." He turned back to Gaia.

The man backed away a short distance, bowing as he went. "Minister, his eminence, the Primus, insisted I return with you."

Kalona threw a hand towel down in annoyance. "This is insufferable. I have a dinner guest, an honored visitor."

Gaia watched the charade with interest. An accomplished politician he may be. *But not an actor.*

"The Primus is aware of your guest, Minister. He summons you, regardless."

"Very well." He pursed his lips and frowned. "My apologies, Gaia. I must leave on matters of the state." He pushed himself upright. "A room has been arranged for you at the Manor. You know it?"

"Yes, thank you. About four streets over."

"I will send someone for you the moment I have news of Terra. A guard will walk you to the hotel. It is not safe for you to be out while the constables continue the hunt. We don't want them shooting you by mistake." They both laughed.

"No. Not on a full stomach." She grinned, pretending to go along with Kalona's story. "I'll stay a while longer. I saw a tray pass earlier, covered in small, beautifully-decorated sweets. If my nose was correct, that is. I think I would like to have a closer look." Gaia patted her stomach and sighed.

"You must mean the dessert tray. It is piled with exquisite morsels designed to tempt those taste buds the seafood missed. Pastries, chokolat, lemon sorbet, mango crush, ice cream, and caramels fit for a king. You may need a carriage to take you to your room. I will have the cart sent immediately. Have fun. I'll see you in the morning, if not before." He flashed his election platform smile and departed.

Gaia picked out the man who was obviously her guard for the evening. He stood stiff and formal near the main entrance. He displayed a nervous energy that she found unsettling. His official epaulets bore a different design than those of the constables.

The mobile tray arrived, and she picked several desserts and savoured small portions of each creation as she pondered her feelings about the situation. The overdose of sugary delights made her feel odd, like she was running at double speed.

So, Kalona is playing a double game. She suspected they had already captured Terra. The minister's ambition drove him to covet the device Terra carried. He could not hope to hide this from Gaia forever. She needed to be wary of an ambush. *How did it come to this? Just who can I trust?* Gaia felt terribly alone. Only one name came to her mind: *Bart.*

Gaia rose and made her way to the door. Kalona had taken care of the account, and the restaurant manager waved her on. She complimented the man on the restaurant's fare and staggered to the door, feeling full. *I hope any attack doesn't involve too much running.* The guard stepped in beside her as she entered the street. *What form might an attack take?* Probably one or two men with stun guns. Maybe even the guard. She pushed her sugar-hyped senses outward, intuiting any sudden changes in the energy around her.

She didn't have to wait long. The cadaverous-looking man she'd seen reflected in Kalona's eyes appeared about a block ahead, walking toward her, one arm buried inside his robe.

Good. Up close and personal. No running. That worked for Gaia. She knew from experience that it was typical of most people to glance down at their weapon just before the attack. That would show her when to move.

The man looked surprisingly relaxed as he neared. *He's done this before.* Ten paces. Her guard stiffened. His breathing changed. His step faltered.

Gaia suppressed a grin. The guard's tell was obvious. His hand moved to rest on the pistol hanging from his belt. *Any second.*

Two feet from Gaia, the walking cadaver's arm swept up. She slid one foot forward, pivoting on the other, steel-like fingers grasping the gun hand. Her momentum pulled the pistol past her as it discharged, the shock wave hitting her unfortunate guard. He buckled at the knees, his pistol dropping from nerveless fingers.

With her assailant off balance, Gaia reversed direction, spinning behind the man, taking his arm with her. His scream joined a loud crack as one of his forearm bones broke. The shriek and crunch mingled in one hideous concerto, resounding off the surrounding marble walls. The cadaver's pistol clattered to the cobblestones. She released her grip and kicked the man behind the knee, dropping him to the ground.

Gaia seized the whimpering man by the hair, banging his face into the cobblestones. She pulled the now-bloody face upright again. "Who ordered this?"

The man spat at her feet.

There would be only a few seconds before the commotion alerted help. Others would come. "Don't make me hurt you. Speak up"

He remained sullenly silent

"Right then. Remember, you made me do this to you." She grasped the broken forearm and squeezed. The man's eyes popped, his ashen face breaking into a sweat. His mouth flapped, but no sound escaped. She released her grip. "Tell me what I want to know. Or I'll break the other one."

"I'll see you dead, cunnis. Dead! You hear me? Dead." The man gasped.

Voices called out. "Magister, we come."

A few minutes. That's all I need. Gaia cursed. There was no time for further interrogation. A whistle sounded nearby. In frustration, she kicked him in the groin and took off running. A glance back revealed the magister curled up in a ball. Passing a small balcony, she leapt high in the air, grasped the balustrade, and hauled herself up. With the added weight of the local seafood, it was a lot harder than she was used to. She belched, feeling instant relief. Lying flat in the half dark, she watched as armed men materialized from darkened streets, confirming to Gaia the breadth of Kalona Juliard's duplicity. People swarmed onto balconies to see what the ruckus was about.

Gaia slunk behind a flapping drape as a small man with round spectacles emerged from double doors and peered over the edge of her balcony. Voices called out. Men ran in all directions. Someone called out for a physician, another for Gaia.

The voice of a chief constable boomed out, amplified by the walls. "Good people of Atlantis. A dangerous fugitive has attacked the magister. She bears the white skin of a foreigner and red hair. Have any of you seen her? Search your homes. Call out if you see her."

With a snort, the small man adjusted his glasses and turned to go back in the house. He froze, staring at Gaia's shoes poking out from beneath the drape. He turned his head to glance down the street and then back to her.

Gaia watched through a narrow split in the drape, her breath held tight in her chest.

"Show yourself." He spoke in a quiet but commanding voice.

Gaia pulled the drape aside, her eyes pleading with the man to remain quiet.

He examined her over the top of his glasses. "Did you really attack the magister? You look too small."

"Yes, I did. He attempted to ambush me, then declined to offer up the information I sought." Gaia remained obscured behind the curtain.

"Humph. 'Bout time someone mugged him. He's a low-life lickspittle, an ulcer on the soft belly of Atlantis." He looked back over the balcony and called out. "You down there."

Gaia's chest constricted with fear.

The small man surprised her. "Keep the noise down. Some people sleep early. Go on. On your way."

Gaia heard a muted grumbling.

"Don't backchat me, Constable. I'll see you on charges."

"Sorry, Senator. My apologies."

"Well, keep a civil tongue in your head no matter what citizen you address." The senator looked up the alleyway, then back to the unseen voice below. "What happened?"

"Someone broke the magister's arm and escaped with his weapon."

"They sound dangerous, indeed. How many of them, did you say?" The senator snickered.

"Just one woman, Senator. She's extremely dangerous. Lock your doors."

"I will, Constable. Good evening."

"Ave, Senator." The sound of sandaled feet receded as the searchers moved away.

"Come inside, maimer of men." He chuckled at his own small joke. "Come. I won't turn you in."

Gaia crawled through the door into a plush but modest-sized apartment.

"I am Senator Willem Campari. You must be Gaia." He smiled at her surprised expression. "I keep an eye on the comings and goings of certain members of the government. Much corruption and power seeking has infiltrated the top layers of our ruling body. It is well known you arrived here today. Not many women with your skin and hair coloring hereabouts."

Gaia stood away from the open window. "Thank you, Senator. It appears I have been betrayed by one I thought a friend."

"Ah, yes. Kalona Juliard. Once a good man. Power has corrupted him. He seeks more. Always more." Campari shook his head and poured a glass of water. "You are trembling, my dear. Are you well? Some water perhaps?"

Gaia waved away the offered drink while keeping watch out the window. "Just shaken. I need to find a … friend. The person I came here seeking."

"Terra? I should imagine Victor has her at Justice Hall."

"Victor? Is that the name of the man who attacked me?"

"Yes. Magister Victor Trombe, head of Intelligens. Toady to Kalona Juliard. A detestable man on his best days." Campari drank the water from his glass and placed it back on the table. "As I said, Victor will have your Terra held at Justice Hall. Humph. Justice. A poor use of the word. Not from Victor. The man is a sadistic pig. I pray he will get his comeuppance one of these days and that I may be there to witness the event."

"Can you tell me where to go, Senator? They don't realize how dangerous Terra is, even without the device she carries."

"Ah. So that's it. Juliard covets this device. The man who would be king. Fool."

"Senator, time is of the essence. Can you tell me how to get there?"

"No, Gaia. I cannot. It is too dangerous. Men search for you everywhere. Victor may be a vile man, but his constables are efficient. They *will* capture you." He smiled. "I can, however, take you there." He held up a hand at her protests. "No one will stop me and a lady of the night." He winked at her. "Here. Put this on." He passed Gaia a long hooded cape with a silk and gold braided sash.

"This is all but the uniform of the Ladies of Leisure. It will make you invisible to the eyes of most." The senator chuckled again. "You are now my private paramour. Discretion is a highly-valued virtue in Atlantis. No one will ask questions." He threw a cloak around his shoulders and opened the door. "Come."

Gaia followed the man outside. The street had quieted from the chaos of fifteen minutes earlier.

"Here. Put your arm around mine. We should appear as a … couple." He took Gaia's arm and smiled. "Hmmm. Pleasing to walk with a woman nearly my own height, for a change. So many amazons about." He stopped and regarded Gaia. "And one so pretty, too. Does an old man's heart good to parade such a beauty on his arm." He pulled her along at a rapid pace, stopping as they reached one of the portals. "A business owned by Kalona won the tender to build all these. The wretched man grows rich on the toil of others. Come." They stepped into the niche.

Gaia tried to learn the working of the device as the senator shuffled the crystals.

"There is …" The two travelers popped out another portal across town. The senator took up the frenetic pace again. "There is talk of larger, more powerful portals to transport goods across town. And even farther afield, to the mainland. Many jobs and trades may be lost. Atlantians grow frightened at these sudden advancements. Too much, too fast. It scares our allies and enemies. Such fear can lead to war. Or rebellion. Of course, only certain individuals benefit from these advances." He tapped the side of his nose and gave a conspiratorial wink.

The senator appeared to have boundless energy for a man of his age and build. He walked and talked with no apparent discomfort. Gaia found herself short of breath trying to keep up with the man. They swung round a corner into a brightly-lit avenue. These were the wondrous lights Gaia wanted to see this visit. They flashed past at a dizzying rate. Gaia slowed, pulling the senator to a halt.

"Is something wrong, my dear?"

"No, Senator. It's just that I promised myself I'd see the Rainbow Bay this trip. Can we stop for a moment?"

"Surely. We should be safe. If we walk up that road a hundred yards, we'll come out next to the lookout. I certainly couldn't deprive a lady of such a treasure."

Gaia followed the energetic senator to the top of a small rise. He heart filled her throat as the lights came into sight.

"Rainbow Bay." The senator seemed to grow six inches with pride. "One of the seven wonders of the modern world."

Gaia stood, mouth agape. Nothing she'd heard prepared her for the sight. The two pincers of the harbour she'd seen by day were lit in a way that made the water of the harbour appear to be phosphorescent, the colours pulsing randomly around the bay and undulating across the water. Like ripples caused by a stone, the colours and patterns moved and bounced off each other, flashing and dimming to no apparent pattern.

"This is the only thing of beauty Juliard's crystal technology has built. Quite something, isn't it?"

"It's incredible. Thank you for bringing me." Gaia sighed. "Guess we better get on with my mission." Reluctantly, she followed the senator back down the road and along several brightly-lit avenues.

"There." The senator slowed, pointing to a dark, brooding building that sat on its own away from the city centre's lighting. "That is Justice Hall. Now what, Gaia? I cannot gain you entrance. And even if I could, it could well lead to your demise."

"Thank you, Senator. I must go alone from here. There may be a way I can enter. I have secrets of my own." Gaia bowed to the senator.

"As do all women, my dear. Travel safe. Return to my apartment if you seek a place to hide." He waved Gaia farewell and departed as quickly as he had arrived.

A strange, foreboding sensation passed over Gaia. She called out before the senator vanished around the corner. "Senator. Don't ask me why, but don't go home. Take a boat away from here as fast as you can go. Do it now."

The man looked at her askance, then nodded. "As you advise, Gaia. So I shall do. Good luck."

CHAPTER TWELVE

Gaia slipped behind one of the many obelisks and inspected the baleful building. She could make out but one entrance, situated at the east end of the structure. A number of guards patrolled there, but none further along. It appeared the Atlantian's had no cause to worry about anyone entering Justice Hall through solid marble walls. Gaia smiled. She surmised they focused their attentions on people trying to escape, not enter.

She made her way to the corner farthest from the entrance, then along the end of the open space, until she moved out of the lit area. The imposing outer wall loomed over her. The last two hundred yards were in darkness, Gaia relying on sparse light spilling across the main open area to guide her. She traced her fingertips along the sand-pitted marble wall. Placing both hands flat on the surface, she closed her eyes, pushing her energy body, her awareness, into the interior of the massive structure.

The energy inside was heavy, oppressive. Many entered, few had left. Atlantis was known for it's benevolence throughout the Mediterranean. This was their dirty little secret. Gaia's mind travelled down sparsely-lit corridors, up and down stairs, searching. Loud voices called to her, drawing her along like a magnet. Terra. Kalona. Others.

Gaia directed her conscious energy to a dark corner of small, high-vaulted, windowless room. Chains, shackles, and other grotesque torture devices she could not identify hung from the ceiling and walls. Four guards lined one wall, their attention riveted on the small huddle of people in the centre. The room stank of stale air, mold, urine, and excrement, apparent to Gaia even in her present pure energy form.

Gaia felt her physical body react to the sights her energy form saw. Victor Trombe, his arm in a sling, stood next to Kalona Juliard, both watching as a third man stroked Terra's flesh with a red-hot iron. She writhed and twisted at the touch, but not a sound left her. The stench of burning flesh overrode all others momentarily. Gaia's body ground its teeth. Seven people, plus Terra in the room. She didn't have the power to deal with them all. Not with the link to Sanctum closed to her.

Victor paced the stone floor. His skeletal body reminded Gaia of a praying mantis with fresh prey. "Come along, Terra. This pain can cease if you just tell us what this device is and how to operate it. Then we will release you."

Victor jerked back as Terra lunged at him. The chains attached to her shackles yanked her backward.

Victor laughed. "No one is coming to your rescue. We can do this all night. Can you?"

Gaia pondered. Why didn't Terra just slip the shackles off? If she were anything like Gaia, she had the ability to escape most devices designed to secure her. Was Terra, like her, susceptible to iron?

Terra looked up, sensing Gaia's presence. She sneered. "Is this your doing?"

Victor spun about, trying to perceive what Terra saw. "Who are you talking to?"

"Gaia. This is her doing."

"Gaia. That gullible fool. She can't help you. It's only a matter of time before we find her." Frowning, he looked around the room again. "Guard, order a sweep of the entire building and the grounds." One of the four guards trotted from the chamber. Victor turned back to Terra. "Once we catch her, she can join you. A happy reunion."

Terra grinned. "Gaia did that to your arm, didn't she?" Terra laughed. "She saw through you, a pimple on the ass of the universe."

Victor pointed to the torturer. "Again."

Gaia closed her eyes, trying to block out the savage image. Something tingled in her mind. *The manacles. There's something special about them. They're stopping Terra from escaping. Interesting.*

"Please, Terra. Tell us what we want to know." The soft, diplomatic voice of Kalona, honed by years of public speaking, begged Terra to comply.

"Very well." Terra pushed herself off the floor. "I need my hands free to show you."

"I don't trust her, Minister." Victor darted off to one side, keeping out of Terra's range.

"We have armed guards here, Victor. She can't escape." Kalona waved the guard closer. "Keep your weapons ready, set to maximum stun. Jailer, unshackle her. Be careful."

Gaia sensed the smile that remained hidden to Terra's tormentors. Even as the jailer pushed Terra face down on the dirty, cold stone floor, the danger signals screamed in Gaia's head. She wanted to call out to warn the Atlantians, but even if she could, would she? These so-called civilized people had tortured Terra. *No.* Gaia wouldn't help if Terra attacked any of them. From her experience, there was only so much Terra could do to these people.

The jailer placed his foot in the middle of Terra's back, pinning her in place while he knocked the rivet out of the shackles. The man leapt back as Terra rose slowly to her feet, rubbing the red welts on her wrists.

Gaia's sense of danger increased. Terra's burns had started to heal the moment the shackles were removed. She had powers beyond those Gaia possessed. *My best chance to take Terra is gone.*

The fourth guard returned and joined the others in a semi circle, weapons trained on Terra. Kalona retrieved Terra's metal tin and stood in front of her, holding it. Terra's pale face and long hair dripped sweat from the shock her body had withstood. Neither Kalona or Victor seemed to notice or care. Their eager, expectant gazes were fixed on the tin. Terra stepped hesitantly forward to take it.

"No," Kalona said, pulling it out of her grasp. He moved it inches closer. "I will keep my hand on this device at all times. Show me what it does." Victor nodded, appearing to approve Kalona's cautious approach.

Terra smiled and folded her arms. "No. I'm free now. Time for you to pay the price of your folly."

Kalona snatched the tin to his chest. "Shoot her! Shoot her!" he screamed.

Terra unfolded her arms and pushed her palms out, facing her tormentors. The four guards fired as one. Terra stood there grinning. Nothing had happened. No bolts of energy, no inert prisoner on the floor. The guards checked their weapons, then tried again. Nothing.

"Get her. Hold her down!" Kalona screeched, backing toward the door.

Gaia could smell his fear. It oozed out of him like foul-smelling sweat.

The guards rushed forward, holstering their ineffective weapons, fingers and arms extended to pull this enemy of the state to the floor. Terra made a small sideways motion with her hands. Behind her, the coals of the fire used to heat the irons glowed white hot. Flames lifted out of the brazier and funneled around either side of her, forming a super-heated barrier between her and the guards.

She blew a short breath, fanning the flames. They expanded outward, consuming the four hapless men in an instant. Though physically outside the ominous building, Gaia heard the agonized screams of the men as the furnace-like flames reduced them to charred skeletons within seconds.

Kalona and his cronies almost made it to the door. It swung shut in their faces with a resounding crash. They tugged with all their might as Terra remained in her spot, whistling an unrecognizable tune.

She rubbed her wrists again, erasing the last of the welts. "Just where do you think you're going? How rude. We haven't finished our little tea party yet. I thought you Atlantians had better manners."

Kalona fell to his knees, retching at the overpowering stench of burnt flesh. Victor continued to bang on the door, calling for help.

Terra's flames receded. She stepped over the smouldering, crackling remains. "You." She pointed her finger at the torturer, then crooked it. "Come here, you." The man clawed at the wall, trying to resist the force that tugged him back to lie whimpering at her feet.

Her eyes blazed with anger. "You want to torture someone? I'll show you how it's done." She grabbed the man's hair and dragged him to the simmering brazier. His strength was no match for hers as she pushed the side of his face against the hot steel. Terra grinned as the man burnt his hands trying to push his melting face away. She released him for a moment. "I guess I should turn the other cheek." She rammed the other side of his face into the brazier, placing a foot on his knees to stop him flailing about. She let him go again and turned her back on him.

"Hmmm. Who next?" Terra advanced on Victor. "I despise men who ambush women. Something special for you, I think." She sidestepped deftly and held out her hand. The still-smoldering torturer let out an anguished cry as Terra snatched the hot poker from his trembling hand. "Thank you. Just what I wanted." She glanced sideways at him. "Nice try. Now wait your turn. I haven't finished with you."

She patted the man affectionately on the face, educing a mind-numbing scream as pieces of burnt flesh detached at her touch. The man fell to the ground, a quivering, whimpering wreck. "Don't blubber. I wanted to show you how to torture." She kicked him. "Pay attention. Have you ever seen what happens if you poke one of these ..." She indicated the glowing, thirty-inch-long poker. "... up someone's fundament?"

Victor visibly blanched, his eyes on stalks. He tried to move, but an invisible grip held him tight. Terra rotated a finger, drawing Victor toward a device to one side. Looking much like the typical punishment stocks seen in villages, it had the usual three holes for head and hands cut from heavy timber, except it was set lower, forcing the victim to bend further.

Victor struggled in vain as his body was bent forward. Terra clamped the top of the stock-like device closed, pinning Victor. Walking behind him, she lifted his robe, exposing his buttocks. "This might hurt a smidgen, Victor. Payback for all the suffering I'm sure you've inflicted on innocents over the years." Terra thrust the poker forward at its soft, puckered target.

Kalona's cries were barely audible behind Victor's blood-curdling shriek.

Gaia could take no more. Her conscious form snatched her back to the relative calm and safety of her physical body. She'd stayed, in the hope of finding a way to recapture Terra. But Terra had far too much power. Gaia was at a loss to explain this.

Voices reached her from the dark. *The guards.* She'd forgotten they had been ordered to search the grounds. She could make them out only as shadows against the backlighting. *Three of them.* One huge brutish shape and two smaller. They didn't know it yet, but their line of approach had Gaia pinned in the corner. One of them, the biggest, carried a longer, shoulder-fired version of their pistols.

She hunkered down in the corner, planning her escape. Her best option would be to wait until the men were nearly on her, as far into the dark as they could go, then release a blinding pulse of light. She could flash out of there while their night vision recovered.

The guards stopped and stared toward the building, perhaps sensing a presence.

Gaia bit her lip as one of the searchers pointed. The man with the shoulder weapon raised it, moving the gun from side to side, as he sought out what his companion had seen. The weapon swung back toward Gaia and fixed on her.

"Come forward with ye hands in the air, or I fire 'pon ye."

Gaia considered her meager options. The three men fanned out, weakening her position further.

"Now! Do nay test ma patience. Move!"

Gaia cursed silently and stood up from her crouch. Slowly, so as not to risk drawing fire from the searcher's weapons, she moved toward them.

"Aye. 'Tis the red-haired woman the Magister seeks." The men spoke excitedly amongst themselves. "'Twill be a bounteous reward we doth share for this capture." They laughed. Two of the men moved toward her, brandishing a set of shackles, as the largest of their group covered them with the shoulder weapon. Their grins vanished as the ground began to tremble.

Gaia staggered as the ground pushed upward, hurtling her to the shattered cobblestones. Bits of masonry tumbled off the top of the structure. Some crashed to the ground whole, others exploded into bits as they struck the hard courtyard.

Like Gaia, the guards ran on unsteady feet, as far as they could get from the crumbling building.

The earthquake gained in magnitude, spreading out from its epicenter at the Justice Hall. Gaia heard panicked voices and screams of terror as roofing tiles cascaded into the streets of Altantis. The obelisks went next, swaying to and fro like metronomes, before succumbing to gravity and toppling. Their falls added to the shaking ground. Masonry became lethal missiles hurled long distances.

Gaia tried to find a safe location to hide, but no one spot seemed any safer than the next. The ground swayed and heaved, making walking impossible. Cracks too wide to jump across appeared as the ground split, one side pushing skyward. The massive columns supporting the front of many buildings began to crack or fall; roofs caved. The lighting dimmed as the illuminating crystals cracked and broke, adding their razor-edged shards to the airborne mayhem.

Gaia could not see beyond the large courtyard she occupied, but the screaming of the populace told her all she needed to know. The whiter shade of the glowing crystals was replaced by the orange glow of hungry fires. Atlantis was crumbling, returning to the earth from whence it came. She knew this event had already come to pass in Bart's time, but she'd never suspected Terra might be responsible, or that she possessed the power to do so. Her soul was equally terrified and sickened by the needless slaughter of innocents. This wasn't their fault. It was Victor's and Kalona's. *And maybe mine. If only I had captured Terra …*

An ominous, primal sound caught her ear. The few people who'd found their way to the courtyard cast their gaze to the east, toward the tall peak of Atlantia. Even in the semi-lit darkness, Gaia could see the fear in their faces. For the first time in recorded history, Atlantia was erupting. In that instant, she prayed the helpful senator had taken her advice and was speeding out of the harbour to safety.

The entire mount appeared to be growing, swelling. Gaia had seen a similar fearsome phenomena once before, on another assignment. A place called Mount St. Helens in the USA. She harboured no hope for the populace of Atlantis. The orange-red glow of several lava flows showed through the dense ash spewing forth from the broken mountaintop. Suffocating ash, carried by wind, began covering the courtyard like grey snow.

Gaia glanced to her left. The wall of Justice Hall bowed, then exploded outward, raining lethal debris and creating a gaping hole in the side of the once-impenetrable structure. Suffocating dust and ash filled the air, irritating her nose and burning her eyes. Rubbing only made the stinging worse. She drew her borrowed cape tight around her head and mouth. Through the billowing dust, something moved. Gaia squinted through blurred vision.

Terra.

She strode from the cavernous breach with a casual air, brushing dust off with a look of disdain. Gaia's stomach churned at the thought of what she might have done to Kalona before she left.

Terra's voice carried to her over the devastation taking place. "Ah, Gaia. I see you stayed for the show. That was a mistake of earth-shattering proportions." Terra began laughing hysterically at her own perverted humor. She turned and pointed at Atlantia.

Gaia lost her footing as the ground lifted. An orange plume spewed skyward from the mountain. Hundreds of red-hot projectiles arced from the centre and began their destructive descent toward the city.

"Terra, don't do this. You've had your revenge. The people don't deserve this."

"Yes, they do. They benefited from the rape of the earth that supplies their technology. They turned a blind eye to the tactics of their leaders." Terra stopped for a moment, as if gathering power to her. Her arms shot out, her fists closing. She pulled the clenched fists toward her, willing the mount to respond to her command.

The swelling mountainside split asunder, responding to Terra's force.

How has Terra done this? Where did such power come from? Atlantis had about sixty seconds of life left in it, as millions of tons of lava, rock, and ash were released in one massive, devastating explosion.

Gaia flinched. The largest of the guards sprawled on the ground at her feet with a ghastly gurgling sound. A moment ago, he had been running for his life through the choking, blinding grey ash. Now he lay dead, the body smashed and burned by a lava bomb from a vengeful Atlantia.

Terra's maniacal laughter reached out from the gloom. "You see, Gaia? It's all so simple. These demonstrations of power are necessary every now and then. This one all the more so, as a vessel to rid myself of your annoying interference. I was wondering how you got here, seeing as the veil is closed for business. But I suspect the professor supplied a method."

Anger welled in Gaia. She recoiled as an exploding lava bomb showered her with sparks.

"Oooo. That one was close. Nearly got you. You know all these deaths are your fault. I was planning a small shake, but a nice big eruption will suit perfectly to entomb your crispy remains for an eternity."

Gaia fell to the ground, shaken off her feet as the earth heaved. A pressure wave rolled over her. Through the darkness of the falling ash, she made out the bright orange-red flash of the nearby volcano. She shuddered. No one on this island would survive the lava and ash billowing out what was left of the top of the crater. Unable to stand on the unsteady ground, she knelt and pulled Bart's small disc from the inside pocket of her jacket. She couldn't stop Terra this time, but she could escape, follow her, and try again.

Her hand clutched the small device tight, willing it to life. There was no response. The laughter came from the gloom one last time.

"So that's how you got here. I can feel it, even through all this muck. If your toy works anything like mine, there's a small fatal flaw you might have missed. I nearly did. But I've had time to play with mine. Ha ha. Someone went and changed the calendar on you. Did you recalibrate to allow for the change? Shouldn't take more than about … oh … sixty seconds. Such a shame. So close. I better be off, before that cloud of super-heated ash reaches us in fifteen seconds."

Gaia frantically scanned her device for the flaw Terra spoke of.

"That's the spirit. Try. Ten seconds left before you fry. What would your Bart call it? Oh, yes. A pyroclastic flow. That's gotta hurt. You could try that 'flash' trick of yours. Won't be fast enough, though. And after the flow, this entire cesspit will sink into the ocean. No one will ever see it again. Let this be a lesson to anyone who fucks with me. Goodbye, Gaia. I'd say it was great to meet you, but …"

A pulse of light from out of the gloom indicated Terra's departure. Gaia's fingers shook as she pushed buttons and received feedback. Terra was correct. She needed to reset the device to allow for the time zone. Somewhere in the future, some scientist had added ten days to the Julian calendar she was working with. Some error in early timekeeping had been corrected, and it threw her device out of synch.

Easy to fix, if I had sixty seconds. Gaia could feel the ground shaking harder and deeper as a gigantic freight train of super-heated debris and gas bore down on her and the centre of Atlantis. *Terra's right. No time.* Gaia clutched the device to her chest and fell to the ground. A searing heat ran ahead of the approaching flow. Gaia's robe began to smoke; the ends of her hair singed. Vainly, she pulled the robe tight around her, fingers dancing across the disc.

Oh, Bart. I wish …

***

"C'mon, you piece of shit!" Bart screamed. The whining of capacitors reached a crescendo, and a red light flashed on the console of the VG^4. *Ready*. Energy surrounded him, as it had the previous three attempts. Something was different this time. The field pulsed with colours, moved, and reshaped as he stretched out with his consciousness.

Urgency. There was a sense of urgency to the field. *Gaia*. He could hear her, feel her. Images flashed through his mind, unbidden. *Pompeii? Vesuvius?* Terror filled his heart. "Oh, shit. She's in Atlantis." A shimmering wall of clear energy materialized in front of him. "This is new." He visualized Gaia. The wall's surface stilled, acting like a crystal ball. Gaia lay curled up on the ground, ash falling, lava bombs crashing around her, showering her with sparks. *Something else. What is she feeling?* "Oh crap."

He saw the wall of ash and flames. He could feel the heat. *Fuck. A pyroclastic flow.* Gaia was so close. He wanted to reach out and touch her. *Yes, that's it.* He pushed an arm through the glistening wall image, his hand touching her shoulder. *I should be there. What am I missing? Why aren't I passing through the vortex? I can do this. Gaia told me I knew how.* "C'mon, Gaia. Move! Get up and jump out of there!" he screamed at the top of his lungs.

***

Bart? Where are you? Gaia opened her eyes. Silence and darkness surrounded her. She tried to move, banging her head against a hot, hard surface. She coughed. *Smoke*. She pulled Bart's disc out from under the robe, the two small LED's casting weak light. *A cave. I'm in a cave. How is this?* She glanced around and coughed again. Her robe was smouldering, smoke filling the tiny chamber she occupied. *What is this? There's no entrance.*

Gaia reached her fingertips out, touching the surface. "Ow." It was too hot for bare skin. Another smell assailed her. *Rubber*. The soles of her Nikes were melting. She banged her head again as a voice echoed, startling her.

"C'mon, Gaia. Move! Get up and jump out of there!"

Bart. His hand touched her shoulder. "Where are you?"

106

There was no reply. Her lungs gasped for oxygen. *All right. Think. Quick. I'm in a cave.* For a moment, she wondered how Bart had touched her, spoken to her. Where was he now? Then his shouted words galvanized her to action. She returned her attention to the device. The red and green LED's both showed green. *Reset. The future. The calendar correction. Somehow, I'm ten days in the future. I'm* inside *the cooling pyroclastic flow. Did Bart do this?* The enormity of the situation threatened to unnerve her. *Jump. I must jump.* She focused on Terra, feeling for her energy. Smoke from the robe and rubber burned her throat.

An energy field opened around her. She could breathe. There was air in here. *Of course. I'm connected to a different time zone. This air is from there.* Sorrow for the villagers nearby, trapped inside this ash without the benefit of a temporal distortion, filled her heart. All dead. Buried under cubic miles of volcanic debris. If Terra kept her word, the entire island now sat deep under the Mediterranean's blue waters. Man would search for Atlantis for the next 10,000 years.

Light. The now-familiar wall of energy materialized in front of her. Taking a deep breath, she prepared herself for what might come and leaned into it.

Multi-coloured lights flashed past. Green grass rushed up at her. She rolled forward on the soft turf, dizzy for a second.

Fed by fresh air, a portion of her robe burst into flames. She tore it off and swung it against the ground. The fire died, only smoke remaining. A flash of movement caused her to twirl around.

Two people, dressed 15th – 16th century Europe, she guessed, stood there gawking. Another voice, familiar and angry called out.

"Witch! She's a witch. Burn her."

Gaia spun to see Terra pointing at her. The two villagers took up the call. "Witch. She's a witch." Other voices joined in. Within seconds, a dozen people, some armed, appeared from all directions.

Gaia glared at a smirking Terra and ran.

All matter is merely energy condensed to a slow vibration. We are all one consciousness experiencing itself subjectively. There is no such thing as death. Life is a dream and we are the imaginations of ourselves.

- Bill Hicks

CHAPTER THIRTEEN

Gaia tugged at the hard, sturdy, rust-encrusted shackles circling her wrists. They cut into her skin, her blood warm against icy, swollen flesh. She sat back against the cold, damp stone wall and considered her options. There didn't appear to be any. She was trapped. All her powers, her abilities, amounted to nothing. Something in ferrous metal blocked or short-circuited the connection to the universal energy she drew from. Right now, she was shackled and caged in that material. Were it not for the metal holding her, she could vibrate her molecules and simply pass through the wall. Or even, at a greater cost to her energy, reshape into a smaller being and slip through a crack, an opening.

But the shackles, the bars, rendered all that impossible. Her energy, her soul, was trapped, facing the potential of a painful, flesh-searing death. Gaia noted an additional reaction to the metal. Where it touched, her skin was red, swollen, and blistered.

She groaned and recalled how close she'd come to escaping. The villagers had proved no match for her speed, but they cornered her when she took a wrong turn down a blind alley. She'd fought them, looking for any opportunity to flee. As the mob surrounded her outside the blacksmith's, she had seen Terra climb onto a ledge to watch the sport.

It had made Gaia more determined, angry. Two lumbering men had suffered crippling kicks to the groin, and the blacksmith received a broken nose when she elbowed him. Then, the crowd had crushed in around her, and she'd been unable to move. Some brute hit her on the head. The next thing she remembered was the painful bruise, a headache, and the stench of the cell she now resided in.

"Psst."

Gaia spun toward a small, barred exterior window behind and above her. "Who's there? Can you help me?" She started as her awareness touched the owner of the sound.

Terra?

"Help you? No." There was a quiet chuckle. "Why would I do that?"

"Who are you?" Gaia asked, but she already knew.

"It's your old friend, Terra. Come to say hello. Or is that goodbye? Hmmm. Be my last chance, I reckon."

"Why are you doing this?"

"To you? Or why did I take Cooksley's machine?"

"Both." Gaia pulled the shackles a short way up her legs and gingerly touched her raw flesh.

"I had to stop you from interfering in my mission."

"Your mission? What do you want with Bart's device?"

"Bart now, is it? He was a good-looking human, I suppose. If you like that sort of thing. Why do you think I'm here, Gaia? What have they told you?"

"That you sought the device for your own ends. That's all."

Quiet laughter reached through the small barred window. "They held back much. Do you even know who I am?"

Confused, Gaia frowned. "A Watcher. Another like me."

"Ha. I am nothing like you. It's interesting they sent you, given the similarity in our names, the mythical roots they spring from. Think about that for a moment, Gaia Hassani: earth mother and assassin. Odd mix. If you're the earth mother, then what, or who, am I?"

A heavy door banged shut, keys rattled. Gaia tugged at the shackles, trying to pull the chains from the wall.

"'Taint no good to struggle, witch. None hath escaped those chains in three score year. Be silent, or it be the whip for ye. Think ye lucky ye perish by fyre on the morrow. Our lord doth bain the rapin' an torture. Least fo likes o me. 'Tis shame." The loathsome-smelling guard leered, rotten teeth protruding between twisted curled lips. "Aye, 'tis shame. I wager ye a tasty

morsel. It may pass my lord leaves a crumb fo me, aft he take wat he desire."
He scratched at his groin and spat at Gaia's feet, then passed on, cursing his
misfortune.

"Made some new friends, I see." Terra's mocking voice sent waves of
anger through Gaia.

"You still haven't answered my question. Why are you doing this? Why
are you being so cruel?"

"Cruel?!" Terra screamed the word. "Cruel. You don't know the
meaning of the word. I've put up with humanity's cruelty, avarice, and waste
for millennia. They will all get what they deserve when I find the right vortex.
You are a pleasant diversion while I wait . . ." Terra's voice trailed away. "I'll
watch them light that fire tomorrow, to make sure you're no longer a threat,
then I'll leave. Despite what you may have seen in Atlantis, even I don't enjoy
the stench of burning flesh or the screams of agony as the flames blister and
melt the flesh from your bones. And you will scream, Gaia Hassani. Far
longer than those fortunate guards I left in Justice Hall. Their fate was swift.
The fire will scorch the flesh and enter your lungs. Your screaming will stop,
but not the torment. And all this will be as nothing, compared to what I have
endured."

Terra gasped for breath, consumed as she was with her anger and spite.

"But why? Who are you?"

"You still haven't figured it out? I thought you were one of the best they
had." Terra snorted her contempt. "Who? I am Terra."

"I know your name. Who? What are you?"

"I told you. I am Terra. I *am* the earth." Terra's voice rose in volume,
moving toward a crescendo. "Or, more to the point, a being manifested from
all the anger, greed, pollution, and violence - all the evil and dark energy that
has collected on this planet. I have endured man's depravation of my body
since time began. I am cometh to deliver the end. Bart Cooksley's device
released me from the shackles that bound me to this sphere of rock. I am the
end of all that has been and all that might have been."

Gaia's knees buckled, pitching her to the cold, slimy floor. Terra's rant
reverberated in Gaia's ears.

Terra panted like a mad dog, the sound made more frightening by the
high, gleeful undertone.

Gaia searched for words, pushing through her stunned senses. "You're mad. What are you planning to do?"

"Mad? No more so than humanity and its excesses. Plan?" Terra's answering laugh sent a chill through Gaia. "It's simple, really: find the one vortex, the one wormhole that takes me back to the beginning."

"The beginning? You can't mean—?"

"Oh, but I can. And I do. The very beginning. That moment a millisecond before the Void reached critical mass and exploded, starting the spread of matter and primeval ooze outward. Then I have the choice. Let it all start again, fresh, new. Or end it. Back to the Void."

"But that will be the end of you as well." Gaia's mind struggled with the enormity of Terra's intent.

"Yes, but such relief. To finally rest, forever. You like my idea?"

"No. You mustn't. There are so many good people. Not everyone is evil or corrupt."

"Your words are nothing to me. Even so, those who claim to be good turn a blind eye as my body is raped, pillaged. Destroyed. No more. It ends."

The heavy breathing at the window slowed and calmed. Gaia wondered if perhaps Terra had gone.

"I'll see you tomorrow, Gaia. At the so-called trial. You should know they have already built the wood heap and stake. Villagers for miles around have heard of the witch who appeared, in strange garb, smoking, from out of thin air. They've been arriving all afternoon, bringing along wood for the fire. Firewood is a scarce commodity hereabouts. But they bring it nonetheless. They're holding a feast tomorrow, in your honour. The biggest event the village has seen in many years. You're the entertainment. How does it feel to be so important?"

Gaia choked back tears at Terra's taunting voice. Never in her existence had she felt so alone, so wretched. Abandoned in some insignificant corner of medieval Europe. A blip on the radar of Earth's history. Not that there would be any history left when Terra was done. Gaia felt abandoned. *No. I chose this path. I chose to leave Bart Cooksley behind.* Her stomach churned. Somehow, the short time with him, the closeness and stolen kisses, made her fate seem all the more tragic, painful. *But I heard his voice, felt his touch. How? Where is he now?*

"You not talking to me, Gaia? Hmmm, I meant to ask. How did you get here? Did that cute professor help you?"

Gaia clamped her teeth together in anger.

"You will tell me, Gaia. If you don't …"

"You'll what, Terra? Kill me? They plan to do that tomorrow anyway."

"I had more creative ideas in mind. You see, I'm still connected to my energy source. All the darkness and negativity. I can change my form. Maybe I'll change into *you* and go back to that moronic professor you seem to like so much. Take him for a roll in the hay. You understand that, Gaia. Sex. I'll ravish the professor as you, take his penis inside me, take his seed, enter his soul, then dump him in a heap, devastate him. Tear down the few good thoughts he has of you before I move on and destroy it all. Am I getting your attention yet, Gaia?"

"I … how can you be so evil?"

"Just doing what comes naturally to so many humans. I am the product of their evil. They rape me every day. Pour chemicals into my innards while they think no one watches. I watch. They dump their waste in my oceans, suck oil and minerals from my body, drop their bodily filth on my soil. How could I be anything but what I am? So what's it to be? The information I seek? Or your precious Bart's opinion of you?"

Gaia dropped her head in resignation. She curled into a ball against the wall and began to sob.

"I want my answer, you weak-minded fool."

Gaia sucked in the emotions that racked her. "I was able to slipstream on your vortex. It remained open behind you, long enough for me to follow. It's why I emerged out in the open, for all to see." Gaia hung her head. "My device was smashed in the chase."

"If I find out you're lying to me …"

"Why would I risk that? I promise. It's the truth. Leave Bart alone."

"Very well. Not that it will matter. By this time tomorrow, you'll be reduced to an obscene piece of charred flesh. All for the amusement of the local fools. Your soul, your essence, returned to the Hall of Souls, the Guf. Even that will cease to exist when I'm done." Terra chuckled. "Ashes to ashes, dust to dust. Your remains will belong to me. How ironic."

"I'm sorry you have become so blind to beauty that all you see is darkness. I pity you, Terra. I may be about to die, but at least I have experienced love and the splendor of the universe around me."

"How dare you pity me." Terra's anger raged in a flash of red reflecting off the dark stone walls inside Gaia's cell. Terra's anger abated, cooled. Her voice took on that mocking tone. "Time I was off. Must get my beauty sleep. Want to look my best for the big event. Oooo, look. You have a visitor. Seems the local lord has arrived to sit in judgment. I hear talk he likes to, how shall I put this, partake of the pleasures of the flesh with the pretty captives. Maybe he'll offer you a deal. I'm guessing you'll be too high and mighty, your head too full of your Bart Cooksley to consider such a proposition. Chances are he wouldn't keep his word anyway." Terra snickered.

"I almost forgot. Considering where we just came from, I thought it fitting to share a human cliché that admirably covers your predicament: 'out of the frying pan and into the fire'. You two lovebirds have fun."

The sound of Terra's retreating laughter and footsteps was replaced by the ominous approach of heavy boots. The door burst open, the rotten-toothed guard leading the way with a flickering torch.

"Here she be, my lord. Pretty lil thing, no? We dun see no hair like thart round ere much."

"Silence, you oaf. Speak when I speak to you." A pair of thick leather gloves crashed against the guard's shoulder.

Piercing blue eyes peered at Gaia through the bars. There was intelligence and cunning hidden there.

"Why is the prisoner still chained? She be no bigger than a hare. You not be 'fraid of her, jailer?"

"'Fraid? O wisp of a girl? Nay, my lord. But I hear tell she led her captors a merry dance. Fast as that there hare. Dun bloody smithy's nose, and two others fearing to use they manhood ever agin."

"So. Some spirit in the woman. It be the red hair. Fyre in yon soul. Well, fyre may be the doin o' her. Unchain her, jailer, but lock your door." The tall, thin stranger turned to the two men accompanying him. "You two wait outside yon door." They retraced their steps back to the hallway.

The jailer's breath was like a sewage pit. Gaia fought the urge to retch.

With big, calloused hands, he fumbled with the rough-edged shackles. Unable to open it, he dragged it, and her, partway across the floor to better light.

Pain raked the raw skin of Gaia's wrists. She bit back a moan.

The liege lord of the village stormed into the small cell, a short, stout stick swinging in his hand. "You pig. I should have ye flayed."

The jailer grunted as several blows rained on his shoulders.

"You 'ave been too long in my father's service, oaf. His ways be finished. Test not my temper. There be room on thay fyre for likes of you."

Gaia remained sullenly silent as she appraised the slim, well-dressed man. Golden curls tumbled past his shoulders. He would have been handsome, were it not for an overly large, pointed nose and almost feminine lips. He carried himself tall, chin high. A man used to his high station.

The jailer knocked the pin out of the second shackle, releasing Gaia's leg. She tried to scamper away, but he caught her ankle with a speed that surprised her. She turned her head from the stench as he whispered to her.

"Ye play nice with my lord, ye may yet live."

All the while, the tall stranger stood, hands on hips, watching. Gaia spied the small, bone-handled dagger that hung from his hip. He seemed to sense her intent and grinned. Unfastening the holding belt, he tossed the dagger to one of the guards at the end of the short hallway. "Kaint 'ave ye be tryin' to stick me, can we, my lady? Jailer, out."

The vile guard glared at Gaia and slunk away.

"Right out, jailer. This be not for your eyes. Go. I will call, should I need your services." His blonde curls swung outward as he spun back to Gaia. "'Ave ye been fed?"

Gaia looked up from her spot, curled up in a ball by the wall. Hunger gnawed at her, overpowering the churning generated by the knowledge of her fate. She shook her head. *Tomorrow is another day. Someone may yet take pity on me, set me free.* She understood more about the human condition in that one moment than ever before. *Hope.*

"Guard, get ye to tavern. Return with hot food." The guard made a short bow and vanished through the door. "My lady, I am Francis de Guerre, lord and benefactor of the surrounding area. How are you addressed?"

Gaia fought the urge to ignore the man. *He may yet be of use. Escape may still be possible.* "I am Gaia."

Francis' head rocked back. "The earth mother. Surely this is some wicked jest. I ask you again, name thyself."

"I am Gaia. It is my name." She uncoiled and stood, staring defiantly at the man who held sway over her life.

"Then you are bewitched. None may bear that name; it is sacred." Gaia saw his eyes pass from her head to feet and back again; saw the light in his eyes.

"This garb you wear. It ... it shows your form for all to see. Scandalous attire." He licked his lips. "You are beautiful, my lady. Yet even in that beauty, I cannot bring myself to speak the name you claim as yours. I will not risk being bewitched as you are."

Gaia felt his eyes taking in the curve of her breasts, the bare cleavage.

"I will not force myself 'pon you. That was my father's way. But we may strike a bargain. Favour willingly given will stand you well tomorrow." Francis walked a slow circle around her.

Gaia could feel his eyes stripping the clothing from her. "You would let me live, my lord? I could leave?" Her stomach roiled at the idea of what he proposed, but the chance at life was tempting, captivating.

"No. That is beyond my power. I have heard recounted the story of your arrival. That, your odd garb and yellow eyes leave no doubt of the verdict. The whole shire has gathered for the verdict. You be a witch, or are bewitched, and must die. We must purge the demon that possesses you by fyre. In return for your favour, I can offer you the garrote, administered before the fyre is lit. 'Tis a far quicker, less painful way to cast off this flesh and release your soul from torment."

"You would offer this way in return for the favour of bodily pleasure. You are no different from your father. He was honest in that he took what he wanted, did not try to strike a wicked bargain." Gaia's anger flushed her face.

"You dare to speak to me so?" Francis stalked to one corner of the cell, turning to glare at Gaia. "'Tis true I bargain; is but a small thing I ask. You are beautiful. I would have you but that I could. I offer a quick death, free of the agony of fyre."

"You offer little, at no risk to yourself. I will have none of your so-called charity, Francis de Guerre. You say what you ask is but a trifle. It is not so. I have not given myself to another, and I will not to you."

"I risk much. I am lord here, 'tis true. But the people would have their sport with you. They would watch with glee as you scream and beg for death. To interfere with that, to allow the garrote, is to risk their displeasure. Such things have brought down more powerful lords than I."

Gaia pivoted slowly on the spot, holding the man's eyes as he circled her.

"You puzzle me, my lady. You give the appearance of being high born. Your garb, your manner of speech, your refusal to ease your passing." He hesitated, then drew away from Gaia. "You say you be virginal. Eh. The most powerful type of witch. I must beware your spell. I feel it now. The need to have you, to break my vow and take you by force. You be witch, this I see." He moved to the cell door and bellowed. "Guard. My dagger."

"So, you will use force. What of your vow?" Gaia advanced toward him.

Unsheathed dagger in hand, Francis met her halfway. "I will not force myself, but I would see if you bleed, whether you be of this earth." He grasped her arm and pressed the tip of his dagger against the skin. It resisted the pressure for a second, then gave under the sharp edge. Blood welled from the small cut. "So. You be flesh. And flesh will burn."

The guard stood, hand on his sword hilt, as Francis wrenched open the cell door. "You will regret your decision on the morrow, as the flames leap high and tear at your tender flesh." He stopped in the opening, breathing hard. He turned one last time. "My guard will bring you good food. Take this one thing from me. It may well be the last meal you ever taste." He slammed the heavy door. "Jailer, tend the lock."

Gaia watched Francis de Guerre, liege lord of the area, march down the dim corridor. She stumbled back into the corner and curled up in her small ball again. *Damn him. To ask for so much from me for so little in return.* It had made her sick to consider his proposal. For her life, she would have made the horrid sacrifice. But not for so little in return. To die regardless after giving something so precious. No. There was but one man she would have given this gift to. And she'd left him asleep on a workbench in 2011.

Gaia realized now, too late, that she felt love for Bart Cooksley. And now she would never see him again, feel his arms around her. Taste his sweet kiss. See the grin on his face as she told another of her innocent stories of misadventure. *He doesn't even know where I am. Or does he? I saw him, heard him. Didn't I? The only possible means of him reaching me, I stole. Stole. Like some common criminal. How could I betray him like that?*

Gaia pulled her arms tight around her knees and rocked as she awaited the delivery of the promised meal, and pondered her fate.

CHAPTER FOURTEEN

Gaia stood at the edge of a large clearing just outside the village, one of the lord's guards on either side of her. Her shackled hands trembled. The previous night's greasy stew that passed as food in the village did nothing to help her quell the urge to throw up. Her knees felt weak, barely able to support her tiny frame.

"Bring forth the accused," the crier demanded, his voice cutting through the expectant conversation of assembled villagers. An eerie silence fell upon the eager throng. All eyes turned in the direction of an imperious Francis de Guerre, seated on a shaded dais at one end of the broad open space. Necks strained to catch a view of the stranger, this witch from who knew where.

Gaia staggered forward, supported at the elbow by the two guards. It was as if she were watching herself. Men and women alike taunted her, spat at her. Young children clung tightly to their mothers' legs as she passed, their eyes full of awe and fear. Adolescents tugged at her clothing, trying, it seemed, to tear off a small memento. Bart's borrowed jacket spilled its lining out of holes torn and cut by grasping hands.

Some were silent as she passed, others vocal. Some touched her hair. One woman cut a piece off and held it up in front of the jeering crowd. Somewhere in all the noise, Gaia heard wagers being made.

"How long will she scream once the fyre is lit?" Men and women alike gathered around the bookmaker.

"How long will it take her to die?" another offered.

She heard bets being placed that varied between three minutes and two hours. *Two hours?* Her head swam at the horror of it. From the varied opinions she could hear, the time depended on the amount of timber on the fire, how it was laid, and the force of the wind. Her stomach spasmed. Bile filled her mouth. She could hold it no longer. What remained of the meal spewed out her mouth.

The crowd cheered and redoubled their taunting. There was sport to be had with this witch.

"Witches' clothing!" someone screamed. The crowd took up the call. The mob surged forward, pushing the guards aside. Little by little, by blackened fingernail and small dagger, they stripped her garb from her. Only the vest's liner remained, the gortex fabric resisting their best efforts to destroy it. Unable to defend herself or even cover her nudity, Gaia suffered their onslaught.

Screams issued from the crowd as sun glinted off drawn swords. The bright steel swung, striking with the flat edge, for now. But the menace was real. The mob reluctantly withdrew with their prizes. Scratched and bruised, hands still bound behind her, Gaia emerged from the throng, into a small area in front of Francis de Guerre. Patches of her pale, freckled skin showed through blood smeared by a hundred cruel hands, the marks interspersed and joined together by rivulets of blood from dozens of cuts and scratches. She was grateful when the guards threw her to the ground, enabling her to curl up and cover her humiliation.

From the ground, she saw the lord stand. "If anyone dares interfere with these proceedings again, I will order my guards to hack those nearest to death. Do you hear me?" His voice was angry, authoritative. A cowed, uncomfortable silence fell. "You, there. Why do you dare approach?" Gaia heard the guards' shuffling feet, but they did not move toward the intruder.

From the corner of her eye, Gaia could make out a tall stranger in a dark brown, full-length cape. The man's face hid within the shadow cast by the hood, but the voice was strong, commanding, bordering on insolent. The man's right hand held a polished staff, as long as he was tall. A giant, compared to those around him. The crowd edged back, cowed more by this monk than the sword-wielding guards. "Would you interfere with the Lord's work, my liege?"

The lord stared down at the interloper. "I would never think to do so, Priest. Yet you would interfere in mine. Explain yourself." Francis de Guerre sounded all powerful, but Gaia detected hesitation.

"It would seem, my liege, this *is* the Lord's business, as you intend to consign this woman's soul into his care in summary fashion. I merely wish to offer her some modesty until sentence is passed and applied." Gaia felt something rough and scratchy on her skin as the man bent and wrapped a blanket around her.

The crowd roared. "A horse blanket!" Laughter mingled with general conversation, the mood of the villagers lightened, less threatening.

It may have been poorly made and flea infested, but it represented far more than mere covering to Gaia. Someone else cared enough to step forward, to help. Not, it seemed, to halt the proceedings, but one friend, anonymous though they were. Her shaken spirits rallied. She would face these accusers strong and determined. This stranger, this monk, brought steel to her spine. She turned her head, in time to see the man's black leather boots carry him a short distance. *Thank you. Whoever you are.*

"Silence. Hear ye. Hear ye. All those assembled here. The trial of this witch is commenced. Who is the accuser?"

"I be the accuser."

Gaia shivered at the sound of Terra's confident, poisonous, mesmeric voice.

"Step forward and name thyself."

"I be Clare Morgen, merchant from Munich." Terra's lie flowed with the ease of a wide river.

"Speak, Clare Morgen. What be your telling?"

"I be near the village square, the day past, when this witch appeared out of thin air, the smoke of her brimstone still about her. I was wicked scared, I tell you. All saw her garb. 'Tis not natural. There be the devil about her."

The crowd roared for blood. "Burn her! Kill the witch! Burn her! Kill the witch!"

Francis de Guerre regarded Terra with a look Gaia could not fathom. He held his hands up to the crowd, waiting for them to quiet. "Clare Morgen, ye not be of these parts. Your word is not bond. Be there other witnesses to these events?"

"Aye, my lord." A man and woman stepped to the edge of the crowd, awaiting permission to advance. Smoke from small cooking fires obscured them for a moment, before the breeze forced a parting in the greasy fumes. The man rubbed his eyes, blinking.

"Come forth, Harold of Lombe. Your bondswoman with you." The two made their way warily, standing in front of the dais a short distance from Gaia. One look from her was enough for them to step back.

"Be not afraid. The witch is restrained. Speak ye. Doth this Clare Morgen speak the truth?"

"Aye, my lord. It is as she sayith. The witch there …" He pointed toward Gaia. "She was not there one breath, then the next breath, was. 'Tis magic, I tell ye. Smoke issued from her. I thought maybe a dragon at first. So frightened, was I."

The mob swelled forward at this new evidence. A wave of Francis' hand saw the four swordsmen advance on them. To his left, a solitary archer nocked an arrow to his string. The message was clear. The front of the mob retreated, compressing those behind. The catcalls and taunts quieted to a sullen, ill-humored muttering.

"What of you, woman? What say you?"

Harold of Lombe's companion looked at Gaia, then at the ground.

"Well, speak up." Francis pointed to one of his guards, who moved toward the woman.

"I seen it, my lord. I dint wan say ill of her, but I seen it. 'Twas the divil's work. All smoke and brimstone. She appear from nuttin." The woman went back to staring at the ground.

"Any other witnesses?" There was silence. "How was she captured?" A dozen voices spoke as one. Gaia listened as varying accounts of the chase were offered. The only areas they all agreed on was that she'd been cornered in the smithy's shed, and a number of villagers had suffered minor injuries in their brave arrest of the witch. Every farmer, villager, and serf for ten miles now claimed credit for her capture. Francis de Guerre shook his head and rubbed his stubbled chin.

He stood and stepped off the dais, his guards forming a loose circle around him as he strode the three steps to Gaia. He crouched in front of her and whispered. "You will now be given the opportunity to tell your story. If you admit to being a witch, I can still allow the use of the garrote to ease your passing. Please. Take this opportunity. I could not bear to see one as beautiful

122

and seemingly well-bred to suffer the fyre. You must admit your crime. Without this confession, the crowd will demand death by fyre. I can appeal to their Christian senses, if you repent."

Gaia saw pain in his eyes, felt the torture of the sentence he had no real option but to carry out.

"Please, my lady. I have never had to pass such a dire sentence before."

De Guerre stepped back and motioned to one of his guards. The man slipped his hand under her elbow and hoisted her upright. With her hands still shackled behind her, the blanket slipped from her shoulders. She saw Francis' reaction to her nakedness, felt his arousal.

A lump moved in his throat, his eyes flicking to something over her shoulder. There was an almost imperceptible nod of his head, then the monk wrapped the coarse blanket about her once again. She wished she could thank the man for this small kindness amongst so much cruelty, but when she reached out to him with her mind, it was blocked. Then he was gone again.

"So, witch. Speak now. Admit thy guilt. Save your immortal soul from an eternity of fyre." De Guerre's eyes pleaded with her.

She shook her head. "I am no witch. I am unjustly accused by a mortal enemy who would see me dead." She tilted her head toward Terra.

"Lies! Lies!" the crowd screamed. "Beware the witch's spell!"

"This may be so, my lady," Francis intoned. "But others saw you. People I know. They have no need to falsely accuse you." In a quieter voice, "Please. Admit."

"I will not. I am no witch. I am Gaia, saviour of souls."

The crowd hushed at the speaking of her name, their sudden intake of breath seemingly simultaneous. A moment's stunned silence was followed by frenzied pushing, stopping only at the sharp swords of Francis' men.

"She's a witch," the crowd roared. "She claims the name of the earth mother. Burn her! Burn her!"

Francis de Guerre's mouth set in a grim line. He turned on his heal and climbed back to the dais. Once again, he raised his hands, silencing the crowd.

Gaia watched the man take a deep breath, then another. "After due deliberation in the matter before me, I find this woman ..." He hesitated and took one more breath. "guilty of ..."

The din of the crowd rose.

" … the practice of witchcraft. She is to suffer death by fyre. Guards, carry out the sentence."

Gaia's knees went weak. With strength she believed had long deserted her, she forced herself to remain standing. Two of the guards closed in on either side of her. They tossed her blanket aside. With rough hands, they grasped her arms and pulled her through the crowd, toward the waiting stake.

She ground her teeth together, trying to fight off the nausea that threatened to render her body useless. The guards pushed forward as men and women alike groped her naked breasts and buttocks, rubbed their filthy fingers between her legs, and spat vulgar remarks. Her breath came in short, desperate gasps. She fought fear and tears of humiliation. Her legs went rubbery. The guards half carried, half dragged her.

The crowd pulled back, many taking up the viewing spots they had staked out earlier. A couple of territorial disputes broke out. Some began to retrieve food and drink from baskets. The atmosphere changed from one of near riot to that of a carnival. Musicians took up a lively tune. The bright sun of early morning gave way to clouds. A breeze picked up from the south.

Gaia knew rain would be too much to hope for. The wind would fan the flames. Perhaps that would speed up the process. She dry retched.

She was filled with disgust at the festival unfolding around her. Men ran about taking last-minute wagers. *These people, these humans.* They would sit there, eating, drinking, and joking as she writhed, screamed in agony, and slowly died. They'd brought their children to enjoy the spectacle.

Perhaps Terra has a point.

Gaia couldn't help thinking, if this had been twenty-first century New York, someone would be selling souvenir t-shirts and polish hotdogs. Her mind flashed to her last New York assignment. If it weren't for her current predicament, she might have laughed at the absurdity of the notion. *I never took the time to try one of those sausages.*

For a brief moment, she thought there might be a chance of escape. The guards knocked the rivets from the shackles and pulled off the remains of her vest. The vest was tossed at her feet as strong hands lifted her high onto the pyre and secured her to the stake, first with leather thongs, then with a chain.

Metal chains. A sob rose in her throat. Her one chance of escape was gone. Even tied to the stake, her hands cruelly lashed around the rough wooden post behind her, she shook uncontrollably. A knot, were a branch had once grown, protruded into her left kidney. She searched the crowd with the futile hope of finding help. *Someone. Anyone.*

Terra stood some distance away, her face no longer smiling. The look was more serious now, perhaps even sympathetic. The eyes of the men ravished Gaia's naked body, their leers and suggestions sickening. Nothing in her experience had prepared her for the abject loneliness and terror she felt.

The guards withdrew to where Francis sat staring at the ground beneath his feet. This was not, it seemed, a cherished part of being Lord.

Gaia sensed a presence. She turned her head to the left. A few feet from the wood pile, stood the hooded monk, watching her. Silent, unmoving, apart from a hand that made the shape of a cross. She imagined he was pitying her fate, praying for her soul. She moved her lips. "Thank you."

He nodded, continuing his benediction.

As much as she wanted this day to never end, for time to freeze and nothing to happen, the waiting ate at her insides. A small amount of bile found it's way into her mouth. She spat, much to the joy of the crowd. *What are they waiting for?*

Most eyes were turned toward Francis de Guerre. It was he who had the final word, a small signal of the hand. The raucous sounds of the crowd diminished, as if someone slowly turned down the volume. The silence was a knife turning in her stomach. Everyone, with the exception of Gaia, seemed to be ready, an air of expectation hanging limp, a flag awaiting a breeze.

And the breeze blew. A subtle, almost missed gesture of the hand from de Guerre. A murmur moved through the crowd. A burly man stooped over a small campfire, an unlit torch in his hand. As the torch blazed to life, so did the crowd. The man looked at Francis de Guerre, making sure. The hand gesture was more noticeable this time, if dismissive. The crowd grew silent again as the man, flaming torch held high, made his way the twenty-five yards toward Gaia.

He stopped short, frowning, as a small girl ran out and placed a flower at Gaia's feet. The child's innocent smile released the tears Gaia had fought so hard to contain. Images of Bart Cooksley flooded her mind.

In turn, Gaia's tears fed the crowd. Some grunted their disgust, as others held up hands for the money from a wager won. The small girl stood, her smile fading, sadness in her eyes. Even at her age, she seemed to know what was coming. Gaia's misty eyes found Terra. Her implacable, heartless enemy turned away, preparing to leave, her attention focused on Bart Cooksley's device.

Frances de Guerre stood and left the dais. Glancing over his shoulder, he frowned. His lips pursed and twitched, his shoulders hitched. He inhaled deeply. Turning to his left, he signaled a green-shirted man who leaned against a tree. Gaia had not noticed him earlier. He jumped and nodded, striding long, fast paces toward the stake.

The crowd became restless. A jeer rang out, then another. The man with the torch looked puzzled, his head swiveling to catch de Guerre's eye. The boos grew louder. People rose to their feet. They stomped thunder into the ground beneath them.

Then Gaia saw it. A thin piece of leather strap in the approaching man's hands. *A garrote*. Sobs wracked her body. She was grateful for the mercy shown, but sad for an end come so soon.

More of the crowd were on their feet now, angry at being robbed of their lingering sport. Gaia's end would come too soon for most. A rock sailed past the executioners head. Francis de Guerre's swordsmen unsheathed and ran toward the mob.

Gaia saw the green shirt pass near her. The man mounted the wood pile. She felt his presence behind her.

A surge of Terra's anger pulsed against her. "Got lucky, didn't you, Gaia? Bye." She had no time to think of a response, as something cut into the skin of her neck, cutting off life-giving blood and oxygen.

Her lungs screamed for air. A rock thunked against the stake above her head, but the executioner kept at his task. She half thanked him. Her body shook, trying to suck in a breath. Her chest spasmed, her eyes and tongue bulged, her body fighting for life. Smoke passed in front of her face, a sure sign the wood pile was now alight.

A sense of peace settled over her struggling body. A giddy, dizzy sense of finality. The tumultuous shouts of a riot broke out around her. Gaia's vision dimmed. Her tears abated.

Bart, I love you.

A warm trickle ran down her leg as muscles went limp. Her body jerked once more, and the grey mist turned to blackness. Deep, soothing blackness.

Alchemy is the art that separates what is useful from what is not by transforming it into its ultimate matter and essence.

Philippus Aureolus Paracelsus

CHAPTER FIFTEEN

Bart was a study of tranquility and calm, a Zen garden surrounded by serene pools of crystal-clear water and gentle sounds of terraced waterfalls. Outwardly, that was true.

To Bart, it was like being in a sound-proof bubble, the slow-motion images received by his optic nerves in over-exposed sepia tones. Colour and sound were extraneous distractions, abstract concepts superfluous to his pinpoint focus. A calm, medative mind held back a tortured body, whose very molecules vibrated with pent-up energy and rage.

The placid pools reflected in his eyes scanned the scene of the battle-to-be one last time. If looks could kill, Terra would vaporize, every last electron, neutron, and proton dispersed instantaneously into the void of space. The first tremor broke through the calm as he registered the shimmering wall of energy that signaled Terra's imminent departure. The tips of his fingers tingled, the left hand beginning to lose grip on the three primed, M84 military-grade flash bangs. Panic shredded his stomach. The bitterness of bile filled his dry mouth, irritating the back of his nasal passages.

Bart's dispassionate eyes watched and waited as Terra vanished in a mirage-like flash. It was almost too late. He'd waited as long as he dared. Terra posed too much of a threat. Rescue would be difficult enough without her interference.

With deadly focus, the executioner kept the pressure on, dodging another missile hurled by the angry crowd. The silent ticking of seconds in Bart's head reached fifteen as Gaia's head fell forward, unconscious. He could still save her. Her heart would continue to beat for some time yet. The danger was oxygen deprivation, hypoxia of the brain. If Bart's first-aid training was correct, there was still time. But he had to move.

NOW!

Like a coiled spring released, the brown cassock came free of him in one wide sweep of his arms, the three flash-bangs propelled, disappearing into the mob. He swung the six-foot bō in a wide arc, cracking the executioners ribs. His first notion, the irrational, emotional one, was to strike the man's head, splitting it open like a ripe water melon. Bart refrained. He knew the danger of a paradox if he killed someone here today. The executioner gasped and fell backwards, taking his evil tool of trade with him.

The flash bangs exploded, their bright arc of light and shock wave stunning those within a wide range, knocking many to the ground. With his left hand, Bart reached into a pack slung over one arm and tossed the hissing, sputtering cylinder into the stunned crowd. Their frozen looks would last but a few seconds. Pop! The tear gas released, a second canister already arcing toward a different section of the crowd.

Shock and awe.

These were followed in quick succession by two red smoke grenades. A few brave or foolish people started toward him, some staggering forward only by their body weight. Many coughed and wailed, their eyes streaming at the magic attack this masquerading priest had unleashed on them. A rock bounced off his ballistic armour. This was one risk he hadn't counted on, but there had been nowhere to hide a Kevlar helmet. The cassock had worked well to disguise his Territorial Forces disruptive camo battle gear. He had worried someone might spot his black leather boots.

The crackling of wood alerted him to a more immediate danger. The torch bearer had lit only one corner of the stack, then fled at Bart's violent presentation. The fire was taking hold of an edge of the wood stack. Bart pulled a plastic drink bottle from his webbing and crushed the vial inside, tossing the reactive mix on the fire. He didn't wait for the result. He jumped onto the smoky, spitting wood stack, slapping Gaia across the face. Her head jerked back, the sharp, gasping intake of air sounding like a symphony. He hesitated for two more seconds, watching as her chest moved of its own accord. Her head bobbed as her lungs frantically sucked much-needed oxygen.

Thank God. I didn't wait too long. Gotta go, gorgeous. I got work to do if we're both gonna get out of here alive.

He leapt off the burning front edge of the wood stack, the hardwood bō cracking an approaching guard on the elbow. The man screamed as nerveless fingers dropped the brandished sword. Bart continued, swinging the bō in fast circles over his head and around his back. He blocked a second sword, before striking the man an excruciating blow on the leg. The man screamed and dropped to the ground, clutching his knee. Swaying back on his hips and twisting, Bart used the bō to send a pitchfork-armed man headfirst into a tree with a sickening thud.

Paradox or not, Bart held nothing back, short of killing people outright. Breathing through the filters in his nose, he advanced toward the spot where the ever-so-merciful Francis de Guerre had been.

Behind him, a loud 'poof' sounded. He swung around to check on Gaia. His homemade chemical fire extinguisher had been 95% successful. Some small flames still licked at the edges of the stack. But he had time. Time to give the lord of the manor a trashing.

His self-indulgent thoughts of revenge were brought home to him in a painful way. The arrow penetrated the ballistic fibers and stopped about half an inch through the metal armour plate. Wincing, he smashed the shaft off the vest with the bō, the tip of the arrow still nudging against a rib. *You stupid prick. Stick to the plan.*

He looked up. The archer was nocking another arrow. Bart's left hand flicked a throwing star from his equipment webbing. The star caught the archer in the shoulder. The bow fell. *Threat eliminated.*

Ya great pillock. Get Gaia, and get the hell out of Dodge. Despite eye drops and breathing through the nose filters, the tear gas was beginning to have an effect on him. He dashed back up the small mound to the fire stake. Gaia hung upright against the stake, limp in the restraints. The rise and fall of her blood-smeared chest swept aside the panic that welled inside him.

A quick glance around revealed a number of spluttering but resolute villagers advancing on him. *Shit. They made them tough in the old days.* He tugged at the chain and swore. A lock secured the end. *Damn it. Didn't want to do this.* He flinched as the arrowhead scraped against his rib.

Bart pulled the heavy Colt .45 automatic from its holster and discharged two rounds at the lock. It collapsed under the attack. He unhooked the shattered remnants and threw them at the remaining villagers, half of whom had turned tail and run at the first shot. That still left seven solid-looking men zeroing in on him. *Fuck you guys. I haven't got time for this shit.* He pushed and tugged at the chain, ducking his head back in the nick of time as a rock flew past. The chain clanked loosely at Gaia's feet.

The flames at the corner of the stack were taking hold again. Bart estimated he had about sixty seconds to free Gaia. *Oh, what the hell.* From his vantage point on the pyre, he swung to face the closest villagers. He raised the .45, his first shot blowing the head off one man's pitchfork. It was enough witchcraft for all of them. They fled to the four winds as Bart holstered the weapon.

He swung the bō around in a wide circle to ensure no one had snuck up on him. His freedom of movement was sorely restricted from the arrow strike. Moving Gaia would be a painful operation. His combat knife made short work of the leather restraints. Gaia's knees buckled, pitching her forward. Try as he might, she slipped to one side, her hand coming to rest near the flames, the skin puckering. *Shit.* He jerked her back. *Ow.* The arrow tip twisted in flesh, jabbing at the rib.

He dragged Gaia's naked body to the ground, away from the hungry blaze. The flames cried out their disappointment. His last act before the fire reached the post was to grab the tatty vest lying there. *Hmmm. This looks like the remains of one of Rebecca's.* He pushed the thought aside and slid Gaia's arms though what was left of the jacket. The vest was hardly adequate for her needs. He wondered for a second why he bothered. His eye fell on the discarded priest's cassock. *Perfect.*

Bart hoisted the now-wrapped Gaia over his shoulder, balanced himself to retrieve his bō, and took off running toward the woods at the north end of the village. Once there, he needed three to four minutes to reset and charge the backpack hidden in the sparse forest. The villagers had fled in the direction opposite Bart's witchcraft, and Francis de Guerre and his remaining guards were nowhere to be seen. The field lay strewn with food, blankets, tableware, and even a toddler one of the villagers had forgotten in their panic. The worst was over.

Although slight, Gaia's weight caused Bart to lean to one side. The arrow head stabbed him with every step. He stopped at the tree line and ran a hand over the edge of the ballistic vest. The hand came back covered in blood. *Shit. I need to be careful. Don't want that sucker puncturing my liver.* He transferred Gaia to the opposite shoulder and moved on.

The backpack lay where he'd left it, about fifty feet into the woods. Ignoring his own pain, Bart lay Gaia on a patch of lichen moss, the bō next to her. He loosened the side straps on the damaged vest and pulled it off. *Damn. The Army's gonna want to know what happened to this.* The damage sustained was sufficient to warrant a new vest, and they weren't cheap. *Maybe Malcolm has a replacement. Better that than a Board of Enquiry.* Bart ripped the Velcro on a pocket of his combat pants and extracted a small field dressing. He casually wiped the wound and slapped on the dressing. "Ow."

Teeth bared, Bart glanced around. The villagers might yet rally and follow. He swapped out the half-empty magazine of his pistol for a full one and holstered it, then patted his pockets. *One more tear gas canister. Two flash bangs.* Satisfied the area appeared clear, he leaned over Gaia. His jaw clenched in anger at the horrid red welt on her neck. *Fucker. Should have hit you harder.* He ran his hands over Gaia's body, stopping at her hand. The skin was blistered in one spot. He gently applied some balm before wrapping it with another field dressing. *Hope you forgive me for that burn, my love.*

Bart sat on his haunches and looked down at her, holding her hand to his chest. "Got ya, babe. Time to go home." He leaned over and kissed her on the forehead. Something cold touched his neck as a twig cracked next to him. Bart froze.

"Get up slowly, witch. Make a false move, and I'll slice your throat to the bone."

Bart did as he was told, his heart and hopes in the pit of his stomach. *How could I have been so careless?*

"Turn. Let me see who dares rout my men and steal the witch from her fiery death."

Bart complied. "Francis de Guerre, I assume. I wondered where you'd got to."

The tip of Francis' sword pricked the skin under Bart's chin. "I am he. What name do you go by?" De Guerre frowned, his eyes scanning Bart's attire.

"Professor Bartholomew Cooksley, at your service." Bart would have feigned a bow, were it not for the gleaming blade at his throat.

"Professorie? You be a learned man?" Bart felt a drop of blood run down the front of his neck.

"I am. Quantum Physics and History." He smiled at the blonde-haired land owner. *Give me the slightest chance, mate, and I'll beat you so bad your own mother won't recognize you.*

"I know of history. What be this quandun fizziks?" He stepped around Bart and looked down at Gaia, his blade leaving a shallow cut as it followed de Guerre's movements.

"One of the sciences. I don't expect you'll understand."

"It be witchcraft by any other name? Where do ye come from? Your garb, as the lady's, is strange to me."

"We come from a country called America." Bart lied, seeing a possible opening.

"What is this America? I've never heard o' it."

"It was discovered by Columbus in 1492, for the Queen of Spain."

"I know of this discovery. But this not be the name given by Columbus. It is named the Indies."

"Yes, that is true. It was called that for many years. It was a land to be fought over for centuries. The Spanish arrived first, then the French, and finally the British."

"Do not mock me, Bartholomew Cooksley. You speak in riddles. You talk of things yet to come. This be the language of the witch, the casting of spells."

"I am no witch. I am a man of science. I, and the lady fair, come from the year 2011." He saw the look of bewilderment in de Guerre's eyes and continued. "We came here seeking a dangerous criminal, a woman named Terra."

"I know no such person. You speak nonsense."

"You know this woman as Clare Morgen, Gaia's accuser at her so-called trial." The taunt spilled out before Bart could stop it.

"Aye - the stranger from Munich. I did not take her word as truth. Others spoke against your lady. Tell me true, how is this?" The tip of the sword continued to press against Bart's throat. De Guerre moved with the graceful fluidity of a practiced swordsman, offering Bart no opportunity for escape.

"It is Terra, Clare, who is the witch. She bewitched the two witnesses to give false testimony, so she could escape justice. She is a cunning and dangerous criminal. She would see my lady perish by fire to advance her plans."

"We will get to the bottom of this. We shall return to the village."

"There's no point, sire. Terra is gone. I saw for myself. She vanished as soon as she was sure Gaia would perish and would be unable to interfere with her plans. You know this is true. Did you not speak to Gaia and find her ... different? Her garb, her speech. Doubtless, she would not bend to your will." Bart felt the pressure of the sword relax.

"What you say is true. She defied me like no other before. She be willful beyond measure."

"Oh yeah. You got that right. She is an amazing woman."

De Guerre was silent for a moment. "Even be she not witch, she hath cast her spell, nonetheless. To allow the garrote was a folly that may yet cost me dear. You saw for yourself the peril the mob can pose, even for I." His eyes darted to Gaia. "You love her? Is this why you risk all to come to her aid?"

Bart eased back from the sword and turned his head to look down at Gaia's silent form. He sighed. "Yes, I do. She has touched my heart. I had to save her from the fate you set her, no matter what the outcome."

De Guerre lowered his sword partway. "I had no wish of this. I am caught in a past set by my father, which demands appeasement of the local people." He took a deep breath, his eyes unfocused, gazing past Bart. "My father was a mean land owner. He reinstated the *jus primae noctis*, the *droit du seigneur*. You understand this term, Professorie Cooksley?"

Bart clenched his teeth and glared. "Yes. The right of first night. The right to sleep first with any new bride." As a test of knowledge, it was a good one.

De Guerre's head tilted, the partial frown indicating puzzlement. "You are indeed a learned man. You are correct. It won him no friends. He took what he wanted, fermenting anger and rebellion hereabouts. As a boy, I was forced to bear witness to this … depravity."

"How is it you are so different from your father, Francis de Guerre?"

"My mother, as strong a woman as your lady, tried to protect me. Our land holding is large, and the income is comfortable. She sent me to Italy to be educated. I understand some of this science you speak of. I have read Galileo and da Vinci. And I had the privilege to meet a visionary named Nostradamus. We live in fast-changing times. Some of what you talk of is not foreign to me. I heard Nostradamus speak of strange things to come."

"Then you know Gaia is no more a witch than your own mother was. She must be allowed to go free, to continue her pursuit of the criminal, Terra. Release us, Francis de Guerre. Do what you know in your heart to be right." Bart reached out a hand and pushed down the sword pointed at his chest. De Guerre did not resist.

"It may be, Bartholomew Cooksley, that I owe you a debt."

"How so?" Bart crouched next to Gaia, his fingers stroking her ashen face.

"The mob did not take well to the mercy I showed your lady."

Bart glared at him again. "I'm sure you thought it was mercy. In my anger, I sought you out on the field. I would have beaten you severely had I found you, Francis de Guerre. Only your archer prevented this from coming to pass."

"I … understand. I have wronged you both. Your lady told me I was no better than my father, and she was right. She indeed has a spell about her. I tried to bargain my mercy for her favours. In the end, I could not bear her to suffer and ordered the garrote. I may not have escaped today, but for your intervention. Your witchcraft." A smile twitched across the man's lips.

"What you call witchcraft, we call modern warfare. More correctly, crowd control. The smoke I used is designed to render the mob incapable, without serious harm. None of your people, or your guards, will suffer any permanent ill effects. I'm afraid your executioner will suffer pain for some months. Bind his ribs tight; he will heal." Bart hesitated. "I wished to kill him, but such a rash action may have a profound affect on my future. We call this phenomena a 'paradox'."

De Guerre nodded. "What of your injury, Professorie? Surely my archer wounded you grievously."

"I'll be fine. My armour stopped most of the arrow." He held up the ballistic vest for de Guerre to see.

"You can understand why many would see this as magic. The ability to stop an arrow, to render men as blubbering women. And that device on your hip. It thunders like the smoky weapons I have seen in larger cities. A firearm?"

"Yes. Five hundred years more advanced than what you have seen. This …" He hefted the Colt into sight. "This is capable of killing nine men in less than nine seconds. I did not use it to that effect today. As I said, anything I do here may alter the future." He slipped the heavy weapon back into its holster.

"Nostradamus spoke of a war where tens of millions died. Were weapons like this used?"

"Yes, and worse." Bart stiffened and turned his head. Voices carried through the woods. "Men call your name, Francis de Guerre. I must be gone. Have I your leave?"

Francis slid his sword into it's scabbard. "My men seek me. You have my leave, Professorie. It would seem to me that you could take it at a whim, should you wish. How will you escape? You have no horses, and my men are mounted. The ones you struck may suffer sulfurous moods and ignore my orders. Oh, I have something of your lady's. The jailer took it from her." He handed Bart a shiny disc shaped object.

VG^2. Bart turned the object over then placed it in one of his numerous pockets. He bowed a thank you.

"You, Francis de Guerre, man of science, are in for a rare treat. Stand back a few metres." Bart checked Gaia's pulse and strapped on the backpack. "Can you help me, please? Lift Gaia."

Bart slung his vest loosely over his shoulder. As a piece of twenty-first century technology, he could not leave it behind. He sighed as he spied his bō. No room this trip, old friend. Francis dropped a limp Gaia into Bart's arms. "Step back, my lord." Reaching round Gaia's legs, he fingered the small hand pad fitted to the front strap of the pack. A whine started, the note climbing.

"What be that?" A frown pulled Francis' fair eyebrows together.

"Building a charge. Storing energy. Nearly there." A readout on the console flashed from red to orange and then green. "Goodbye, Francis de Guerre. You have proved to be an honorable man." Bart borrowed his final words from pop culture. "May you live long and prosper."

Bart concentrated on the lounge in his home. He imagined the smell of fresh coffee, the feel of the leather couch against his back, his feet on the coffee table. On the wall, he could see a calendar. His mind focused on the date. He heard a gasp next to him as the air in front of him shimmied and swirled. A hole opened. "Goodbye, Francis."

Bart stepped forward, entering the hole. His body bent, twisted, molded like plasticine. At the edge of his consciousness, he saw his bō. Francis pushed the tip into the vortex and let it go.

Bright, pure white light surrounded Bart. Then nothing.

***

Terra cursed vociferously. "God-damned useless piece of crap." Once again, she'd missed her desired target. *This device of Bartholomew Cooksley has design flaws. Worse, it takes a full day to recharge.* She was stuck in her present location for an entire, tedious day. Bored, she wandered aimlessly around the Viking village, causing mischief.

Each jump seemed to land her in random locations, each associated with some major event. It was as if the energy generated with those incidents had left an echo in time and space, a nitch she dropped into. She had to laugh. Many of the occurrences were her doing. Attempts over the millennia to shake up mankind, to issue warnings.

Pompeii, Krakatoa, a major earthquake in 1900s California, and one she regarded as some of her best work - the total annihilation of Atlantis. Eventually, she hoped, the incident she sought would pull her. *Then, revenge.*

Terra's vitriolic temper flared again. *The humans who rape me continually won't even know what's happening. A millisecond of bright light, then an eternity of nothing. And for me, it will be time to sleep. Blessed, everlasting sleep.*

For everything that ever existed.

CHAPTER SIXTEEN

From nothing, came blackness. Pure, deep, pitch dark.

Gaia's senses registered nothing. Then pain. It penetrated her being.

This is not possible. Those waiting in the Hall of Souls, the Guf, feel nothing, hear nothing, sense nothing. Yet I feel pain and see, albeit darkness. If I feel, then ... her essence struggled to find the words, to form an understanding.

I think. I feel. Therefore ... *I am.*

Am what? And this pain. What is it? The darkness diminished, a line of subtle light moving across some sort of barrier. A wall. Excitement pushed the pain aside. *A car. I can hear a car. Its headlights. That's the light. Where am I?* Somewhere nearby, the car passed by, the room returning to darkness. But not as dark this time. Eyes. I can see. She felt wetness, something running down her cheeks.

Tears. I'm alive!

Gaia trembled. Her senses began to feed information back to her. Blurred, non-sensical at first, but something. *Anything.* A breeze wafted across her face. Heavy curtains rustled, and light spilled from beneath them, then vanished as they settled again. Hairs stood up on her neck, reacting to the coolness of the breeze. Such beauty, she thought. Such simple, yet divine sensation. *I live.*

Gaia floated in a tepid pool of recollections. *I'm alive. How is this possible?* Vague memories, dreamlike perceptions stirred in her. *Touch.* Something cool and damp on her head. Gentle, warm caresses on her skin, her arms, her legs, her ... She felt her face go hot. Touches everywhere, in every public and private niche of her body. Yet the sensations were ... pleasant, loving. Not the rough, humiliating violations of the mob.

The mob. The fire. Oh, god. Am I burnt? What am I? If I'm burnt, shouldn't I feel more pain? She flashed hot, saw images of her tossing, feverish body. *Where am I?* She tried to scream it, but her throat squeezed off her voice. *Pain.* Excitement gave way to panic. She tried to move, but her body failed to respond. *Do I have a body? I must. I feel it.*

She tried harder, pushing out toward one source of her pain. *A hand.* Fingers twitched. The hand felt tight, constricted. It brushed against her hip. Rough. Scratchy. An image of a blue blanket flashed past. She moved the hand again, turning it against the tender skin of her hip. *A bandage. That's it.* The hand stung, the pain increasing as she closed fingers, the skin stretching. An involuntary groan slipped from her chest. *A sound. Someone else. Where?*

Snoring. There's a man here. She swallowed and grimaced. Her throat was tight, tender. *The garrote.* Her stomach churned, her body bending upward and back, twisting to escape the blurry image of the thong slipping over her head, tightening around her throat. The memories, sensations of the following seconds made her retch again. The snore responded, a loud snort issuing, then settled back into a rhythm.

Gaia moved her hand again. It ignored her at first, then edged its way to her face. The fingers danced across her damp cheek. The room seemed brighter now, her eyes adjusting. She breathed slowly, deeply, amazed at the comfort this gave her. A soft, light fabric rested on her. She pushed it back, surprised to find herself naked. Small red marks stood out at intervals. Strange welts criss-crossed her torso. *The mob.* She remembered their wanton, fevered attacks on her body, the tearing of clothing, and the brutal groping as she was dragged to the stake. But the welts? A recollection flooded her awareness. *The iron chains.*

The quiet in the room hurt. Gaia felt threatened by it, didn't trust it. Surely there should be more sound. After the loud, angry mob, it seemed unreal, artificial. Was this some sort of torture? A reaction of the mind, before the pain of the fire set in. *No. There is someone else here.* She forced her head to turn toward the only source of noise.

A figure sat slumped in a padded chair, a blanket pulled up to the neck. Or was it a cassock, a priest's robes? *The kind stranger. No, that can't be.* The anachronism of a sixteenth-century priest and a twenty-first-century car bewildered her. Gaia squinted, trying to see more detail. Another car, more headlamps. Illumination moved across the room like a spotlight.

Bart!

Even the constriction in Gaia's neck couldn't hold back the sob that wracked her. "Bart." The word tore at her throat, forcing its way, raspy and hoarse, into audible life.

The sleeping figure jerked in the chair. His head shook, fingers raked through unkempt hair. Bart looked around the dark room, yawning, stretching.

"Bart." The tears flowed freely as Gaia croaked the name again.

Bart shot out of the chair as if someone had applied a cattle prod to his back. "Gaia, Gaia. You're back. I was so worried. I thought I'd lost you." Words spilled out of him in a torrent, disconnected, tender. He sat on the bed next to her, taking her good hand in his.

Even in the meager light, Gaia could see the tiny glistening drops rolling down his cheeks, before being lost in the stubble of many days' growth. Her heart felt fit to burst. Soft lips brushed the back of her hand. She murmured.

"Sshhh. Don't try to talk. Your throat is swollen." Fingers brushed like butterflies across her face, down her bandaged neck.

Regardless, she tried to ask the questions that tore as a wildfire through her mind. *How? When? Where?*

"Sshhh, I said. Now's not the time." He kissed her hand again and left the room, returning with a large mug. "Here. You need to drink something. It'll help." He put a hand behind her head and eased it forward, tipping the mug to let the odd-tasting concoction trickle into her mouth.

The first swallow burnt.

He turned the cup once again. "More. Drink."

The second sip was soothing, cool. She looked at his glittering eyes. Something small and wet dropped off his face and landed on her shoulder. In her mind, she saw a slow-motion sequence, a splash.

Bart sniffled and wiped the back of his hand across his face. "Got a cold, sweet thing."

Gaia sipped more of the mixture. *Honey and …?* She didn't bother trying to figure it out. Bart put the empty mug to one side and sat there silent, smiling. Gaia reached both hands out and took his, cradling them to her face. "Thank you."

"Sshhh. I won't tell you again."

A laugh welled up inside her at the mock rebuke. It hurt her throat, but it felt good.

"Now you; sleep. I'll see you in the morning." He stood to leave.

"Stay. Please," she rasped.

"Of course." He moved toward his chair.

"No, here. Hold me." She patted the bed next to her.

Bart stood rooted to the spot, seemingly unable to decide which way to turn. He came back to the bed and lay down next to her.

"Closer."

"I'm already right next to … oh. I see." Bart slid off the bed, lifted the sheet off her naked body and slid in next to her, still clothed.

Gaia smelled his unwashed body, felt the bristle of his chin against her cheek. Bart's arms encircled her, pulling her close. She rolled on her side, feeling his body mold to hers, one hand on her stomach. His warmth filled her with a glow she'd never experienced before.

"Thank you." Cocooned in the safety of Bart's arms, sleep took her.

***

Bart fussed about Gaia. From one of the closets, he produced a luxurious bathrobe. He left the room for a few minutes and returned when she knocked on the wall. The trip from the bedroom had been an easy one for Gaia, cradled in Bart's arms. He fluffed up a pillow to place behind her on the La-Z-Boy lounge chair. Now she sat, feeling like a queen must feel. She smiled wryly. *The attention Kalona received in the restaurant.* Her eyes followed his every move.

Bart's modesty, now that she was awake, seemed moot to Gaia. The dressings and balms over her body told a story of their own. This man, this Bart Cooksley, had bathed her from head to foot twice a day and had dressed her infected wounds and scratches, some of them in intimate, delicate areas. She smiled as she saw him now, embarrassed if her robe slipped open.

The familiar smell of Bart's coffee machine comforted her. She longed to speak to him, shower him with thanks. Every time she tried, her throat screamed its displeasure. Then a scolding would follow from Bart. He had finally got angry and told her to "shut up." So now she sat listening to the stories he told as she drank an unusual tasting beverage Bart had prepared her. A mixture of yoghurt, banana, egg, honey, oranges, and strawberries, he claimed. And a little ice.

It was delicious. Gaia found her strength returning. She had to suppress a laugh when he began cooking some bacon and eggs for himself. Partway through, he realized he was burning flesh and ran about in a fit, hiding the unfinished food and spraying scented aerosols.

Gaia could see he was horrified at what he'd done, and she tried to put on a brave face. She found it funny, but a melancholy settled on her for a time after that. She'd forgotten it by the time he delivered the next soft meal for her.

Seeing her annoyance at not being able to talk freely, Bart set up a keyboard interface to the huge LCD television in the lounge. This became their main mode of communication, with Gaia's husky voice barking at Bart when she became frustrated.

Bart began by telling Gaia everything he could remember, from the time he found her and the device gone.

Gaia typed. "I'm sorry. I'm a wretch, a common thief."

"There's nothing common about you, Gaia."

"Why did you come after me, and how? I didn't deserve your help."

Bart screwed his mouth up as he considered his response. "I did it for two reasons. The first, I was already seeing changes, paradoxes. I worried they might threaten the rest of civilization. After all, I started all this with those damned devices."

"What happened? What changed?" Gaia glanced around the room and nodded.

"See? I didn't fix the door or the room; they fixed themselves. That was cause for concern." Bart tilted his head.

"You said two reasons. What was the other?"

Bart stood silent for what seemed an eternity. "You, Gaia. I came after you. As for how…" With Gaia's eyes riveted to him, he paced the length and breadth of the lounge, recounting the tale of the third machine and the problems he'd encountered trying to build it, the difficulties he'd had finding her.

Gaia typed. "If you concentrate more on the emotion and feeling of a place, rather than physical characteristics, it should work better."

"That's exactly what happened. It was my third or fourth attempt. That's when I sensed you in Atlantis. Actually, I thought it was Pompeii at first. I can't believe I'm privy to what actually happened to Atlantis. Anyway, I couldn't get to you, but I saw you. I was able to touch you."

"And that saved my life, Bart Cooksley. It threw a temporal field around me and nudged me ten days into the future." Gaia explained the phenomena of the correction to the original Julian calendar. Bart nodded. "It gave me enough time to follow Terra. But, as you know, it was out of the frying pan …" She stopped typing and clamped a hand over her mouth. The incident of the bacon had arisen again.

Bart shook his head and grinned. "After the Atlantis attempt, I tried something different. I meditated before I tried again. I was able to see where you were and make preparations, ensuring I arrived before the trial. It took a couple of attempts, but it got easier each time."

"I saw your boots, Mr. Monk, and didn't realize. I was so scared." Gaia grasped Bart's hand and pulled him to her for a kiss. "Thank you," she rasped.

Bart wagged a finger at her, pointing at the keyboard. She smiled. "How did you get me out, Mr. Monk? There were so many people there, and the soldiers."

"Ah. Among the many things I do, I'm a territorial infantryman. A part-time soldier. Underneath the brown cassock …" It took Bart another ten minutes to explain the actual rescue, his injury, and the encounter with Francis de Guerre.

Gaia's keyboard clicked. "You're hurt? Show me."

"I'm fine. It was minor. You're the one who got hurt. I was worried your fever would never break. After all I did to get you back here, it looked like you would die of an infection. I've been bathing and dressing your wounds since …" Bart's face went red. "I'm sorry. I had to bathe and dress all of you. Everywhere."

Gaia ignored Bart's embarrassment. "Fever? How long have I been here?" Gaia's hand's started to tremble.

"You've been out of it for three days. Your body had a weird reaction to the metal of the chains and shackles." He crouched next to her, touching her face. "I guess iron is your Kryptonite. Most of the welts have almost healed now. You'll be fine in a few more days."

"I need to go. I have to stop Terra. And what's this Kryptonite? I don't understand."

"There's a make-believe comic book hero called Superman. Super strong, super fast, super . . . well you get it. Superman. Kryptonite is the one thing that can weaken and kill him, like metal does to you. Anyway, you're too weak to go chasing after Terra. You need rest."

Gaia's body shook as she tried to stand.

"Gaia, stop it. It's not the end of the world if you leave her for a few days." He tried to ease Gaia back into the chair.

"No, you don't understand, Bart." She grabbed her throat at the burning pain.

"Gaia, don't try to talk. You'll hurt your throat. Use the keyboard. Please."

Gaia relented, slipping back into the chair. Her fingers flew across the keyboard. In short, clipped sentences, Gaia told a shocked-looking Bart exactly who and what Terra was, and her intentions. Bart collapsed onto the couch as Gaia told him how she came to be, how she escaped because of Bart's device. "She will cause the end of the world if I don't stop her." Gaia's head dropped. "I don't know if I can. I don't know how. She is the earth. If everything here is part of her, what, then, could kill her?"

"So we need something not of this earth. Perhaps a weapon edged with some meteor or mineral." Bart paced the room, absentmindedly scratching his chin. "Moldavite, perhaps. Or some cosmic force? Solar radiation? No, she's used to that. Oh god. What the hell do we do?"

"Not we, Bart. Me. This is my task. She's dangerous, even for me. How could you hope to best her?"

"Hey there, missy. Hold on a minute. She's not invincible. She can't fight hand to hand like you can. If I could get close enough with the right weapon . . ."

"She won't let that happen. She's aware we know about her now."

"No she isn't, Gaia. She thinks you're dead, remember? And she thinks she can beat me. It might be enough. She might get cocky. From what you've told me, she's overconfident, arrogant. And you're not ready. You need more rest." Bart went silent for a moment, his eyes flitting about as he thought. "Strategy and tactics. We deliberately show weakness and draw her in. I go after her as the angry, vengeful, careless lover."

Gaia felt the heat rising in her face. "Well, Professor Cooksley. After the last few days, you probably know more about my body than I do."

"I … um … I did what was necessary to make you well. I … I had to make sure you were clean, sterile."

Gaia grinned at the stammering Bart and tapped away at the keyboard. "I know. I thank you for everything you've done for me. I'm sure you were a perfect gentleman the whole time. Not like those …" Her fingers dropped off the keyboard.

"Hey. I just had an idea. It's a tad corny, but it might work." Bart's teeth showed through a broad grin.

"Tell me."

"It's corny, so don't laugh." He screwed up his face, then blurted out. "Silver bullets."

"What? Make sense."

"Silver bullets." He turned the whiteboard over and drew on the back. "In every vampire movie, there are only a few things that can be used to kill the vampires. A stake through the heart, cutting off the vampires head, and direct sunshine. Or silver bullets. Actually, silver bullets are probably for werewolves, but … whatever."

"Won't work. Silver is one of her elements, Professor." A notion stirred in her mind.

"Don't you mock me, young lady. I was speaking metaphorically. I get some bullets cast with Moldavite inside. They will fragment on impact, releasing the foreign mineral. I just have to get as close as twenty-five to fifty yards." He paced excitedly back and forth. "Yes. It could work. And I only need fragments, not large crystals. So much easier to get." He strode to the kitchen to make a fresh pot of coffee.

Gaia sat quietly, considering the idea. She'd encountered guns on previous assignments, so she had a passable knowledge of their workings. She typed her thoughts and waited for Bart to return. "How long will this take? We must get after her. Soon."

"Actually, no." He handed Gaia a steaming mug. "I almost forgot to tell you. I only worked this out after you stole the second device and absconded. The original prototype has the bad equation *hardwired* into it's ROM chip. She'll never get to where she wants to go with that device." He punched the air.

"Yes, but ..." Gaia hesitated. "Once she realizes, she could come back here for one of the newer devices. She must suspect by now that you have another. We can't leave her out there. She's messing with things, causing paradoxes. The longer she's free, the angrier and more meddlesome she'll become."

"I know, but we have time. And Terra has a weakness. It's brilliant. I should have realized sooner. Everything has a weakness of some sort, no matter how big or strong. Yours is iron, Terra's is extra-terrestrial matter. Or antimatter, if it comes to that. Not that we can lay our hands on any."

"And what's your weakness, Bart Cooksley?"

"Mine? Fine blue cheese, good coffee ..." He paused. "And cute, red-haired women."

"In that order?"

Bart chuckled. "Most definitely not."

"Coffee first, then?" Gaia's lips twitched in amusement.

Bart leaned over the chair and kissed Gaia. She slipped an arm round his neck and held him there, enjoying the warmth of his lips, their closeness of spirit.

"Hmmm. You are feeling better, aren't you? Would you like to try standing?"

Gaia nodded.

Bart slid his arms under hers and assisted her out of the chair, then held her as she steadied herself. "Look. Nothing wrong with you. You've been faking it to get attention."

Gaia swayed on her feet for a second. She waved Bart's hands away and, using the couch as support, made a circle of it. Her legs worked fine, she decided, and made a second wider circle without support. She grinned as she came back toward Bart. And tripped.

Bart caught her in his arms, her head against his shoulder. Gaia made no attempt to pull away.

"You did that on purpose, didn't you?" Bart pulled her closer.

Gaia shook her head, unable to look him in the eyes as she smiled. She let him draw her in. He smelled so good after his morning shower and shave. Gaia hadn't made it that far yet. She put her arms around his neck and gazed up at her beaming hero, tilting her head back to accept his kiss. This one made her head spin. The heat of his body against hers was as much as she could take. She felt herself shiver. Her stomach fluttered with a sensation new to her. Gaia was aware of a hot flush on her chest as warmth spread from her loins.

She leaned back, her hips pressed against Bart. He appeared … rattled, she thought. So many things had happened to her in the last week. So many new sensations, new feelings. Some of them had been terrifying, painful. Others, like the ritual with Nigel, exciting and seductive. The ones with Bart were tender, sensuous. She'd never felt desire for a man before. Was this what stirred in her now? A longing to be closer than anything physical touch could offer. A need for more.

Gaia wondered if these were the feelings Bart had told her about. Feelings that lead to the love making, the physical union of man and woman. His fingers caressed the small of her back, sending minute electric shocks up her spine. She felt powerless to break away from him. She was a fly in Bart's web. He only needed to come and take her.

Bart kissed her on the forehead. The spell broke.

"You do seem to be feeling better." He released his hold on her. "I have to go out and get supplies. There's fresh coffee on the counter and nibbles here." He opened two cupboards, displaying an array of unfamiliar objects. "Don't eat all of these at once; you'll make yourself sick. There's juice and milk in the fridge, along with more of your current drink of choice." He pointed out a large lidded container in the fridge. "Just pour a glass full into this," he put his hand on a large glass-bowled device, "and push this button for say, fifteen seconds. Then pour and drink."

Bart vanished from the room. He reappeared in a bright yellow button-down shirt with black palms printed across it, and shorts. A pair of sunglasses sat amongst his curls. Flashing a smile, he jingled a set of keys. "I won't be long, my dear. Get some more sleep. You need to heal and recharge."

"You're abandoning me?" Gaia's happy little world collapsed inward on her. It felt to her like her facial muscles followed, her smile and eyebrows pulling inward. She knew Bart had to leave and that he'd return, but she wanted him close now.

"Don't give me that puppy dog look. I'll be back soon. Right?" He pulled her near again.

Gaia basked in the glow of his closeness. The small kiss he left on her cheek wasn't enough, but she let him go. Her heart twinged with his loss as he disappeared into the garage. She stood there with her arms wrapped around herself, until the sound of his car faded behind the closing door. An emptiness engulfed her, the void filled with sadness. She bit her lip and turned to the kitchen. Finding nothing of interest in the cupboards, she made her way back to the super-king-sized bed.

The robe lay discarded on a chair as Gaia slid naked, back under the soft, comforting sheets. She felt safe here; a smooth, linen cave. An echo of something past called to her. As hard as she tried, it stayed hidden, buried. She pulled one of the huge down pillows in with her, snuggling up to it. Sleep came once again.

Russell Turney

CHAPTER SEVENTEEN

Bart glanced at his shopping list as he parked outside the grey, nondescript concrete block warehouse. He checked his watch. *Malcolm should be here by now.* Bart locked the Range Rover and made his way to a small side door. He knocked, then looked up at the almost invisible security camera and smiled. A buzz indicated the door was unlocked.

This was only the second time he'd ever been to this building, the last in a row of identical, bland commercial premises. Malcolm didn't allow too many people here. This side of his business operations were not to be found on any company register or lease agreement. Ostensibly part of his importing company, this small building was more of a hobby.

"Bart, long time no see." The burly ex-rugby player chuckled and offered a hand devoid of the pinky finger. A hunting accident, he claimed.

Bart wondered if some of the people he ran with had something to do with the severed digit. He never asked, and Malcolm never offered.

"What brings you to my corner of the woods? You after more of those grenades?"

"No, although I might top up on those next trip. They work a treat." He cast an eye around the warehouse. "I need some specials - hand loads."

Malcolm regarded him through bushy eyebrows. "That all? Why the cloak and dagger, then? Let me guess. Another of the famous Cooksley experiments."

"Sorta. Look, if I tried to tell you, you wouldn't believe me anyway."

"Hmmm. Nothing different there, then. As secretive as ever, eh? What ya after?"

Bart placed a small cardboard box on the bench. "I need half a dozen .45 auto rounds and half a dozen .303 rifle rounds."

"That don't sound so odd." Malcolm's eyes scanned him. "There's more to it, isn't there?"

"Yeah - custom loads." He looked at the box and sighed. "I need each round to be embedded with fragments of this." He opened the box, revealing what looked to the casual observer to be several rough chunks of green glass. "Forty-two fragments in each round. Exactly forty-two, Malcolm."

Malcolm picked up the box and examined the contents. "Not glass, I'm guessing. Some sort of … hmmm … crystal, would be my guess. This is weird, even for you, Bart. You realize this stuff will probably screw the barrel of your weapons. Gouge them out after only several rounds." He looked in the box again. "Of course you do." He nodded his head. "You only want six of each. Disposable weapons, special ammo. Man, you better keep my name out of whatever you're doing, mate."

"No worries there. I don't even know your name, Frank." Bart grinned.

"Frank? I deserve a better alias than that." He shook his head. "So what is this? Some sort of Kryptonite-type deal?" Malcolm laughed. "As if."

"You nailed it, Malcolm. That's exactly what it is."

"No need to be sarcastic now, Bart. I said I'd help. Any other special requirements? You want through-and-through or splatter?" Malcolm's face lost it's smile, the eyes cold and hard.

"Splatter. As explosive as you can." Bart set his lips tight.

"How much time I got?"

"Need them sooner than ASAP. What are your thoughts on this?"

"I can possibly do the .45s today. I was thinking dum-dums. Messy as fuck, but super effective on centre of mass. Do not get caught with these. They're against every rule in the book." He shook his head. "Man. It sounds like you got yourself into some serious shit."

"You said a mouthful. How long for the .303s?"

"I don't have the casings here. A day or so. I can build the rounds in the meantime. Seeing I've got more time for those, I was thinking something a little different. How serious is this? You're not squeamish, are you? And why .303s? They're a bit long in the tooth, mate."

"End of the world serious, Malcolm." Bart held up a hand at Malcolm's raised eyebrows. "I kid you not, mate. Super serious. And no, for what I gotta do, I'm not squeamish. The target has already tried to kill a lady friend of mine twice, both times by incineration; I got no qualms about this. As for the .303s, I trust them. The design's been around over a hundred years. Heavy hitting and reliable as fuck. If you can see it, you can hit it with those suckers." He screwed his mouth up and added wryly. "Millions of dead axis soldiers attest to their effectiveness."

"For sure. Hmmm, a woman. Figures. You sure you're doing this for the right reasons?"

"It's more than just the woman." Bart took a breath. "None of this will ever come back to you, mate. No one will even miss the intended target. Officially, they don't even exist."

"Okeydokey. Something clandestine, eh? I know nothing. Now, the .303s. How would some frangibles sound?"

"You can do those?"

"Shit yeah. Just add in whatever that is." He pointed at the box. "They'll take the leg off a horse. Hit the body, and they'll leave fragments for ten yards. As I said, very, very messy." Malcolm looked at the box again. "You want me to smash that up as well?"

"Yeah. Hopefully I got you enough for the shards. You know how to get hold of me?"

"No problem. I'll drop the .45s off within the day. Ya got my money? I trust you, but in this business … well … Not all my customers make it back." Malcolm tilted his head and grinned. "Do your best to survive, Bart. I like your style. Hey, did that small disc I made for you work out okay?"

"Yeah. It worked a treat. Work in progress on this current job, you might say. Can't tell you more than that, sorry." *You're as trusty as they come, mate, but time travel might just bend your brain a tad.* "And ditto, mate. We must get together for a beer when this is over." Bart handed across a thick envelope for the purchase.

Malcolm leafed through the notes in the envelope. "Cool. I'll get the .45s to you later today, the .303s as soon as I can. You'll be home?"

"Should be. If not, leave them behind the cactus on the back porch." Bart shook Malcolm's hand again. "Hey, you got any military ballistic vests?"

Malcolm eyed him warily. "Should have some next week. Call back." He shook his head and grinned. "Always good to do business with you, bro. Take care." Malcolm tucked the envelope in his back pocket. "Keep your head low."

"Will do, Malcolm. Will do." Bart grinned.

***

The distant hum of cars and singing of the local birdlife filtered through Gaia's sleep. She rolled over and stretched, squinting against the sunlight reflecting off the beige walls. Another night gone. How long have I slept? The bed next to her was empty, save for the pillow she'd dragged in. A quick check of the room revealed no Bart. Hollowness echoed inside her. Why had he not joined her again?

She pulled the bathrobe about her, intent on finding Bart. Bright colours caught her eye. Someone (Bart, she surmised) had left some garishly-coloured parcels on the end of the bed. Gaia's curiosity got the better of her. She picked up the first one and shook it. A small card, addressed to her, dropped out. Excitement replaced the emptiness she felt. Shaking hands held the card as she read it.

"Dearest Gaia." She sat on the edge of the bed. *"I bought you some presents. Something every beautiful woman needs, especially you, after recent events. I hope I got the sizing right. When you're done with these, look in the right-hand side of the large, mirrored wardrobe in the bedroom. All my late wife's clothes are still there, as you already know. Pity about that jacket. ☺ Help yourself. She was a similar size but taller. Love, Bart."*

Gaia leapt off the bed and attacked the parcels with a gusto that surprised even her. It was so exciting, opening mysterious presents. The first shreds of paper flew over her shoulder to reveal another wrap inside, this one labeled Victoria's Secret. Who is this Victoria, she wondered, ripping the second layer open. A spasm tightened her throat as the contents spilled onto the bed.

Gaia held the red and black laced lingerie against herself. They looked close to the right size. But there was more. She knelt on the carpet next to the bed and opened the next parcel slower, almost reverently. Plainer, more practical than the first, the items were gorgeous, nonetheless. Two more packets revealed a third set, these a soft silky material. Gaia rubbed them against her skin. She didn't think she'd ever felt anything so luxurious. She wanted to try them all on. She decided she should bathe first, before wearing these gorgeous, delicate items. A final box held a small number of obviously cheaper, more practical items. Gaia put on one of these perfectly-fitting sets and rummaged through the wardrobe for some outerwear.

Oh, Bart. Thank you.

Gaia found a pair of jeans that fitted nicely, once she'd rolled up the legs three inches. She danced crazily in front of the mirror, holding up different blouses and t-shirts. She finally selected a sequin-covered t-shirt. Something practical to wear around the house. Bare footed, she ran out into the kitchen to hug Bart.

Her shoulders slumped. A note sat on the kitchen counter, next to the coffee machine. Another note. *I want the real Bart. Where are you?*

"Hi, Babe. Didn't want to wake you. Have to work a half day at the uni. Be home late afternoon. Then we need to get ready for you know who. Kiss. Bart."

Gaia frowned. *You can't leave a girl presents and abandon her.* She made herself a coffee and raided some fruit from the fridge. She spent the next few hours touring Bart's house, poking in cupboards and acquainting herself with the working of various implements. She squealed with delight when she worked out how to make the shower run properly.

Dashing back to the bedroom, she grabbed her new red and black underwear and bathrobe and ran back as fast, not daring to turn the shower off, in case she couldn't get it going again. She learned how to operate the mixer by touching it, but this device seemed to have a mind of its own.

Gaia spent twenty minutes luxuriating under the hot water, washing away the worries and aches of the last few days. She ran shaky fingers through her wet hair, pushing it back, removing the worst of the tangles. When her body dried, she slipped into her new underwear and modeled for herself in the mirror, before wrapping her trusty bathrobe around her. A smell she couldn't identify wafted from the kitchen.

Bart. Bart's back. Excited, she ran the short hallway, then slowed, making a more dignified, demure entrance into the lounge. He turned and smiled. She ran the last ten feet and threw herself at him.

"Whoa, whoa. Did someone miss me? Hmmm, you smell good. Did you figure out the shower?"

"Yes. It was wonderful. I feel so much better." She wrapped her arms around Bart's neck and pressed herself against him. "Thank you for my lovely presents. You smell good too. Have you showered?"

"Yes, at the uni. In case you were still asleep when I got back. I didn't want to wake you. Your voice - it's almost healed. Let me have a look at your neck." She stood still as he examined the red welt circling her throat. "Man, you heal quick. Amazing. So, your presents. Did they fit okay? I wasn't quite sure of the sizing."

"They're perfect. Here. See?" She stepped back and opened her robe.

Bart's face flushed bright red. His eyes tried to look everywhere except at Gaia. "Hey. What did I tell you about displaying yourself like that?"

Gaia felt crushed. "Don't you like looking at me? I just wanted to show you the lovely new things you bought. You think I'm ugly, don't you? I'm horrid after all those other people touched me. That's it, isn't it?" She turned away from Bart.

Bart reached her in three long paces, throwing his arms around her from behind. "No. No, Gaia. It's just ... well ... I like you, but I hardly know you. And you know so little about humans, about men. I don't want to take advantage of you." He squeezed her tight to him, feeling her sobbing. "Don't cry. I'm sorry. C'mon, turn around. Show me. I promise to look."

"You don't think I'm ugly?" Gaia sniffed.

"No. You're the most beautiful woman I've ever known." He stroked her hair, sniffing the clean, apple fragrance.

"I thought you'd be happy to see me dressed all pretty. I'm sorry. I'm not used to being human. All these strange emotions that flood me sometimes." She leaned her head back on his shoulder.

"Don't be silly. You're definitely not ugly. But you're going home after all this is over. And I'll still be here, without you. I ... I don't want to lose you. You can't imagine how that feels. So I've been trying not to get too close to you. Do you understand?"

Gaia wrapped her arms around Bart's arms. "Yes. No, I'll miss you too. I don't know what's going to happen. I'm ... I'm so confused. I want you near me. I miss you when you're not here. I want you next to me in bed." She pressed against Bart. "Can't we just do this a bit at a time?"

"Gaia, I like you. I don't want to spoil this, for either of us."

Despite all Bart's protests, Gaia could feel a response from his body nudging the small of her back. One she recognized. She'd felt that energy before, in Nigel's car. She linked her fingers with his as she thought about all the things he'd told her that first night, her first sex talk. Gaia wanted Bart close to her. She remembered the incredible, heady sensation that emanated from Nigel as he released. She made her decision.

She eased Bart's arms loose from around her and guided one hand inside her robe, feeling his fingers on her bare skin.

"Gaia, what're you doing?"

She felt Bart's body twitch against her back. His fingers trembled. "I don't want to go back out to face Terra or return to Sanctum without this joy. Would you deny me this?" Touching the edge of Bart's thoughts, she saw what he wanted without invading his mind. She slid his hand up to her breast. Goosebumps stood up on her skin. The nipple hardened at the slight touch, the sensation somewhere between pain and ecstasy. Gaia shivered. A quiet gasp escaped her lips.

Bart's hot breath warmed the back of her neck. She let herself mold to the shape of his body. Her heartbeat pounded in her ears. Muscles twitched randomly in her stomach as Bart's other hand caressed her there. She felt her own breath coming in uneven pants as she pressed her buttocks against him. His mouth brushed the flushed skin of her neck.

A shudder shook her to her feet as his lips found the side of her neck, small soft kisses dancing along her jawbone and up to her ear. She wasn't sure if her body would explode or collapse.

He smelled of soap, clean and fresh, his cologne intoxicating but not overpowering. Gaia turned her head toward him, the kisses making their way across her cheek to the edge of her lips. The robe slid open as Bart's soft touch explored the curve of her hips, the line of her ribs, and the soft contours of her belly.

Gaia felt hot, flustered. She licked her lips and gasped. She wanted Bart to touch her, to caress the uncomfortable yet incredible feeling low in her abdomen. Bart slid his hand from the front of her breasts around to her back, where his fingers manipulated the clasp. The tightness around her chest eased. Her breath came faster as she waited, in exquisite agony, for the hand to return to her breast. Bart did not disappoint her. She groaned at his touch, the fingertips as butterfly wings on her nipple.

In her mind, Gaia laughed. Her new underwear hadn't stayed on long. *Victoria's secret must be the effect lace has on men.*

Gaia ground her hips back against the hardness she felt behind her. She slithered a hand between them, toward his penis. It responded to the touch of her fingers. She squirmed, unable to keep her hips still. Her most private of places was hot, wet. Bart's fingers brushed across the front of her panties. She whimpered. This was torture. Divine, beautiful torture.

Hurry! She grasped Bart's hand, forcing it past the elastic, down to the coarse red hair hidden beneath her panties. His fingers paused there for a moment, playing in the small forest, then moved on. She gasped, knees shaking at the slick wetness, the gliding of his fingers over soft, yielding flesh. A heady, sweet mustiness mingled with his cologne. The finger fluttered, and she moaned, her mouth seeking his. Waves of incredible, intoxicating pleasure pulsed though Gaia, reducing her to jelly.

At that, Bart scooped her up in his arms.

As Gaia held tightly to Bart's neck, he whispered, "Be careful what you wish for, Gaia Hassani."

She purred her answer as he carried her to the bedroom.

CHAPTER EIGHTEEN

Gaia ran her fingers through the sparse hair of Bart's chest. She tingled, from the tips of her toenails to the ends of her red tresses. Her breathing and heart rate had slowed from the orgasmic high of fifteen minutes earlier, the toe-curling climax still fresh in her mind. It was the nearest thing Gaia could think of to their two souls being joined as one.

She had been totally unprepared for her body's response to Bart's touch, the tender yet passionate strokes, the astonishing final invasion of her core. Not a word had passed between them since he swept her up in his arms. For her part, she still tried to comprehend and order the jumble of thoughts and sensations that had assailed her senses. For now, she basked in the glow emanating from her abdomen and a brain-chemical-induced kind of drunkenness. She floated, giddy and sated.

Bart had been everything she'd hoped he might be. Her dream, her fantasy, had become real, tangible. Beautiful. The reality of his lovemaking was far from the intellectual idea of love, the bare physical, sexual coupling she'd heard him describe many nights ago. His talk had done little to prepare her for the aftermath, the feelings that poured from her heart, the closeness she felt with this man.

Gaia snuggled closer, aware that Bart had not taken his eyes off her since their shared climax. She understood now what she had asked of him. To leave him now and return to Sanctum was unconscionable. To take this joy, his heart, from him this way and leave … Yet she had no choice. She must return. Those were the rules.

"I'm sorry," she whispered.

His fingers stroked her hair. "For what?"

"For forcing you into this. For taking part of your heart when I know I'll have to leave you. It was not fair of me. I didn't understand what I was doing. Will you ever forgive me?"

"First off, you didn't force me. I chose to go along with you. Yes, you have taken a part of my heart. But you had it already. It will be agony to lose you, to see you leave. But at least we shared this moment, this time together. The memory of tonight will never fade. I'll always remember you, my petite space lady." He nuzzled her neck, his lips educing a new set of shivers. Bart chuckled. "My Barbarella."

"Stop trying to make me feel good. You knew what I was doing to you, and you let me. Why would you put yourself through such pain?" She rolled away from Bart, feeling him spoon up behind her.

"Yes, I knew. And I chose to be with you. I chose to enjoy the moment, to take what time I could with you. It's what you asked of me. Don't spoil this moment. Treat it exactly as you said – moment by moment. You have given me something precious. I'm never going to forget you, Gaia Hassani."

Gaia rolled back to face him. Her hand traced the small lumps of his spine. "I … I'm going to miss you, too. More than I thought I might. I'm sorry. There are so many competing feelings racing round inside me. I don't know how to control this body sometimes."

"That's part of being human, Gaia. There is no controlling it, or its complex feelings and emotions. Sometimes, it's about the letting go. Welcome to Earth. Welcome to the human condition. And welcome to love, Gaia." Bart kissed her, brushing her teeth with his tongue.

"Ohhh. What are you doing?"

"Well, miss. There are a huge number of variations to the sensual acts that two people can perform. We only covered the basics the first time." He grinned.

"Bart, do you trust me?" Gaia slid her hand down his stomach, coming to rest on his manhood. She took it in her hand, caressing it.

"Ah, yes," he squeaked as she stroked him. "Why do you ask?"

"There is something I want to show you. You need to trust me." She could feel him hardening to her touch.

"I trust you. It's nothing kinky, is it? It appears I've awakened a monster in you. Oooo."

"What is kinky? I don't know this word. And what is this monster you speak of?"

"Sex. You enjoyed it, and, going by what you're doing to me, you want more."

"Oh yes. It was wonderful. I understand. You mean something in me wants more of you, yes?" Bart's hardness filled her hand. "You want me?"

"Yes, of course." He kissed her hard.

"Then trust me." She pushed him onto his back and straddled him, guiding him inside her. Her eyes closed, a small murmur escaping as she leaned back, taking him fully.

"You little vixen. Oh god. Yes, I trust you."

Gaia leaned forward, her elbows resting on either side of Bart, moving her hips against him. "Is that good? Am I doing this right?"

"Oh, god yes. Better than you know." Bart ran his fingernails gently down her back.

Gaia leaned over and kissed him, her passion mounting, small moans issuing from her. "Let me … know when … you're ready," she panted.

"Oh, you'll know. Soon."

Gaia worked her hips in a circular motion, pushing back at the same time.

"Oh god. You … I …"

Remaining on her elbows, Gaia brought her fingertips to Bart's head, thumbs touching the temple, the fingers spread out behind his ears. Feeling her energy building to a peak, she connected to Bart's. She felt their energy ebb and flow, pulsing backward and forward. Her lips twitched in amusement as she saw the look of surprise on Bart's face. "You ready?"

Bart didn't need to answer, she could see it, feel it, as their energies stopped pushing and joined. Gaia closed her eyes and pulled with her mind, merging their souls in the ether between them. She felt Bart twitch and let go, let her orgasm pulse over both of them, sharing hers, feeling his.

Gaia heard Bart's sharp intake of breath, felt his back arch as their combined energies rippled through him. Groans and words spilled from his mouth, but not in any language ever heard on Earth. He spoke in the language of souls, ancient beyond measuring. Gaia responded, stifling a giggle as she saw they were floating two feet above the bed. Through the intoxicating sensations that washed over them, Gaia heard something. *An echo? No.* It was gone again. *Maybe it was nothing.* She pushed, seeking, then pulled back, puzzled. *A barrier.* As if their joined souls shared a secret not available to even her.

Kaleidoscopes of shape and light pulsed through and around them, flashing outward to the walls and returning, crashing into each other, exploding and reforming anew. She felt the transfer of energy as Bart's semen issued forth into her, the released life force emitting primal emanations captured deep inside her, then shared through their soul link.

The peak of the wave passed. Gaia surfed the sensation, riding it beyond its normal, human limits. Bart shook, his eyes rolled back in his head. Gaia held on tight, refusing to let him miss one second of the ride, feeling the wave curl and crash upon her, rolling her off her imagined surfboard.

Trembling, Gaia eased their terrestrial bodies back to the bed. She kissed Bart, then studied him. He was still shaking, his body spasming. Only Gaia's weight, mounted on his hips, stopped his body from jerking its way off the bed. She leaned forward again and reconnected to Bart, brushing against his soul, speaking soothing words. His shaking eased, then abated. To Gaia's relief, his eyelids fluttered open.

"Sshhh, just breathe. Relax, my love." She kissed his face, his lips, feeling the heaving of his sweaty chest slowing. She swallowed, then blew several times, easing down her own heightened breathing. Gaia rested her hands on Bart's chest to steady herself, as the room revolved slowly around her. She wiggled her bottom against Bart's still-full erection. "Oooo. Wasn't that enough for you?"

Almost in response to her words, it twitched and began a slow deflation. Gaia pouted, then leaned forward to kiss a now focused but still silent Bart. She held his face and kissed him noisily. "Was that a bit much? Are you all right?"

Bart's voice came back hoarse, an echo of the soul still present. "I'm fine. Better than fine. Wow. I ... wow." He shook his head, blinking hard.

"You sure? I didn't frighten you?"

"No. No, Gaia. I … man, I can't find the words. That was incredible. Look at me; I'm still shaking." They both started laughing. "Phew. What did you do? I've had some good sex before, but … man, that was something else." Bart entwined his hands with Gaia's.

"I did two things." She pecked him on the cheek. "I joined our energies first, so we would share the pleasure of our flesh." She snuggled down on top of him and nuzzled his neck. "Mmmm. Very pleasant."

"It was extraordinary. But it was more than just the sex, the orgasm. Hey, don't squeeze like that, you'll … too late."

Gaia giggled as she felt Bart's limp penis fall out of her. She rolled off him, leaving a leg lying across him.

"You minx. You're getting the hang of this whole sex thing real quick." He laughed. "I still got a few things to show you that I know you'll enjoy." He ran a finger from her neck, down her front, to the thatch of coarse red hair. "Two things. You said you did two things. C'mon, spill."

"Spill?"

"Tell. Go on. Tell me what you did."

"Well, once I'd joined us energetically, I waited until we both reached the peak, you know, the point of no return." She giggled again and twirled a finger round one of his nipples.

"I know. Hey, behave. I need a rest, you nympho. Finish your story."

Gaia faked a pout and continued. "I pulled your soul partway out of your body and merged it with mine."

"Is that what the weird noise was?"

"You must mean the soul speak. It sounds peculiar to human ears; they're not designed to receive the frequency. Well, it's more than sound. I can't explain. There is nothing in any of the human languages to describe it."

"Yet, somehow, I understood a portion of it. Not in my head, but … out there, between us. It was like I knew you, from before."

Gaia ran her hand over Bart's chest. "That's not possible. We have never met. I'd remember." She smiled, but inside, her mind was in turmoil. She recalled the barrier, the thought that their two souls had conducted a secret conversation. *Why? I should have access to all of it. Why can't I see Bart's soul records?*

"Well. I'm not so sure about the soul thing, but you can do the shared energy thing again sometime. That was wild. I've never felt a woman's orgasm before." He frowned. "Man. Never thought that phrase would ever pass these lips. I just want to lie back and sleep after that."

"Don't. Please. Stay awake and snuggle with me. You don't have to talk. Just hold me." She laughed. "After I get back from the bathroom. Just be a minute." She rolled out of Bart's arms and dashed to the ensuite.

She returned a few minutes later, leaping onto the bed and bouncing on it next to Bart before settling down against him.

Bart rolled into Gaia, planting a juicy kiss on her. "I love you, Gaia Hassani."

"I love you, too, Bart. Please, don't let me hurt you."

***

A rhythmic thumping noise forced its way through a crack in Gaia's sleep. She blinked back the sunlight and rolled over, her arm seeking Bart. She propped herself up on her elbows, eyes sweeping the room for her missing lover. Not finding him, she rolled on her back and thrashed her legs and arms in a good-natured mini tantrum. *He has to stop leaving me alone.*

The thumping continued, changing note and tempo. Curious, Gaia slipped out of bed, shrugged into her trusty robe, and went in search of the source. She found it and Bart in the garage, where he was practicing his kung fu against a defenseless wooden dummy. She sighed as her sweaty, muscular, bare-chested lover beat the bejebbers out of the stoic dummy. Sensing her, he turned his head and smiled, before redoubling his efforts.

Show off. Gaia retreated to the ensuite and ran herself a shower before donning another of her Victoria's Secret ensembles. The red set she consigned to the laundry basket. She pulled the sequined t-shirt on over bare skin and donned the overlong jeans again.

A sweaty Bart tried to steal a hug and kiss.

"Ewww, don't you dare." She pushed the grinning Bart away, allowing him the kiss alone. "Shower, you brute. Then you can have a hug." She smacked his bottom as he slipped past her, then stopped, puzzled. *Why did I do that? Is it appropriate?* She shrugged and moved on. To the sound of running water, she brewed fresh coffee as she had seen Bart do numerous times.

"Getting you trained nicely." Bart rubbed the towel through his curls. He came up behind Gaia and kissed the nape of her neck. "You sort the coffee; I'll make some pancakes. Then we need to talk." He flicked the towel at a fast-moving Gaia, missing by a decent distance.

***

Bart sat back in the deep couch, put his hand over his mouth, and belched.

Gaia eyed him, her jaw working on her last pancake.

"Phew. I think I made too many, but I didn't know how hungry you might be." He frowned, looking at the few leftover pancakes from what had been a huge pile. Crumbs and blobs of maple syrup and whipped cream dotted the coffee table. Gaia seemed to be a bottomless pit.

"Yummy." She licked syrup from her fingers and settled back into the couch next to Bart with a sigh. "I'm full." She grinned and laced sticky fingers with his, the other hand covering her mouth in an attempt to disguise a long, strident belch. She flashed a toothy grin.

"You did well with that knife and fork." He squeezed her hand. "I didn't think you'd manage. At the beginning, you looked like me the first time I tried chopsticks. How do you do that?"

"Do what?" She leaned forward and scooped some leftover syrup up, slurping it off her finger.

"Learn stuff so fast. Knives and forks, computers, the shower." He opened his mouth for a finger load of syrup offered by Gaia.

"I don't know. I just have to touch something, hold it for a minute, and I know how to use it. Let me show you. Get a book from your library. Go on. Anything at all."

Bart frowned and eased himself off the couch. He selected a hard-covered version of *Lord of the Rings* and bought it back, sidling up next to her again.

Gaia took the book, placed it in her lap, and put a hand on top of it.

Bart watched as her eyelids fluttered, then closed.

She was silent for a moment. "Hmmm. Interesting. Exciting. A whole different world. Ask me a few things from the book." She grinned cheekily.

"Right oh, miss. He flicked through the book and selected a page at random. "What is the name of the bad guy? And what are his nine kings called?"

"There's two bad people; Saruman and Sauron. The nine are called Nazgûl, the ring wraiths. Try again." Her smile widened.

"Something a bit harder, perhaps." Bart retrieved a book on Quantum Physics. Then one on advanced Calculus. The result was the same each time. She knew the answers to whatever he asked. She frowned while handling the Physics book. When he asked her why, she responded by opening the book.

"This equation is wrong." One eyebrow lifted, daring him to prove otherwise.

Bart considered the selected equation. "Oh my god. You're right. I think it's a typo, but it is wrong."

Gaia had her head tilted to one side, smiling. "Told you."

"Can you do this with anything?"

"Yes. Well, everything I've touched so far. Something to do with universal shared consciousness." Gaia collected the dishes off the table and walked them to the kitchen.

"You might need to explain that. It sounds like it would line up right beside Quantum Physics, but …"

"It's simple, really. Everything ever built, thought, or done resides in a huge collective library, a part of the Akashic record."

She paused for a moment, puzzling over the memory of their joining, Bart's blocked soul record. "I can usually access the information by touching something. A bit like a computer download. For instance, I only needed to touch your coffee machine for a moment to know how all coffee machines work. Sometimes it almost seems like too much information, so I filter." She loaded the dishes into the dishwasher, turned it on, and grinned. "See. Dishwashers the world over, solved."

"Man. That's gotta be so handy. Hey, I have an idea. See if you can read one of these." Bart handed her a movie DVD.

Gaia held it for less than thirty seconds before she burst out laughing. "Funny. Did that really happen?"

Bart glanced at the label; *Ghostbusters*. "No. Most movies are made up. We call it fiction. That was a comedy, a funny story. Here, try these."

Over the next hour, Gaia worked her way through Bart's entire DVD collection. A couple of times, she stopped to cry at a weepy chic flick Rebecca had slipped in. By the time she finished, she was running around the room and ducking behind the couch. She pointed a finger gun at Bart. "Bang, bang."

Bart chuckled. "Let me guess. *Beverly Hill's Cop?*"

"Excellent." She turned and pointed at him again. "C'mon punk, make my day." She holstered her finger gun and wiggled her hips. "I see why you liked Barbarella."

Bart had to laugh. "All my secrets revealed. Which movies did you prefer? Comedy, romance, action, horror?"

"The ones that were funny and warm."

Bart nodded his head. "Ah, romantic comedies. Okay, today's film session is over. I think next time I'll give you some documentaries to watch. Real life, animals, history." He went quiet for a minute. "If there is a next time." He glanced over his shoulder as something occurred to him. "I'm gonna get you to handle a couple of devices, in case Terra turns up suddenly." Bart left the room and returned a short time later with a long case and a locked tin. He unlocked the tin and pulled out his Colt .45 automatic. "Here. I want you to know how to use this."

Gaia frowned and walked to where he stood. "I know what this thing does. I've seen one before. Is it really necessary that I know how to use it?"

"I think so. Once I get the special rounds I ordered, this gun should be able to stop Terra." He placed it in Gaia's hands.

"It's heavier than I thought it would be." She pushed a button to eject the magazine, then racked back the slide to ensure it was empty. She took up a stance and aimed it double handed at Bart's television. "Bang."

"Gaia, sometimes you are just a wee bit scary." He took the unloaded pistol and placed it on the counter top. He glanced at his watch and frowned. "I also want you to try this." He unzipped the long case and pulled out a scope-equipped .303 Le Enfield.

Gaia treated it the same as the pistol, ejecting the magazine and working the bolt to ensure it was safe. This time though, she placed a hand on the door jamb, using the hand and forearm to support the long-barreled weapon.

"Well done. That stance will give you much better accuracy over a distance."

Gaia tossed the rifle back to him.

"I think you need to filter out all the television and movie references when you learn some of your new skills. You're picking up some bad habits." He jumped at a loud knock at the door. "Shit." He slid the weapons behind the kitchen counter.

The knock repeated as Bart strode to the door and threw it open. "Mate, I expected you yesterday." He slapped Malcolm on the back.

"Yeah, sorry 'bout that. Had some problems with the castings. The first two attempts came apart. It's those damn crystal fragments. I had to jacket them. So, I got your .45s for you. Be another day for the .303s. Sorry." He handed a small box across. "You'll be here?"

"Should be. Otherwise …" He spun and beckoned Gaia over. "You can leave them with this lovely lady. Gaia, this is … Frank."

"Pleased to meet you, Gaia." Malcolm held out a hand and winked at Bart.

"And you, Frank. Bart, is that the best name you can come up with?" She flashed them a wide grin and retreated, leaving them both open mouthed. She deliberately tuned out from them but still picked up snippets of their conversation.

"… got a live one … cute … you dog … got you pegged … tell me about it." She leaned over the counter and smiled as they both looked over at her. Then the visitor was gone. Bart returned to the counter, tossing the box in the air and catching it.

"What you got there, cowboy?" she asked, blowing the smoke off the end of her finger gun.

"Humph. Sounds like you already have a pretty a good idea." Bart placed the box on the counter and retrieved the Colt. "What we have here, my dear, are some Terra wreckers."

"What is a Terra wrecker?"

"Each of these babies …" Bart thumbed the first round into the magazine. "… has forty-two shards of Moldavite in it, as we discussed."

"We discussed Moldavite, yes. Why forty-two?"

Bart did a dance, waving the magazine in the air as he chanted, "I know something you don't know." He stopped as he completed a turn and found Gaia staring at him with her hands on her hips. He cleared his throat.

"Forty-two is a power number. In Japanese, it's bad luck; the numbers pronounced separately sound like the phrase 'unto death'. In ancient Egypt, there are forty-two gods who ask questions of the dead before they can pass on. And, most importantly, forty-two is the answer to the meaning of life, the universe, and everything in *The Hitchhikers Guide to the Galaxy*. It's a cult book …" His voice drifted off as Gaia's jaw dropped.

"You're nuts, Bart Cooksley. Placing your faith in a piece of fiction." She shook her head.

"No more so than some of the things you can do. Think of it as my curse upon Terra. I have cast a spell to assist in her destruction." Bart stuck his jaw out, defiant.

"Fair enough. What you say is true. Sometimes it is the belief, the power we put into something that makes it work. So. I must get close enough to use this pistol of yours to kill or injure Terra."

"No. I'm going."

"You cannot. This is my task. Terra is fast and dangerous. She has powers even I know nothing of. No. I forbid you to go."

"You forbid me? It's not up to you, Gaia. I choose to go. You're not strong enough to face her yet." He raised his hand to halt her protest. "Yes, you are better. But making love with me is a long way from tracking a beast and destroying it. I can do this. I'm a soldier and a hunter. I've tracked animals before."

"Never one as clever, as cunning, or as single-minded as Terra. Please, you can't. I …" A tear ran down Gaia's cheek. "I beg you. I don't want to see you killed." She threw her arms around Bart's neck.

"And I don't want to risk the same with you. I will go. I would rather perish fighting Terra, trying to make you safe, than wait here worrying."

"All right. We both go. Between us, Terra will not stand a chance." Gaia pulled Bart close to her.

"No. I won't hear of it."

"It's not your choice. You just said it yourself. I don't belong to you. I choose to go."

Bart unlinked Gaia's arms and stalked away toward his workshop, slamming the door behind him. Gaia sniffled, then stormed off to the bedroom. It was time to organize better clothes and shoes. A few minutes of searching in the wardrobe, and she stopped, listening to the dull thumps as Bart beat up the long-suffering wooden dummy.

After ten minutes, the noise ceased. Gaia sat, alert, on the edge of the bed. A creak of hinges warned of Bart's return. She straightened herself and thrust her chin out, ready.

"Right. We both go. Meet me in the workshop. I want to double check all the circuits on your device." He spun on his heel and vanished through the door again before Gaia could utter a word.

Gaia reported as ordered. She kept her gaze averted, refusing to look Bart in the eyes. Her sly peek to the side told her Bart was doing the same. The first half of his tests were done in a brooding silence.

"Yours is fine. Fully charged," were the only words he uttered.

Gaia stayed, watching as he checked the larger VG^4 unit. Bart nodded his head after checking the battery charge, then powered up the unit. The familiar humming began to build.

"Hang on," he said. "What's going on here?"

Gaia couldn't resist moving closer to see what was happening.

Bart powered the unit down again, all the time looking at his watch. "Gaia, sweetheart."

Gaia's frost thawed. "Yes?"

"Can you take your device and hide it somewhere? Anywhere."

"Why? What's going on?"

"Please, just do it." The sweetness of his voice turned slightly acidic again.

Gaia pressed her lips together and pushed past him, returning a minute later. "Done. You grumpy bum."

"Can you just can it for a minute? Please." He left the room, all the time looking at his Timex watch. Beaming, he returned a minute later, carrying Gaia's disc.

"How did you find that? I …" She frowned, watching the smirk flitter across Bart's face. "Well?"

"My watch. I used my watch."

"What?" Gaia grabbed Bart's wrist, twisting it to look at the time piece. "How?"

"It's a Timex Expedition. It has a compass. The devices are putting out a magnetic field the compass is attracted to. Hang on." He powered off Gaia's tiny device and turned on his VG^4 again. "Yes." He punched the air, then moved around the room, checking his finding. "Do you know what this means?"

"No." Gaia couldn't help but be caught up in Bart's new enthusiasm.

"It means I can track Terra. As long as I power down my unit, my watch will tell me which direction to Terra, well, to her VG device."

"Our units, you mean." Gaia tried to look tough, but Bart swept her up in a hug.

"Yeah, yeah. That's what I meant."

"But doesn't your unit take a long time to charge? What if you get stuck, need to leave in a hurry?"

"It'll be fine, Gaia. This is great. It gives us an advantage. We can track her now. Woo-hoo!" He squeezed Gaia tight.

Give me matter, and I will construct a world out of it!

— Immanuel Kant

CHAPTER NINETEEN

Bart lay quietly, watching the slow fall and rise of Gaia's chest. Dim light from a quarter moon illuminated parts of the room as Bart eased himself out of her arms and slid from the bed. The carpeted concrete slab floor soaked up any sound as he crept from the room. He glanced at the coffee machine and shook his head. *The aroma might awaken Gaia.* He closed the door to the workshop and turned on a small work bench lamp.

He ran through the mental checklist he'd made many hours earlier. A voice tugged in his head, questioning his decision to lie to Gaia. *She did the same thing when she stole the disc device.* Yet, it didn't make him feel any better. He laid the heavy Colt .45 on the bench and unscrewed the watertight back cover of the VG^2, then disconnected the tiny power cell before reassembling it. *Sorry, sweetie. Don't want you tryin' to follow me.*

Carefully opening a locker on the back wall, Bart extracted a heavy jacket and wrapped it around the VG^4. He flipped the power switch, the humming of the capacitors barely audible. It took sixty-seven seconds. The green LED flashed ready. Bart drew in a deep breath and took the console in his hand, concentrating on Terra. This was a reconnaissance mission, and he pushed his mind, but not his body, to where she was.

Bart shivered, a little of Terra's location touching him. Snow drifted lazily though his vision, drifts eight feet high piled up to the left and right. Nothing appeared to move here. He pushed harder. Barbed wire, miles of it. Dull street lights flickering, an emaciated dog hiding, shivering with cold and fear. Bart jumped. Hungry eyes sought the dog. *Wolves.* A small pack of them darted from shadow to shadow. A sign, the words meaning almost nothing to him. Чернобыля. *Okay. It's Russia, or the Ukraine.* The final image as he pulled away; a huge dismal grey building, steam rising from tall stacks. *A power plant of some sort, perhaps.*

Bart powered down the VG⁴ and scratched his chin. *Russian winter. Shit. Hope I've got enough gear.* He returned to the wall locker and piled all the clothes there on the floor. Stripping off his bathrobe, he worked his way into four layers of New Zealand winter hunting clothes. *Hell, how bad can it be? I'll only be there an hour, tops. Kill this bitch and get the heck out of there. How much colder than Waiouru can the place be? But there was that winter training accident some years back. How many dead?* He shivered.

He flashed back to the barbed wire. Military? High security, at least. The voice in his head spoke again, and he listened. He squeezed into the hammer-repaired ballistic vest, then donned the storm-proof outer jacket. *Christ. I feel like the bloody Michelin man.* He moved his arms about, getting a sense for how restricted his movements were. *Okay. No hand–to-hand stuff, except …*

He stifled a laugh. *If she punched me hard in the chest, she'd break her hand on the armour plate in the vest.* He pushed the thought aside as he forced thermal-clad feet into fur-lined boots. Grabbing hold of the bench, he hauled himself to his feet. Bart stopped, listening to the sounds of the house. Nothing stirred. He hoisted the backpack over one shoulder, then returned it to the bench. Having adjusted the shoulder straps, he tried again, this time managing to push a contorted arm past the second strap. *Almost there, Barty boy.* He felt the weight of the pistol in his hand, considering his options. Six Terra rounds and three plain. He wondered if maybe he should stagger them in the magazine. But then, Terra was his primary target. *Please, let this go smoothly.*

A thought far more important flashed through his mind. *Please, let Gaia stay when this is over.*

Bart sighed and checked his Timex, hitting the power button on the VG⁴ at the same time. He nodded as the needle swung to face him. He double checked all the layers of clothing overlapped and slid a pair of snow goggles over his eyes. He pulled the fur-lined hood over his head and fastened the front closed. *There ya go, mate. Ya probably look like a bloody Eskimo spy. Raiders of the Lost Igloo.*

Shit. He checked back in the locker, dragging out a pair of sturdy gloves and fitting them to his hands. Bart fumbled with the pistol, sliding the rack back and setting the safety. *Locked and loaded. Ready as I'll ever be.* A green light flashed at the edge of his vision.

Look out, ya cosmic bitch; Flash Gordon's on his way.

Bart gritted his teeth and stepped into the mirage-like image in front of him.

With a flash, the window shut behind him.

***

"Fuck it's cold." Even through the cover over his face, breathing was painful. Bart stamped his feet and flapped his arms against his body, trying to generate some heat. *Fifteen bloody minutes, and I'm friggin' freezing. Jesus. Where the hell am I? Where the hell is Terra?* He forced his way through a snow drift and leaned against a tree, out of sight of a passing truck. *Decidedly military looking.*

The mission was spiraling downhill, fast. Following the compass in his watch, he'd made it all the way to a bridge crossing a wide frozen river. The sign Чернобыля once again presented itself, leaving Bart none the wiser. The small amount of Russian he'd learned years earlier, for a planned trip to St. Petersburg, was of no use.

Until, that is, he wiped some snow off the corner of the sign. The logo there was known the world over. A yellow and black circle, the colours alternating like heavy spokes. That symbol and the solid-looking guard post and gate at the river crossing told him all he needed to know.

It also told him his compass would be useless. The magnetic field generated here was magnitudes larger than Terra's device. *A nuclear power plant.* He pushed more snow off the sign. It pointed back up the road to another town, Припʹять. This time he remembered enough of the Cyrillic letters to put a name to it. *Pryp'yat'. Oh, crap.*

A chill, colder than the arctic winds around him, descended on his soul. He knew what the other sign said now. *If Gaia is right, and my devices open vortexes near major events, I'm fucked. I need to get out of here, fast.* Чернобыля made perfect sense now.

Chernobyl.

Bart forced freezing fingers to activate the power up sequence. He glanced about. He could feel eyes watching him. *Close. Just past the tree line.* His hand dropped to his pistol as a howl issued from the trees, followed by more.

Damn it. Wolves. I'm outa' here. He twisted his head to see the control console and cursed. *What's taking so long?* The LEDs had yet to pass the red mark.

Shit. Shit. Bart realized in a flash what the problem was. *The cold. The battery is dropping voltage in these temperatures. At this rate, it's gonna take ten minutes to charge up.* He pushed off the tree and clambered through the snow bank, to the road. *Keep moving. Stay in the open. If those wolves attack, at least I can see them.* He glanced back over his shoulder and saw something that sent cold tentacles of terror up his spine.

Terra.

The wolves had emerged from the tree line, advancing toward him in a tight arc. As in all wolf packs, the alpha was directing. Only this alpha had yellow eyes. Bart stumbled forward, desperate to make open ground. He ducked around a stunted tree and tripped. Snarling wolves were close. Numb fingers fumbled with the safety of the pistol. He stood again and then saw what he'd tripped on. A cake-tin-sized box.

VG¹!

His heart thumped so hard he could barely breathe. Terra had obviously left the device behind when she'd changed into a wolf, a shape more suited to these conditions. *Shit. I wish Gaia had warned me about that. Did she even know?* He gave it no more thought, firing two of his precious rounds into the device, shattering the circuit board and power cells. *Now you're stuck, you bitch. Mission partly successful.*

The howl from the alpha wolf almost paralysed Bart, its note primal, vicious. It vibrated in his head. He forced shaking legs across the road, glancing at the console again. Four more LEDs to go. His initial pessimistic guess was wrong. Four to six minutes. Head down, he almost missed it. The first wolf leapt off the top of the snowdrift at a full run. Bart swung the muzzle up, the round catching his attacker in the back leg.

The momentum of the animal knocked Bart off his feet. He fell hard on the compacted snow, driving the wind from his lungs. It was all he could do to keep hold of his pistol. *Keep going. Don't stop*, a voice in his head screamed. It wasn't the first time he'd been winded. His kung fu master made sure his students knew the sensation, understood that, while uncomfortable for a moment, it didn't mean death or total incapacitation. In that instant, Bart considered it to be one of the most valuable lessons of his training. Gasping for air, he rolled, trying to get to his feet. They slid out from under him, a powerful pair of teeth clamped tightly around his boot. The wolf tugged at the boot, snarling. Bart twisted, placing the pistol at the tip of the wolf's nose, and fired.

The animal didn't even whimper as the dum-dum round exploded in its head, splattering blood and brain matter for yards. Bart scrambled backwards on his butt along the slick surface, distancing himself from the remaining wolves. He counted six in all, two dead or wounded. One hung back, as the other three nuzzled and licked at their injured mate.

Flashes of light five hundred yards away diverted his attention. A siren sounded. Alerted by the gunfire, armed men spilled out of the guard houses at the river. *Shit. This just gets better and better.* He swung his pistol back to the alpha wolf. *Two special rounds left.* The animal stalked back and forth, at what Bart considered maximum accurate distance. *She knows. Fuck her.* He bent his leg, the knee acting as a rest for his hand.

Sitting on the frozen ground, the cold penetrating his body, Bart took careful aim. Both hands and the knee supported the pistol, the chill in his body causing it to shake. He tilted the gun higher, allowing for the distance, and squeezed off a shot. Snow erupted on the ground just in front of the wolf. It darted one way, then circled back, snarling. It howled, the other three wolves looking up, ignoring their now-dead companion. Bart squeezed the trigger again.

His target yelped, a spray of blood showing where the bullet clipped the skin, then passed on. *Fuck.* He dropped the sights, emptying his last few rounds at the more imminent threat, the three wolves closest to him. Two dropped and the third howled and limped away. Bart struggled to his feet. He holstered the pistol, his hands too numb to attempt to load another magazine. They were useless against Terra anyway. It was time to go.

He glanced at the control console. One LED from ready. A zipping sound startled him, followed by a thunk, thunk. Bart hunkered down as bullets kicked up icy fountains out of the compressed snow of the frigid roadway. From the direction of the bridge came the familiar, sinister sound of the ubiquitous AK47. He was beyond the maximum accurate range for this weapon, but it only took one round. Bent over to present a smaller target, Bart ran, away from Terra and the bullets that buzzed past him.

The blinding snow that now whipped around him, impeding his progress, came out of nowhere. The accompanying wind blew so hard, Bart found himself moving backwards, his boots sliding on the icy road. The sound of gunfire vanished, muffled by this sudden, extraordinary blizzard. He tried to turn, to fight his way through the wall of white. It seemed to follow him, stopping his escape as surely as barred walls. Beep. The console signalled full charge. Bart grasped it, triggering a portal, focusing all his will on getting back to Gaia.

A fur-clad Terra walked out of the blizzard in front of him.

"No!" she screamed, directing a burst of energy at him. The pulse hit the vortex, bending the shape of the shimmering wall, distorting and shattering the delicate, tenuous cosmic connection before passing through, knocking Bart off his feet. A bubble formed around the fractured vortex, squeezing, caving in the edges. Bart's insides churned. With a heavy heart, he hit the power switch, hearing the declining whine as the VG^4 powered down. He staggered to his feet, trying to distance himself from Terra. He needed time to destroy the VG^4. It would take too long to power up again.

Terra stopped as the bubble fluctuated and began to collapse in on itself. Bart guessed it was a bullet that affected the bubble's integrity. He never saw it, only felt it, suspecting that it passed through the shimmering wall of energy before striking him a mallet-like blow in the back. The bubble imploded, a massive force pulsing outward. Not even Terra was immune from its effect. It blew her backward into the snowdrift and cleared the blizzard she brought with her. From his position on the ground, Bart saw the progress of the wave, blowing the few street lights as it rippled away from them.

He tried to move, but his back screamed. He surmised the standard-issue 7.62mm round used by the Soviet troops had smashed through part of the VG^4 and hit his vest-protected back. It failed to pass through the ballistic armour, but that didn't stop it from hurting like nothing he'd ever felt. Bart tried to stand again, rolling onto his knees, preparing to push off with his hands. He paused, teeth gritted through the pain in his back, the enormity of the events unfolding dawning on him. He recalled some of the reports and debriefs from the Chernobyl disaster.

Partway through a routine test, an unexplained power surge hit the plant. *But how? This is a paradox. How can I have caused something I already knew happened?*

The weight of the problem seemed to hamper his efforts to stand. His boots slipped, and he fell forward again. *Cold. So cold.* He tried again.

"Where do you think you're going, asshole?"

A boot kicked his feet out from under him. He landed face first, the fur-lined hood barely cushioning the impact on the ice. White stars flashed in front of his eyes. Then, someone was on him, pulling at his equipment. He rolled over, arms flailing in an attempt to throw off his attacker.

It felt like a punch. A sharp stabbing pain between the armour plates of the vest, just beneath his bottom-right rib. He tried to move, but his torso refused to respond. His cold, aching hands fumbled for his combat knife. It was gone. He coughed, tasting blood in his mouth. Then the pain hit. Sharp, intense. Debilitating. He pushed for breath, wheezing. Panic welled up inside. His eyes struggled to focus. Terra stood over him, her hands smeared in blood. A fearsome howl issued from her. Something responded from the nearby woods.

Terra straddled Bart, her face near his, her cold, lifeless, yellow eyes boring into the very core of his being.

"Does it hurt? I think you'll find I've punctured a lung and liver. Shouldn't take you much more than about fifteen minutes to die. Not sure what will get you first. Will it be the wolf pack I just called? Or maybe you'll bleed out or drown in your own blood."

Bart was aware of the returning blizzard swirling around them. They were in what he thought was the eye of a hurricane. *So peaceful, quiet.*

He felt Terra working the straps of the VG⁴ off him, rolling him over to pull it free. "Will you look at that. They missed. Just clipped the casing. Thank you, Bart." She leaned forward and kissed him, then rocked back and laughed. "Now, this time, stay dead, will you? I'm sick of killing you and your lady friend." Terra leaned forward, her breath rancid. "You do know your precious Gaia burned to death? Such a shame." She cackled.

Bart felt the familiar tightness round his head as Terra probed his mind. The gloating look vanished from her face, replaced by anger.

"That fucking bitch is still alive? You interfering asshole."

Bart bit back the grunts that fought to escape as a frenzied Terra landed blow after blow with her boot against his ribcage. *I won't give you the satisfaction, you slag.* Only the vest saved the ribs from shattering and caving in on him. Terra stopped and turned her attention back to the VG⁴.

Bart spat blood at her. "You never …" He sucked in another breath. "That won't take you …"

"It doesn't need to, Bart. Just as far as Gaia is enough. And the other device. VG² was it? Looks like I need a new battery for this, though. Might be tough to find one round here, but I will. Then it's hello, Gaia - goodbye, Gaia. Wherever she goes, I'll follow. There is no escape." She howled again, calling the pack. "As for you … you should learn to die when I kill you. You've been a pain in the ass."

"You've never tried … to kill …"

"Oh, but I have, Bart." She smiled and patted his cheek with a blood-smeared hand. "Except you weren't driving that night, were you? A bit tipsy. So that silly bitch of yours, Rebecca was it, was at the wheel, sitting where you were supposed to be. Oh, poor Barty. You didn't know." Her taunting laughter sucked the spirit out of Bart. She kicked him again.

"I've had plenty of time this last week to rid myself of you. But you've proved rather resilient. I wish I'd known that cow, Gaia, was still alive. I'd have made a special effort, a double. The two of you could have held hands as I snatched your meaningless lives away. No matter. It seems a hands-on approach was much more effective."

Bart's stunned mind tried to order the information. It didn't make sense. It would mean his life was already a paradox, another path. *How?* Try as he might to fight her, to resist, his body relaxed, submitting to the cold that wrapped its icy fingers around his soul.

"That's it. Relax. It won't be long now. I can't wait to tell Gaia the good news. I'd better be off. The bullets those fools down there are firing won't kill me, but they hurt like hell. Hmmm, that's odd. What did you shoot me with, you prick? It went straight through the flesh, but the wound won't close. What? Cat got your tongue? Never mind. In a few minutes, it'll be the wolves that have it. Goodbye, Bart. Sleep well. I'll send Gaia your best regards."

Bart closed his eyes, feeling himself floating away. *Gaia, my love. I'm sorry. You were right.* He forced a hand to feel his right side. The hilt of his knife protruded exactly where Terra had said. *It's no good. The VG⁴ is gone.* He could feel the blood pooling on the ground, warm and sticky for the moment. It would freeze within minutes. Terra's blizzard still spun around him. In here it was silent, save for the sound of wolves sniffing him. Something tugged at his boot.

Bart opened his eyes and stared at the stars visible through the eye of Terra's artificial storm. A shooting star flashed across his dimming vision. The taste of blood filled his mouth. Between bouts of coughing, he made a wish.

Gaia, I love you. I wish I'd had the chance to spend my life with you. If you can hear me, I tried, but I failed. Terra's coming. Watch out.

Then he closed his eyes and let the cold take him.

***

Gaia jerked upright in the bed, a pain stabbing at her abdomen. Her breath formed a mist in the frigid air of what should have been midsummer heat. Shivering, she rolled over to cuddle up to the warmth of her Bart. Her arm floundered about in the half dark, finding nothing but cold, empty sheets. Gaia couldn't stop her teeth from chattering. *What is going on?* She dashed into the lounge, immediately hit with a wall of summer heat.

She could hear her heart pounding in her ears as she rushed back into the still-freezing bedroom. "Bart! Bart!" Gaia screamed. "Where are you?" Silence filled the chilly air. She tore her bathrobe off the stand and hurried back into the lounge. A quick inspection of the house revealed nothing. No Bart. Yet his car was there. She doubled back to the workshop.

Noticing the open locker and her VG^2 sitting on the bench, Gaia re-searched the house, paying particular attention for Bart's pistol and backpack. She winced at the pain in her side, opening the robe to look. An angry purple bruise had formed on the right side, just below the bottom rib. As she stood there, she realized the frigid air had somehow followed her, the workshop windows beginning to fog as the chill met the outside heat.

"Đă¢ ŶΛ Əơьıψ Нϧὠ."

Gaia staggered, the deep, ancient echo of soul speak resounding in her, the connection to Bart never completely broken since they had merged. Fear tightened its cold tentacles around her heart. *The bruise, the pain… they're Bart's.* Somewhere, his soul hovered, preparing to release its hold on his mortal flesh. "Nooooo!"

Gaia wrapped her hand around the VG², trying to find Bart. Nothing happened. She pushed every button, turned it over, shook it. Nothing. *Oh, Bart. What have you done?* She put one hand on either side of it and closed her eyes. She tried to force a smile at Bart's pathetic attempt to stop her, but it cracked, the corners of her mouth bent downward. *So. No power module. Not a major problem.*

Cupping the unit in her hands, Gaia focused her internal energy on the device, her body rocking as the unit pulsed into life. The process was not without its risks. Cut off from Sanctum, Gaia could not quickly recoup the energy extended. An aching hole inside her warned she would need a lot more yet. She reached out, searching the ether for her love. Cold, driving snow swirled in her head.

She started. *There. I see you. Hold on. Please.* A shimmering wall formed in front of her. "Bart." She could see him now, motionless, lying in a spreading pool of blood. Wolves circled, tugging at his clothing. Gaia let out a blood-curdling howl that made even Bart's inert body jerk. The wolves ran, tails between their legs. Before Gaia could savor the small victory, a voice hammered at her head like a thousand woodpeckers

"Ñž 'Ωij Σὰ ŒΨ." A transparent, wraith-like hand extended from nothingness, wrapping its spindly, bony fingers around Bart.

"NO, Thánatos. You cannot have him. **Hёş mį'nĕ.**"

The spectral hand pulled back, hovering, twitching, over Bart's still form. A sound like metal tearing hurt Gaia's ears. "Ựệȓŷ ŵệŁ⫪ . Ɓut hear me, Gaia. Even your power cannot hold back death forever. Ì Şhæȉl' ŘĘȚûȓŋ." The voice receded, the ethereal hand following.

Gaia took her hands off the time device, begging, pleading that the connection remain. The mirror-like wall shimmered and held. Gaia pulled the cord from her robe and lashed one hand to the workbench. The other, she brushed against the vortex, feeling the intense cold. Taking a deep breath, she reached through.

Razor blades of cold sliced into her bare skin. Ignoring the pain, she curled her fingers around Bart's belt and pulled. Her shoulder joints creaked, tendons strained. Bart slid a few inches and halted. Gaia screamed as she tugged at him again, gaining a few more inches. Her arm numbed, savage needles of cold stabbing her unprotected flesh. "Please, Bart."

"**Èõãã ѡḰІΟш.**" The sound came out of nowhere, from no one. As Gaia pulled one last time, Bart's body became weightless. Gaia fell over backward as he sailed through the vortex, landing with a dull thud on the floor next to her.

The vortex closed with a snap. Gaia unlashed her arm and fell on top of Bart. She placed a hand on his chest, feeling no movement, no warmth. Gaia ripped the combat knife from the sucking wound, then eased his outer jacket off. Numb fingers ripped at the Velcro straps securing his vest, throwing it to one side. She ripped off the buttons of the next layer and sliced up the centre of a thick wool base layer with the bloody knife.

Gaia's heart caught in her throat as the still-seeping wound came into view. She put her ear to his chest, heard nothing. "Nooooo!" She pounded on his chest. "Bart! Pleeeease. I love you. You can't die!" His body lurched to each impassioned blow. The eyes remained closed, his chest still. "Nooooo, Bart." Gaia lifted Bart's hand to her face, tears running freely. The first fell from her long lashes. Time slowed.

The tear hung suspended, gravity pulling it downward in inches. A speck of light reflected off the glistening surface of the salty vessel of love lost, before it accelerated onward, landing with a silent splash on Bart's chest.

Bart's body jerked upward with a raspy intake of breath. He gurgled, bubble-filled blood dripping from the corner of his mouth. Gaia felt a sense of absolute calm settle on her. No outside sounds intruded on her as she laid one hand on the wound and the other over his left lung. She closed her eyes and took up a chant, the words unknown to her, yet dancing off her lips as if she had spoken them a thousand years. Each tear she shed hit its fleshy target. Bart's body reacted.

Gaia tilted her head, and the tears ran down Bart's side, mingling with his blood. The bleeding slowed as her tears frothed and bubbled over the wound, slowly sealing it. Gaia swayed, her energy flowing out, ever out, her normal source of replenishment cut off, denied her. The tears flowed like a stream, each one contributing Gaia's love to the healing process. Bart's breathing, still raspy, settled into a steadier rhythm.

Gaia felt giddy. A golden halo of light surrounded their two bodies. All the sleep, all the energy she'd accumulated since her fever broke streamed out of her and into Bart. His eyes fluttered, then opened, unfocused at first. No longer tears of loss, Gaia's tears of happiness and love flowed uninterrupted.

CHAPTER TWENTY

It took Gaia four hours. Still in shock, Bart had regained consciousness long enough for Gaia to help him to his feet and walk him to the bed. Near exhaustion, Gaia lay next to Bart, her arm draped wearily over his heart. Her own breathing became harsher than his, her energy nearly drained. She pushed off him and piled blankets and duvets on her shivering lover. He lapsed back into a deep sleep almost immediately.

Gaia sat on the edge of the bed with her head in her hands. Bart was alive. She'd got to him just in time, as Thánatos arrived to take his soul back to the Guf. That Thánatos had yielded his prize to her was a matter of grave concern. Thánatos dealt in souls, the currency of the dead. *How did he know who I am? Does he come for me soon?* And his cryptic message about her powers. She recalled the moment she had touched Bart's soul, the lack of information available to her. Yet Bart had said she was familiar to *him*. It was as if everyone knew more about her than she did. *Is someone, or something, hiding my own history from me? How? I didn't think it was possible.*

Gaia wove an unsteady path to the kitchen and brewed a fresh coffee. She needed the hit she'd come to enjoy. Bart was alive, his wounds closed, but he would still require attention. She needed to be there for him. *At least for now.*

Blowing over the surface of the hot brew, she made her way back to the bedroom. Some colour had returned to Bart's face. It would be days, maybe a week, before he would be fit. Loss of blood and trauma had taken a toll. Bart's body would need time to heal. Gaia felt sleep tugging at her. It would take her weeks to recharge fully. The healing she'd poured into Bart's shattered lung and liver had all but depleted her. She sipped her hot drink, stroking his face tenderly.

Bart shuddered, muttering. "Terra. Wolves."

"Sshhh. You're having a bad dream, my love."

Bart's eyelids fluttered opened, the eyes rolled back, showing the whites. A hand grabbed Gaia's wrist, spilling hot coffee on Bart's arm. There was no reaction to the hot liquid. "She's coming for you, Gaia. As soon as she fixes the device. Run. Hide. NOW."

Gaia leapt off the bed, the coffee cup arcing through the air. "Terra. She's coming?" Gaia prodded Bart's chest.

There was no response.

"Bart. Is Terra coming here? How long? What's wrong with the other device?" Gaia shook Bart, to no avail. Lost in panicked thought, Gaia paced from one end of the house to the other. She wanted to sleep, to curl up next to Bart. *But if Terra is coming for me, I need to leave.*

A loud knock at the door jarred Gaia from her somber musings. Every fiber in her tired body screamed, doing its best to prepare Gaia for action. For Terra. She stared at the door for a moment and sighed. *Terra won't knock.* Gaia dragged weary feet to the door and swung it open.

Bart's strange friend stood there. "Hello ... Frank." Gaia tried to smile as she remembered the lame name Bart had invented for this man. "Bart's not available at the moment."

He smiled back. "That's all right. Gaia, was it? He asked me to drop these off as soon as they were ready." He handed a small cardboard box across for Gaia to take.

"Thank you. I'll let him know as soon as I see him."

Frank frowned. "You all right? You look a little pale."

Gaia blinked at the bright sunlight. "I'm fine, thanks, Frank. Bit of a hard night."

"Ah." He rotated his hand, imitating drinking from a glass. "I'm guessing Bart's sick in bed." Frank's wan smile broadened.

"Sick. Yes, that's it. It'll be a few days before he's recovered." *How does this man know Bart is sick?*

Frank chuckled. "You're good for him, Gaia. He hasn't tied one on for a while. Ever since ..." He glanced away. "Let him know I called. I couldn't give him the amount he wanted. Ran out of the material he provided. Later." He turned and disappeared down the pathway.

Gaia had questions for Bart. What was 'tie one on' and what did his friend mean by 'ever since'? She locked the door and dragged her feet back to the kitchen. She absentmindedly shook the box as she poured another coffee. An image of its lethal contents flashed through her head.

She ripped the box open. Three deadly-looking rounds lay on the bench. Gaia's head jerked up. She had a plan. Enough chasing Terra. Gaia would lay a trap, wait for her. Gaia gritted her teeth. And a backup plan, a fallback. Something ... inescapable. There was time for that later, time to think as she waited.

Yes. She had it now. She needed somewhere secluded, where this final, brutal encounter would affect no one. She spent ten minutes on Bart's laptop, finding a suitable location and checking the average weather conditions. Almost every place, every location, had people nearby. Gaia decided; a spot deep in Siberia, one hundred years ago. It would be perfect. Gaia would go there and wait. Terra would follow; she had to. She wanted the VG² and a chance to complete her twisted plans.

Gaia searched for and found Bart's gun safe. His four number combination was no match for her, even in her weakened state. She unzipped the long case, hefting the bulky weapon. The three rounds made a metallic sound as they slid into the short magazine. Gaia worked the bolt, chambering the first of the rounds, and set the safety. She knew it wasn't safe to leave the weapon like this, but if Terra turned up, she might not get the time to load. Now all she had to do was flip a small lever, point, and shoot.

Gaia carried the antique .303 into the bathroom, propping it against the wall as she stripped off and stepped into the hot, soothing shower. She put her hands against one wall, leaning forward as the water massaged her head and trickled down her back. Such a simple pleasure. She would miss this, and Bart, when she returned to Sanctum. If she got there.

No matter what happened, Terra had to be stopped.

By any means available.

***

Gaia checked over her outfit. Most of Rebecca's hiking gear fit well, except for the overlong pants and her boots. Three pairs of socks helped, though the boots felt odd to walk in. Gaia's internet search told her to expect temperatures down to zero Celsius this time of year. Tropical compared to the weather Bart had encountered.

Gaia recovered Bart's oversized camouflage outer jacket and pulled it on. Still damp from melting snow, the garment dragged her down, but she needed the camouflage. She put her hands inside the pockets. *Yuk.* Her body reacted to the cold stickiness of blood. But there was something else there. She gritted her teeth and pushed the hand into the pocket again, reemerging with the blood-smeared power cell for her VG².

Gaia nodded her head in thanks to the universe for this gift. She wasn't sure she had the energy left to power the unit and then complete her assignment. Carrying the old .303 Lee Enfield with her, she checked on Bart, then moved to the workshop. Gaia found herself impressed with the craftsmanship of the VG². The casing appeared to be hand made from aluminium alloy machined from a solid block. The two pieces fit together so well, she had trouble breaking the seal. There was obviously a trick to this. Frank flashed into her mind. *He made this casing.* There was more to him than she took in at first sight.

It finally popped open, revealing electrical components set in a black epoxy, holding them firm and offering protection from moisture. She wiped off the power cell and reconnected it. The two halves clicked back together far easier than they had come apart. She tightened the screws and ran her hand over the unit, sensing it respond to her thoughts. She felt better now. Finding the power cell boosted her confidence. She dropped the unit in her pocket and cradling the rifle, headed for the kitchen. There was one final task. One she considered of utmost importance.

Gaia set the coffee machine to make a fresh brew and washed out a thermos she'd found in the cupboard days before. It might be many hours, she surmised, before Terra appeared. Or seconds. She clenched her fists and picked up the heavy rifle again.

It was a good weapon, she decided. Old, but capable. It told her its name. *Betsy.* Named after a grandmother, by a proud man a century before. It spoke to Gaia of dead deer and pigs, of the bush and warm, happy campfires. It had a sinister side as well. An ex-army weapon, it knew how to kill men. She saw images of four men in odd, square-shaped helmets a half century earlier. Only one had survived this weapon's caress. It saddened her to think she would use it to kill another human.

Nỗ. The voice screamed from deep inside. *Not human. In human form, like you. You must kill her. Without feeling. Without mercy. You must do this, Gaia.*

Gaia jumped, snipping off the safety and swinging the long muzzle around the room, her eyes sweeping every corner. She let out a long, slow breath. Resetting the safety, she laid the rifle near at hand. Gaia poured steaming, aromatic coffee into her thermos and added cream and sugar. Remembering the effects of the sugar-laced desserts in Atlantis, she added more. The thermos went into a pocket inside Bart's voluminous jacket. Gaia slung the locked rifle over her shoulder, took a deep breath, and walked to the bedroom.

One last look. One last chance to be close to Bart. She sat next to him on the bed, stroking his face. His breathing, slow and steady, calmed her. Gaia lifted his left arm and removed the Timex. She needed the compass. She was setting a trap for Terra, and every assistance could help.

Gaia kissed Bart on the cheek. Tomorrow, he would wake feeling sore but alive. The wound was as healed as she could manage under the present constraints. As much as she wanted to stay and nurse him, she couldn't. Terra, and the fate of the cosmos, called. Gaia would go, comforted by the knowledge that Bart's body would do the rest. "Goodbye, my love. I'll miss you."

She left the bedroom, stopping long enough to glance at the note she'd written earlier. In the lounge, she turned in a slow circle, taking in the now-familiar shapes, colours, and smells of Bart's house. *I could have lived here.* She patted the breast pocket of his jacket. *I hope you don't mind, my love.* Nestled safely there, sat a treatise on Quantum Physics, written by one Professor Bartholomew Cooksley, MSc Hons, PhD, CRSNZ. Gaia had resisted reading it so far, by either of the methods she knew. It was something special, for later.

Gaia checked the rifle for the *nth* time. Locked and loaded. She put a hand in her pocket and fingered the small aluminium disc. It sprang to life, an obedient dog waiting for directions. Gaia pushed down the emotions that threatened to immobilize her and triggered the vortex. The shimmering mirage floated in midair, waiting for her.

Gaia took one final look, breathed in the smells one last time, and stepped into the portal.

***

The first birds took up their dawn chorus. The sweet sounds drifted into Bart's consciousness. He rolled in the bed, flinching at two separate pains, one in his back and the other in his side. His eyes flew open, his brain registering the familiar sights, sounds, and scent of his own home. He shifted a hand down his right side, feeling the skin there. *A scar. How is this possible?*

Gaia. You amazing woman. That hand couldn't reach, so he swapped, feeling a lump in his back. *Ow. Big bruise there.*

He rolled back the other way, snuggling behind the sleeping form, his arms encircling her. *Pajamas? Those are coming off as soon as I feel well enough.* He smiled, nuzzling his lips to her neck.

"Hmmm. Now you're in the mood. I tried to wake you hours ago. You've been dreaming all night. Kept pulling the blankets off me. So, who's Gaia?"

Bart chuckled. *In a mischievous mood, eh?* Still, there was something odd about her voice. Taking a firm hold on her shoulder, he rolled his love on her back. The soft, slightly-cherubic face of his dead wife looked up at him.

"Rebecca? You're here?" Instinctively, he reached out and stroked her curly brunette hair, running the fingertips over the curve of her ear. Her deep brown eyes twinkled between long curved lashes. A heady dizziness overcame him. *Rebecca. My love.*

"Excuse me, Bart Cooksley. I live here, remember? Wife." She waved the wedding ring in the air.

Current reality caught up with him. He recoiled in shock. "No. That's not possible. I saw … I saw . . . You didn't make it."

"Bart, you're not making any sense. That must have been what you were dreaming about." She reached under the sheets. "Why are you wearing your clothes in bed? Off. I want you, lover."

190

"No. This can't be happening." He repulsed his pajama-clad wife, sliding off the edge of the bed with a thunk.

"What is the matter with you, Bart? You're behaving really weird." She reached for him.

Bart ran from the room, grimacing at the ache in his ribs where he'd been shot.

"You're beginning to piss me off, Bart. Come back and make love to me, now."

Bart leaned on the kitchen counter, shaking his groggy head. This just couldn't be happening. He glanced around the lounge, his jaw dropping. The colours, coverings, furniture. Everything had changed.

Rebecca yelled from the bedroom. "Get back here now, Bart Cooksley!"

Sweat dripped off his brow. The effort of moving even that short distance exhausted him. He fingered the jagged four-inch scar below his ribs. Gaia was no cosmetic surgeon, but it didn't matter. He was alive. *But where? When?* He emptied two glasses of water down his throat and stood there gasping. Leaning back on the counter for support, he pushed his brain to try to figure this out.

Which of my lives is real, and which is the paradox? For almost two years he'd struggled to cope with Rebecca's loss, dreamed about her, begged for her to come back. The moment he'd moved on, Gaia came into his life. *Is Gaia even real?* The scar said yes. Yet Rebecca lay in his bed, calling for him.

Feet stomped around the bedroom. She peeked around the door.

"Don't think you can come crawling back later and expect to get lucky, mister. You owe me an apology." She vanished again.

Bart heard the sounds of the shower running. *What the hell do I do? I love them both. I can't make a decision, not now. And how much of this is real? Shit. Workshop. Check the workshop.* He hastened across the room, lurching into the doorjamb. He supported himself, waiting until his head stopped spinning. *This is real. Symptoms of blood loss.* He pushed open the door to his workspace and froze in the doorway.

Pieces of shredded clothing lay strewn across the floor. A huge pool of blood smeared with foot and handprints took centre stage. Red handprints dotted the bench top. *Gaia. Where are you?* Bart staggered to the bench, slipping in the still-wet blood. He pulled open a drawer and extracted a dog-eared scrapbook. His hands trembled as he flicked through the pages, stopping at a newspaper clipping from 2009.

His stomach churned, dry retching. The newspaper clipping was from the local paper, a copy of Rebecca's obituary. *This can't be happening. It defies all the laws of time and relativity. This is a paradox within a paradox. Shit. Shit. Shit. I can't have Rebecca's death notice and her. It's not possible.* He shoved the book back in the drawer as the shower stopped running.

Bart propped himself against the bench, blinking his unfocused eyes. *What the hell do I do? Where's Gaia?* The wave of nausea passed, and he glanced around the room. *No, Gaia. Please, no.* The VG^2 and his camo jacket were missing. *She's found the power cell. Too damn clever for her own good.* He lurched to the gun safe, swinging open the unlocked door. His .303 was missing.

Rebecca's voice carried from the bedroom. "Bart, what's going on here? Some of my clothes are missing."

He ignored her, his mind stuck in a deep, dark hole. A squawk from the bedroom intruded on his thoughts.

"Bart, what the fuck is going on?" The volume of Rebecca's voice increased by the word. "Why is there a note from a woman in our bedroom? Who the fuck is Gaia?" Cold eyes bore into him. "Are you cheating on me? You fucking asshole!"

A note. Gaia left a note. Clutching his side, he tottered toward the door.

"I want an explanation …" Rebecca froze in the doorway to the workshop, her face ashen at the sight of the blood. The note dropped from her hand, the hand sweeping up to cover her mouth as her body retched. She turned and ran for the bathroom.

Bart placed a hand on the wall for support and bent over for the precious note.

"My dearest Bart. Don't be angry with me. I wanted to get some sleep, recharge a little after fixing your wound, but I have to stop Terra. You said she was coming for me. I couldn't let you be there when she did arrive. ☺ Your friend came back with the three special rounds you ordered. So I've set a trap of sorts. Betsy (that's the rifle's name) and I have gone to a deserted spot next to the river Podkamennaya in Siberia, 1908. I chose this spot so no one else will get hurt. I'll set up a hide and try to get some sleep while I

wait. It'll all work out. You'll see. I love you, Bart Cooksley. I wish things could have been different. I'll never forget you. Love, Gaia."

Bart read the note four times. He slid down the wall he'd been leaning against, head held in his hands. *I love you too, Gaia.* His head came up as a pale-faced Rebecca returned from the bathroom. He'd loved this woman once, still loved her, and would have given his all for her. But she was dead. This Rebecca wasn't real. She was an abomination, a ghost. A zombie.

"Bart. This ... I ... I can't take this. This is too weird, even for you." She walked into the bedroom. "I'm going to spend a few days at my sister's."

Bart sat where he was, unable to move or think straight. He stared at the wall across from him. Rebecca walked past him with a bag in her hand. She said words, but none of them penetrated. He heard the garage door opening, closing, and the sounds of her car driving away. He sat still. The ache where his heart used to be was infinitely more painful than the wounds he'd sustained. Gaia was gone. A hole opened up and swallowed him. *Why didn't she just let me die? I wouldn't feel any pain now. Wouldn't suffer the death of a thousand cuts never seeing her again will inflict upon me.*

Siberia, 1908. Something about the date gnawed at him. *1908?* Bart unwound his stiff body and crawled across the wool carpet to the coffee table and his laptop. As the machine booted up, he glanced across at the coffee machine. *Probably not a good idea just yet, Bart. Stick to water until you're better.* He logged on and Googled Siberia, 1908. Nothing. Not a single item returned. Yet something nagged at him. He shook his head, reeling at the dizziness the action caused.

"Gaia, my love. Be safe."

Quantum theory thus reveals a basic oneness of the universe. It shows that we cannot decompose the world into independently existing smallest units. As we penetrate into matter, nature does not show us any isolated "building blocks," but rather appears as a complicated web of relations between the various parts of the whole. These relations always include the observer in an essential way. The human observer constitute the final link in the chain of observational processes, and the properties of any atomic object can be understood only in terms of the object's interaction with the observer.

— Fritjof Capra

CHAPTER TWENTY-ONE

Gaia cast her gaze around the silent, brooding landscape. Stunted trees stretched across the horizon for as far as she could see. *Not an ideal site for a trap.* Trees in this part of the land were thin and weak, with little in the way of shrubbery or ground litter to provide cover. She sighed. The lack of concealment applied for her as well. She trudged a short distance to the dominant piece of ground, a small mound that offered a wide range of sight. This would do.

Moving in a circle, she collected fallen branches and dragged them to her high spot. She lined a natural hollow in the earth with the moldy-smelling leaf litter and bark, then linked larger branches together to form a makeshift roof. Gaia slid into her hide, checking the landscape in each direction. Not satisfied, she wriggled back out and collected a few more branches, stacking them around the base as a wind block and rifle rest. Back inside again, she nodded to herself and checked Bart's watch and rifle.

The compass needle hovered in a tight arc pointing magnetic north. She switched on the VG^2 for a moment, smiling as the needle swung toward the device. Then she settled back to wait.

Seeing the sun had a few hours left in the sky, Gaia pulled her bulky gloves off and rubbed her hands together. She moved a little of the leaf litter to make herself comfortable and dipped inside her jacket for Bart's book. She resisted the initial urge to scan the book, instead flipping it open to read it. Every few minutes, she put it aside to check the compass and scan the horizon for movement. The first cup of coffee slid down almost unnoticed as weariness forced its cloying, somnambulant grasp over her.

***

Gaia's head nodded forward. She blinked her tired eyes, her hands searching for her precious coffee thermos. She twisted the lid and frowned. Enough for two more small cups. Very small. The futility of her trap weighed down on her. *Sixteen hours so far, and no sign of Terra.*

Gaia began to question her strategy. *Perhaps it would have been better if I chased Terra again. No. That hasn't worked.* Terra seemed to be ready for her each time Gaia arrived. She twisted her stiff body, stretching tired muscles as much as the confines of her hide allowed. She stifled a yawn and looked out over the endlessly-silent landscape.

Huh. Something moved. It made a change from the nothingness of the previous hours. Some distance away, a lone wolf meandered along, sniffing the ground, stopping every now and then to look about. Gaia smiled. *Wolves. Such beautiful primal beasts.* She glanced down at her watch-compass. Tentacles of ice crept through her bloodstream, revealing themselves as a shaking in her hands. The compass had swung eighty degrees, in the rough direction of her furry friend.

Gaia fought the urge to snap shoot. Instead, she took deep, slow breaths, shifting the old .303 in even, deliberate movements. She squirmed her body around to point toward where Terra should be. Making a minor adjustment to the telescopic sight, she slowly swept the area. *Nothing.* Except the wandering wolf.

Gaia blinked her eyes and tried again. *There. A glint of something, a reflection of the rising sun, about a thousand yards out.* She squinted, twisting the focus ring on the scope. *Nothing.* A cloud moved on, letting the sunlight glint again on … a brass buckle. Gaia could just make out an old backpack, with it's thick webbing and brass fittings.

She took a deep breath. What was this bag? Could this be the device Bart used? She looked again, frowning as she swept the barrel across the area. *Where are you, Terra?* Gaia eased the rifle down and stared out over the landscape. Her tired mind tried to put the pieces together.

The backpack lay close to where Gaia had arrived. The only living thing between that spot and her was a wolf, sniffing the ground, working its way in her direction. Gaia watched, motionless, as the animal picked a path among the trees, scanning left and right as it went, searching for something or someone.

Gaia swallowed the scream of anger that tried to emerge. She shrugged her shoulders and drew the stock of the rifle tight to her. A small twist of the scope brought the wolf into sharp focus. *Terra. It has to be.* Calming her breathing, Gaia eased the safety off, her finger sliding along the outside of the trigger guard. Gaia would have sworn the snick of the safety was no louder than the sound of her breathing.

The wolf looked up, nose sniffing the air. Yellow eyes seemed to peer directly at Gaia, piercing her soul.

Terra.

Gaia squeezed the trigger, feeling the heavy weapon recoil against her shoulder. She kept both eyes locked on the wolf. A tuft of fur flew off it's back, the bullet continuing on and striking a tree a few feet beyond Terra. *Damn it. High.*

Bullet and wood splinters exploded back from the tree, striking the side of the animal before it had a chance to react. Gaia worked the rifle's smooth bolt action, ejecting and chambering a new round. A yelp, followed by a blood-curdling howl reached across the gap, stabbing painfully at her ears. The pitiful wail reached inside her, scraping at her already-raw nerves. It felt like Terra was trying to paralyze her. Gaia pushed hard, striving to drive back the effects of Terra's primal cry. Hesitantly at first, she compelled her sluggish limbs to react to her command. The rifle tracked right, seeking the wolf. Gaia's control returned as she spied the limping animal. *Good. Injured.*

Massive black clouds churned in the sky, blotting out the sun. Flashes of lightning arced between them as they gathered together at a rate outside the norm of nature. Wind began to tear at the tops of the trees, bending them as it raced to ground level. Gaia tried to keep the obscured wolf, Terra, in her sights. Terra wove back and forth, working her way toward Gaia by degrees. After zigzagging four times, Gaia realized there was a symmetry to the evasive tactic. Eight steps in each direction.

She swung the rifle ahead of Terra, counting her steps. The rifle recoiled again, Gaia working the bolt as another yelp reached her over the screaming of the wind in the trees. She steadied herself and stared down the tube of the sight. *Damn. I overcorrected.* The wolf, Terra, was within two hundred yards now, limping from the first shot. Gaia tried to smile as the wolf turned again, moving from left to right. Half her tail was missing.

The seriousness of her task precluded any levity. Gaia had one round left. She jumped as a lightning bolt struck the tree nearest her hideout, splitting it. The two halves hung suspended before slowly falling away from each other. Smoke and the heavy smell of ions hung in the air momentarily, to be whipped away by the encroaching wind and driving sleet. The wind shredded the flimsy roof of what had been her home for the last half day, swirling the debris to the four points of the compass.

The chilling, sleet-laden wind searched out every crack in her clothing, every exposed piece of skin. The sudden drop in temperature shook Gaia, the sleet now hail, cold, hard, stinging. She tried to locate Terra, the wolf, but the darkness was almost total. Gaia hunkered down as low as she could in her shallow hollow. The wind seemed to know where she was, focusing its wrath on her. Even with the hood to Bart's extra jacket pulled up over her head, her ears and nose stung, the cold, razor-sharp teeth of frostbite nipping at her body.

Gaia rolled into a tight ball, tucking her face inside the folds of Bart's jacket. Her teeth chattered, her body shook uncontrollably. What little strength she had left was being sucked out of her by the cold, merciless wind. Terra was going to freeze her into submission, or death. Gaia felt so tired, so sleepy. Her eyes fluttered closed. *Peace. So peaceful.* She drifted on a leaf, warm sunshine filling her.

Ĝæîȧ . Ŝẖë đ̦åŵ̦ş ńæ̦. Ŗ̄ēŝị̦şt.

The words shocked Gaia alert. *Who?* She curled numb fingers around Betsy and lifted the muzzle, pointing it in the rough direction of Terra's approach. The cold bit deep, sapping her. Heavy eyelids fluttered again. Light. There was light. Gaia's head flopped forward, then snapped back, fighting sleep. The wail of the wind was distant, a window of silence and light where she lay. A shadow passed in front of the light. Gaia squeezed Betsy's trigger, feeling the recoil, hearing the crack as her last hope, the universe's last hope, left the barrel.

"Ŝč̦æëèèè"

The shrieking was like nothing Gaia had ever experienced. It tore across the bleak landscape. Gaia tried to cover her ears, but the scream penetrated every crevice of her body, tore the very marrow from her bones. It seemed a combination of fingernails on a blackboard, tearing metal, a glacier carving, and young girls screaming, all mixed and amplified beyond human comprehension. Gaia writhed in agony, even as the screeching receded and faded. *Surely even the Wraiths of Tolluk Morre would waver at such a sound.*

Gaia rolled onto her back. Her body no longer shook. Numbness, calming and hypnotic, replaced any pain. She fought to keep her eyes open, her mind drifting between the two realms of her existence. All thought of resistance, of survival, were gone. *Let me sleep.*

Something warm splattered on her cheek. A boot kicked her ribs. *Pain? I don't care.* More blows, more pain. It forced open a tiny window of consciousness. *I've failed. She still lives. Leave me alone; I want to sleep.*

Terra's voice reached inside Gaia's barrier of oblivion.

"Wake up, you bitch. I've come to kill you."

***

Bart jerked awake, the only light in the room his laptop's screen saver. He pushed himself upright on the comfortable leather couch. "Ow." The healing bruises on his back and ribs screamed protest. "Bugger. I was hoping some of this was a dream." Moonlight peaked out from behind heavy clouds, casting beams of light and dark across the lounge. "What the fuck…"

Using the couch for support, Bart forced himself upright and stumbled to the doorway to the garage. Light blinded him as the room's lamps responded to the flick of the switch. "Holy shit." Bart shook his head and blinked hard, trying to focus his vision. As if to confirm what his eyes were seeing, he turned and opened the garage door. *My car is back. Or did it ever leave?*

Running a hand along the wall to steady himself, he made his way to the nearby workshop. No change. A pool of dried blood covered the floor. Yet, the entire lounge had returned to the way he remembered it, the way it had been the night Gaia first turned up at his door. An uncomfortable thought nagged at the edge of his consciousness. Stopping in the kitchen for two more glasses of water, Bart made his unsteady way back to the couch.

He logged back into his laptop and reran the previous evening's Google query. This time, the answer came back different.

"Nooo, Gaia. No. Pleeeeease."

He hoped it was a coincidence. He pleaded with the universe for it to be any other day. Maybe a different location farther up, or down the river. But he couldn't escape the pain eating him alive.

The first page of results for Siberia 1908 had all come back different this time, all the answers the same. One pivotal event. One devastating outcome.

Tunguska.

***

Gaia pushed weakly at the hand searching her jacket. *The disc.* A chuckle of triumph carried to her between gasps of pain from Terra.

"Finally. So much fucking about for this one small toy. How does it feel, Gaia? To have failed again." A grunt of pain mingled with the gloating.

Sharp stabbing pain in Gaia's ribs dragged her back from sleep. Her eyes opened.

"Ah, so you are still awake. Just in time to die. With any luck, I'll go straight from this tender moment with you to my desired destination. But just in case …" Terra doubled over, then stood straight again, her face pale and drawn. " … I'll make sure you're dead this time."

The air around them was calm, as a hundred yards away, the wind circled at hurricane force. Trees cracked and tore from the ground, joining the devastation that churned like some demonic debris-filled spin cycle. Gaia managed a wry smile as she watched Terra examining the VG². Blood dripped from numerous small body wounds, doubtless caused by the back-blast splinters of the first bullet.

Gaia gasped as Terra turned to look at her. Most of Terra's left arm was gone, only the shoulder joint remaining.

"What're you looking at, bitch?" Terra's boot connected with Gaia's ribs again. "Look what you did to me." Terra teetered backward. "Shit. Just as well this will *all* be over shortly. Whatever you put in those bullets is stopping my body from regenerating. Shame you're such a lousy shot." Terra staggered again, struggling to maintain her balance.

Terra stuffed the VG² in her pocket. "How does it feel to be the one who let down the entire human race?"

Gaia hovered between nausea and sleep. She had no more weapons, no more ideas to stop Terra. She'd failed. Not just humanity, but the entire universe. Terra would kill her and then depart for her destination. Within a few minutes, the entire universe would be a void. Nothing.

"You can't do this, Terra." The words squeaked through ice-cracked lips.

"You just don't see the big picture, Gaia. I have to. How long before man spreads out from here and infects other planets? Because that's what they do. Infect. They're a virus, consuming the host at even the cost of their own existence. A cosmic, human-sized Ebola."

Terra grimaced as she dug deep into her jacket, the one good hand emerging with a wicked-looking blade. "Time for you to die, Gaia. How fitting you should go the same way that impotent soldier of yours did." Unable to lean over, Terra crouched next to Gaia.

Gaia found her smile, something to hold on to, be it briefly. "I saved him, Terra. He got to live a few more hours. You're not as effective as you think you are."

Terra snorted, tossing the knife in the air and catching it blade side down, ready to stab Gaia. She shrugged. "Doesn't matter now, does it? You'll be dead in a few seconds, and there are no more devices to chase me with." Terra gazed over her shoulder, her expression tired, face drawn tight with pain. She pointed the knife at the swirling typhoon. "The backpack is in that. Even if you somehow survive, it's confetti now." She raised the double-edged blade and slashed downward with all her weight toward Gaia's chest.

Gaia tensed, feeling the blade strike her. It hurt, but not as much as she thought it might. Instead of tearing, rending flesh, she felt a dull ache.

"What the fuck." Terra pulled the arm back and stuck the blade in the ground next to her. "What you got in there, bitch?" A shaking, blood-smeared hand unzipped Gaia's inner jacket and clumsily rummaged round inside. "A book. A fucking book. Is this what you carry as body armour these days, Gaia?" Terra glanced at the cover and sneered. "Huh. Bart Cooksley. You sentimental cow. You brought a book by Bart. It saved you once, but not the next time." Terra threw the book over her shoulder and reached for the knife.

I'm sorry, Bart. I tried.

- $E=MC3$.

What?

- $E=MC_3$.

The equation, and something Bart had said at the house, ricocheted round inside Gaia's head. He'd been commenting on Einstein and variations in matter and theoretical antimatter. Bart had got it wrong, but … YES!

The warm glow of hope radiated outward from Gaia's heart. A reference from Bart's movie collection popped into her head. "Terra, what we have here, is a failure to communicate."

Terra frowned, the knife poised over her head. "Communicate this." She raised the knife higher.

"I have a present for you, Terra." Gaia turned away so she couldn't see what lay in her hand, the only thing she had enough energy left to manifest. Five grams of pure energy, held in a vacuum. Five grams. A mere teaspoon full.

Terra's gaze flicked to the tiny energetic mass in Gaia's hand. "NOOOOOOO!" The instant her eyes observed the swirling mass, it quantum locked, moving out of theoretical existence, into actual physical being. A millisecond later, the vacuum surrounding it collapsed.

The five grams of antimatter reacted to the matter around it. The annihilation of the antimatter released energy out of all proportion to the mass it contained.

Gaia felt no pain, no pleasure. The instantaneous release of energy vaporized everything for a square mile, the shock and heat waves reaching out another forty miles in all directions.

Gaia felt herself floating between time and space. *Time to return to the Hall of Souls.*

Goodbye, Bart. I did it, my love. I saved everyone, everything.

Everyone except me.

I love you.

CHAPTER TWENTY-TWO

Bart sat with his head in his hands. Red-rimmed eyes stared at a spot on the blank wall. He wiped a tear from his cheek. *Gaia, why Tunguska? Did you even know?* No one had ever figured out what happened that day, June 30, 1908. The region was so remote, it was a decade before the first expedition even tried to reach the area. They'd failed, the next major attempt many years later.

The most popular theory; a comet had broken up in the atmosphere. The airburst explosion destroyed eighty million trees and over eight hundred square miles of forest. Nothing stood upright there even thirty years later. Other theories included a micro black hole. Or an antimatter blast. Or ... So many theories. None of them changed the actual outcome.

Bart sniffed. He had to admit, as a solution to Terra, it was eloquent, if somewhat heavy handed. He forced himself to stand. "Whoa. Earthquake." Glasses rattled on the kitchen shelves as Bart eased himself to the floor between the couch and coffee table. A mug fell off the kitchen counter, smashing on the tile floor.

Gaia's mug. It felt like the broken shards stabbed his heart, a wave of nausea and sorrow spreading outward to reach every extremity. Bart hadn't felt this wretched since Rebecca's death. And now it was happening all over again. Gaia walked into his life less than two weeks ago, but it felt like he'd known her forever. The earthquake slowed and stopped. Bart started to rise.

"Shit. Déjà vu. I hate that." Another thing that reminded him of Gaia. He wondered what change had taken place. He realized he knew. *Tunguska.* The ripples of Gaia's success were reaching through time.

"ĐŪČҚ"

The deep guttural sound seemed to pull his arms out from under him. Bart face planted on the soft carpet. "Ow." He rubbed his sore nose. The house began to shake again. Except ... Bart noticed none of the glasses rattled. He poked his head around the end of the couch in time to see the front door bending. He pulled his head back. Boom. The door blew inward, as it had the night Terra visited. "Oh shit. Not again."

Pieces of timber and glass sprayed across the room, Bart's favourite couch upending on top of him, providing a handy shelter. Bart lay motionless, fearing Terra might yet enter. There was silence. He waited another minute, then hauled himself slowly out from underneath his makeshift bomb shelter. *Humph. Now the house is back the way it was. Gaia was successful.* Bart's eyes misted with emotion. *Oh, babe. I loved you. I miss you.* He took a deep, painful breath. *Damn it. Sick or not, I need a drink.* He started toward the kitchen.

"Oh shit. This just gets weirder and weirder." The shards of Gaia's coffee cup lifted slowly off the floor and swirled in the air above the counter top. Bart backed away as the coffee machine joined it. Before he'd backed as far as the couch, every item on the counter was spiraling like a slow typhoon. Cups and glasses leapt out of cupboards and joined the melee of spinning kitchen equipment. "Where's a bloody camera when you need one."

Bart began to shiver. Frost appeared on the glass fronts of the kitchen cupboards. Snow started to fall in his kitchen. Bart stood there, his jaw reaching for the floor as the swirling mass turned to a miniature blizzard. He backed up farther. Pictures and diplomas rattled on the walls. The circle of debris widened.

A dull thump sounded from the kitchen. Everything stopped, suspended, frozen in space. Not a single plate, cup, glass, or snowflake moved. Bart edged toward the strange phenomena, feeling a wall of intense cold as he approached. He blinked.

Gravity reached out and clawed all the items to it. Plates, cups, and glasses smashed on the tile floor and granite counter top. Bart scratched his head. *My bloody coffee machine better not be broken.*

A whimper from behind the kitchen counter tore at his heart, his hopes, galvanizing him into action. Debris crunched under his slippered feet as he lurched around the counter.

"Gaia! What has she done to you?" Tears poured down his cheeks as his heart threatened to burst with love for his little space girl.

Gaia lay curled in a ball amongst the broken crockery. Bart knelt next to her, running his hand over her trembling body. Frost covered her face and clothing. Bart scooped her small form off the floor. By sheer will power alone, he carried her to the bedroom. "Gaia, wake up. Talk to me. Don't sleep. Wake up." There was no response to his impassioned pleas.

Bart stripped the frozen clothing off her and wrapped her in blankets and duvets. No expert on hypothermia, he knew from the training given to his Territorial Army unit after a training tragedy that it was dangerous to try and heat her up too quickly. Gaia lay ashen-faced. Bart ripped boxes out of the bedroom wardrobe, searching feverishly until he found the stored winter electric-blankets. He laid the blanket on the bed and turned it on low. Stripping, Bart unwrapped Gaia and crawled in with her, snuggling up tight as he rebundled the duvets and electric blanket around them.

"Man, you're freezing." Bart shivered as his body adapted to Gaia's temperature. He gritted his teeth and snuggled tighter. He knew of nothing else he could do. He couldn't take her to the hospital. *How can I explain her condition or who she is? She could die on the way.* For now, he cuddled. Every half hour, he slid out of the coverings and took a hot shower, before returning to his homemade cocoon.

Bart kept the electric blanket on low, on the outside of all the wrapping. It's warmth penetrated gradually. Bart hoped and prayed he was doing enough. After three showers, he had to stop. They were leaving him giddy. In the excitement of seeing Gaia again, he forgot he also needed to rest and recuperate. He talked to her, kept a constant flow of encouragement flowing in her ear.

"Hold on, Gaia. Come back to me. I love you." He wasn't sure whether she heard him or not, or when he fell asleep, or how long he slept. He didn't know what woke him. He lay there silent, listening to the steady breathing of her tiny form next to him. *She feels warmer.* He eased himself partway out and examined her in the light creeping in from the lounge.

Her face had more colour, her lips no longer blue. As he stroked her cheek, she murmured. So quiet, he almost missed it.

"Bart?"

His heart flip-flopped. He slid from the bed, returning with a mugful of warm water and honey, Bart's answer to every ailment. Gaia's eyelids fluttered but stayed closed as he helped the healthy mixture past motionless lips. Finished with his ministrations, Bart slipped back into the duvets, put his arms around her again, and slept.

***

"Thanks for that, Liz. I'll be back on Monday." Bart replaced the phone in its cradle and sighed. Three days of sick leave, two lectures missed. Liz would take care of it all for him. Glass and crockery crunched under foot. He grabbed the broom from its hiding place in the cupboard and swept a path through the debris. He stooped and picked up the coffee machine, examining it for serious damage. The base showed a crack, but the main body appeared intact.

He plugged it in and covered his face as he threw the switch to turn it on. A lack of buzzing or acrid smoke convinced him to add some water and coffee grounds. He shook the almost-empty can. Between he and Gaia, the level in the tin had dropped rapidly. Time to buy some more, especially if he could convince her to stay. He chewed on his bottom lip as he considered how. She'd always told him she had to go once she'd dealt with Terra. Why and how she came to be here at all puzzled him. Everything he'd read or heard suggested she would have been vaporized by the cataclysmic explosion in Tunguska.

He set that worry aside for the moment and concentrated on pushing the bulk of the broken kitchenware into a single pile in the corner. A bin and new front door would come later. After coffee. After more cuddles with Gaia. He sipped his hot beverage from the one remaining mug. As he wandered back into the bedroom, his shocked hands almost dropped it.

A golden aura surrounded Gaia and her linen cocoon. Two ethereal figures, one male, one female, stood next to the bed, the golden light flowing from them to Gaia. One of them turned and smiled.

"The veil is open again, Bart. Gaia will survive." The male turned back to face Gaia. "It is safe for you to approach. You can benefit from the flow of energy once again available to Gaia. Lie with her." His head twisted again. "Do you trust Gaia?"

"Yes, I do. But who are you?" Bart regarded the two tentatively. Both of the visitors bore no hair, their craniums completely smooth. Oddly, it didn't detract from the female's beauty. He guessed their ages to be in the seventies, but he realized they could be thousands of years older, that what he was seeing was just a projection of sorts, something designed to mesh with his standardized view of a humanoid form.

The tall man spoke first. "We are Elders, Gaia's guides and mentors if you will. I am Medus. The female form is Savanha." Both bowed as one. They glanced down at Gaia. "We are here to help Gaia heal, and you, if you so wish.

Savanha spoke. "Join her." Her voice had the same soothing effect as his mother's when he was a child. She waved a hand, indicating Bart should lie next to Gaia. "As soon as she awakes, she can do this herself." The two looked at each other for a second, their yellow eyes radiating warmth. "You have been a friend and protector, Bart Cooksley. Gaia needs one like you."

Bart moved to join Gaia, then stopped. He knew these people, these spectral beings, weren't actually real, weren't there, yet he hesitated to strip off to share his body heat with Gaia.

"Now's not the time to be shy, Bart. Gaia needs you, needs your love."

Bart dropped his clothes on the floor and squirmed in under the covers. He wrapped his arms around Gaia, warmed and comforted by the golden ray encircling them. He winced as the first touch of the energy caressed his injuries, then found himself relaxing, even feeling a little drunk. The site of his wounds tickled. He fought to stay awake, but he was tired.

So tired ...

***

"Bart ... Bart."

The voice tugged him from a deep, peaceful sleep.

"Bart."

He blinked his eyes open in the sunlit room. The pain in his body was gone. He felt better than ... before the recent events started. Bart stretched and twisted his neck. No pain, no giddiness. He marveled at the two visitors' healing power, yet wondered if he had imagined them.

"Bart."

The voice was Gaia's, but it was Rebecca who stood before him. He turned his head to find Gaia still asleep on the bed. Before he could say anything, or react, Rebecca spoke again.

"I'm not real, Bart. Not this time. We can't turn back time, return our lives to where they used to be. You know that better than most."

He sat up in the bed, removing the hand that was caressing Gaia's hair. "If you're not real, why are you here?"

"Gaia summoned me. This is her gift to you. She wanted to give you one last chance to speak with me."

"This is not fair, Rebecca. It's taken me two years to find a way to live without you."

"I know, my love. I watched over you, unable to help or comfort. I know how you have suffered. And now another love has come into your life; Gaia."

"And, like you, she will leave, taking my heart with her. Why is this happening to me? All the women I love die or leave. In some ways, death is easier. It's not as if you chose to leave me. But Gaia will."

"Do you truly love her? Enough to give your life for her?"

"You know I do. If she hadn't intervened, I would already be dead."

"Then tell her, Bart. Tell her you want her to stay."

"I have, I did. She says she has to leave." He wiped his face with the back of his hand.

"That was then. Tell her again."

"I … I will. I miss you, Rebecca. But, when you returned the other day, it frightened me."

"You don't need me, Bart. You love another. And she loves you. Tell her, Bart. Tell her …."

Bart reached for Rebecca's hand, but her misty figure faded to nothing. She was gone. Gone from his life and now only a memory in his aching heart. He gazed down at Gaia sleeping in his bed. The pain in his chest far exceeded what he experienced when Terra plunged the knife into his side.

Rather than disturb Gaia, he re-dressed and took his cold coffee back into the lounge. He sat on the edge of the leather couch and let his misery overcome him.

***

"Medus. Savanha. Where am I?" Gaia pushed partway out of the snug nest of duvets. She looked around the room, orienting herself. *Bart's. I'm at Bart's.* "Why are you here? Why am *I* here?"

"Greetings, Gaia. The council is pleased to hear of your success and your return to health. Your healing is almost complete. With Terra gone, we were able to reopen the veil. All your healing abilities are intact."

"Bart. What of Bart?" Gaia's head pivoted wildly, seeking him.

"He is healed, physically. His heart is another story."

Gaia hung her head. "It was cruel of me to let him so close. I do not deserve his love."

"Yes, you do, Gaia. And so ... you must choose." Medus and Savanha glanced at each other and smiled.

"What do you mean?"

"Your sacrifice to save the humans did not go unnoticed. Or unrewarded. You must choose. Return to Sanctum or stay here with your Bart Cooksley."

"Stay? It is forbidden." Gaia stared at Medus and Savanha in turn.

"Not forbidden. It is merely discouraged." Both elders smiled.

"But I thought ... it is always said ..."

"Yes. It is a secret we reveal to few. You are not the first. Many before you have made this choice, Gaia. Always for love."

"I can stay? Truly?" Gaia held trembling hands to her mouth.

"Yes, you can stay. I think your Bart would like this. Yes?"

"Yes. I ... I hope so. I wish it so. What will happen to me?"

"Nothing. You are trusted beyond all others. You will retain your powers. The first thing you will notice is your eyes. They will attain normal human pigmentation over a short time. Which colour, we cannot say. Also, you will heal rapidly but age slowly. I'm sorry. Bart will age and die while you still remain young. This is the price you pay in staying, the price to be with him. Only when he dies may you return, not before." The two elders looked at each other. "Choose wisely, Gaia Hassani."

"What must I do?" Gaia sat up, back straight.

"There are three steps. You tell us here, now, you declare yourself to Bart, and he must declare his love to you."

"That's all? Nothing else."

"Correct. It is not as easy as it sounds, Gaia. Look deep inside yourself. Do you truly love this man? Do you wish to spend a lifetime stuck here on Earth, with him?"

"Yes. Yes. YES."

"Then the first step is taken." The two elders spoke as one. "Good luck, Gaia. Live long. Live happy."

"Thank you. Thank …" The two elders vanished before Gaia could finish. She leapt out of bed and ran to the door, stopping as she realized she was naked, not something that would have troubled her a week ago. She looked around the room. Not seeing her robe anywhere, see darted into the bathroom and took one of the huge bath towels out of the storage cupboard.

Wrapping it almost twice round herself, she stopped to study at herself in the mirror. The sensation in her stomach was one foreign to her. Fear.

I am Gaia. I am frightened of nothing. Yet I am scared to ask this man if he loves me, if he would have me stay with him. The terror of rejection sent shivers through her. *Is this what all humans suffer? Surely the emotion of love should be pleasurable, not this pain, this terror.*

Gaia splashed cold water on her face and cupped more in her hands to drink. *What I wouldn't give for a decent coffee right now.* She swallowed. *I have to do this. For better or for worse.* She took a deep breath and willed stiff legs to carry her to the lounge doorway. *One room at a time.*

She leaned against the door frame, gathering her scattered courage. She peeked around the door. Bart sat, leaned forward, head on the coffee table. "Hi."

Bart lifted his head and turned to face Gaia. "Hi."

Gaia surveyed the room, taking in the smashed door and broken crockery. "I love what you've done with the place."

"A little post-apocalyptic redecorating. Seemed to fit the theme of the last week." His smile seemed drawn.

"I … thank you for saving me. Again. How did I get here?" Neither of them moved from their spots.

"I only thawed you out. I have no idea how you got here." His eyes darted to the floor, then back to Gaia. "Thank you for what you did to me, for saving my life." A deathly silence hung in the air between them. "I suppose you've come to say goodbye."

"I ... no ... I mean ... Is that what you want? For me to go?"

"It's what you've always said you'd do." Red-rimmed eyes glared at her. "If that's what you must do, then go." Bart's anger rolled over her like a tsunami.

Gaia fled back into the bedroom, Bart's anger jarring every crevice of her being. *I thought he might love me. What a fool I was.* She stood facing the window, taking one last look at the trees and flowers of the garden. Time to go. Time to return to her real life. She wiped a single tear off her cheek, took a deep breath, and pulled herself upright. Chin set firm, she put her hands out in front of her, palms upward, and closed her eyes. Within seconds she would be home, back to Sanctum, where she would feel no pain, no grief. *No love.*

Sobs wracked her.

She joined her thumbs and index fingers together to complete the process. She sensed the connection, readied herself for the uncomfortable surge that accompanied the disintegration and separation from her earthly form. She moved to disconnect. Nothing happened. She tried again. Two strong arms held her back. "Bart?"

"Don't go. Please. I'm sorry. Just stay a little longer. Please." Bart's arms pulled her close.

Gaia refused to turn. She couldn't face him. "You told me to go. Why would I stay?"

Bart rested his chin on Gaia's shoulder. His eyes stared listlessly at the ceiling. "I was angry. Angry that you would leave me alone here after all we've been through together. I ..."

She felt the tremor in Bart's arms.

"I can't imagine going on without you here. I want you to stay. I love you, Gaia."

A surge of energy exploded outward from Gaia's chest, filling her with warmth she could not describe. She twisted against him, reaching up to hang her arms around his neck. " I love you, too, Bart Cooksley."

All the pain, the tension of the last week vanished in that instant. Their lips brushed, tender, loving. Gaia felt her body melting, only Bart's grip and her arms around his neck keeping her standing.

Bart's fingers stroked her back. "Look at the pair of us. Sniffling and carrying on like a pair of love-sick teenagers." He squeezed her tight. "So how long can you stay? An hour? A day?"

Gaia pushed back a loose strand of hair from Bart's face. Her voice trembled with emotion. "Forever." She felt his body stiffen.

"Please, don't tease me, Gaia Hassani. How long?" Bart's eyes searched hers for the truth.

"Forever, Bart Cooksley. I can stay forever. Would you like that?" The words tumbled out broken, choked.

"I ... yes. Of course. Yes." Bart smothered Gaia with fevered kisses. "I just ... I mean ... I thought you had to return."

"So did I. The elders gave me a choice. Return to my natural state ..." Gaia nuzzled his neck. "... or a lifetime with you, puny human that you are." She poked him in the side. "I chose my puny, beautiful, flawed human."

"Flawed. You cheeky tart. Why flawed?"

"You don't keep your promises, Bart Cooksley."

"What do you mean?" Bart looked down at Gaia, his brow furrowed with a frown.

"You promised to show me other forms of lovemaking. You didn't."

Bart scooped Gaia off her feet, carrying her towel-wrapped body the last few feet to the bed. "I'll take care of that right now, miss." He stopped, cradling her. "I love you, Gaia."

"And I love you, too, Bart. Forever."

Epilogue

Elders Medus and Savanha swept their energetic hands over the portal, closing the connection to the earth realm.

"Do you think either of them knew?" The question was a shared thought, more a dialogue than a query.

"No. Not that it would have made any difference to Terra. She had lost the capacity to reason. So many eons trapped inside one planet."

"Others have spent longer in theirs."

"Yes. But the Earth inhabitants have proved especially trying. We knew it was a risk to seed them there. Their intellectual advancement disconnected them from their spiritual roots. They became avaricious and self-serving. And their number grew too large. It was only a matter of time before Terra cast them off again, reshaped the surface, and reduced their numbers, as she has done before. Cooksley's device couldn't have happened at a worse time. Freeing her portended far worse an outcome."

"But she is gone now, consigned back to the Hall of Souls. It will be many millennia before we see her here again. Another of Gaia's children has taken her place, as it was always meant to be."

"It is a difficult task to kill one's own child. I think He was wise to withhold this information from Gaia. As for the future, she will become aware of the new child that grows within her in due course."

"Another child of those two souls will be a great day for Sanctum."

"It is a secret as great as any we have kept."

A subtle vibration reached across the cosmos. "The council of forty-two gathers. He calls. We must go. Will He ever reveal his true plans to us?"

"I doubt it. He hides many secrets. This much I sense. He feels safe now, with Terra gone. If she had managed to complete her task, even He would have perished. Sometimes, I think He is not as all-powerful as he wishes to appear."

"I agree. He cannot see what transpires on the earth realm without our help. It is forbidden to him. That is strange. As if there were another, more powerful than He."

"I sometimes think He feeds on the energy of Earth, the negativity."

"Ours is not to question his orders. We serve. We protect the earth realm from outside influence. It is His bidding."

"He must never be allowed to know of the soul that inhabits Bartholomew Cooksley's body. His rage would be frightful beyond telling"

"No. Never. He will be angry enough that Gaia has chosen to remain. He covets her and her power. And yet, He fears her."

"Yes. If she were ever to rediscover her true essence, return to her original form …"

"Do you think she knows?"

"Of her beginning? It is not possible. He has kept her in human form so long, she has forgotten. Of Bartholomew Cooksley? No. No. Yet somehow, they are together again. All His scheming has come to nothing. All she would need to do is research her name on the humans' Internet. If she were to believe what she reads, His world would crumble before Her might."

"We must never speak of this again. If He ever discovered …"

"Agreed. Silence. However, Gaia and Bart may yet prove valuable to us. Their combined abilities are … impressive.

"Again, I agree. We should think more on this.

"He calls again. We *must* go."

"So it will be."

Epilaugh

Professor Bartholomew Cooksley,
in a lecture to students, November 2011

"When talking of the nature of atoms, of the widely-accepted structure of matter, it is normal to think in terms of Neutrons, Protons, and Electrons. I postulate there is a fourth building block, whose distribution in the known universe appears restricted solely to the planet Earth. This category is disproportionately represented in the samples tested. It is the smallest in size and number, yet it has the greatest effect on the nature of matter and humanity.

I call this fourth category a Moron.

This particle masquerades under many other names and sub types ... redneck, hillbilly, politician, salesman, drunk driver. The names are numerous, and none are mutually exclusive.

Morons fall into two major sub groups:

The *positively* charged, that *repel* intelligence of any sort and ...

the *negatively* charged, that *attract* intelligence, often resulting in a genre known as assholes – Morons that should know better."

More books from Rule of Three Press

Russell Turney
Hitmail dot com

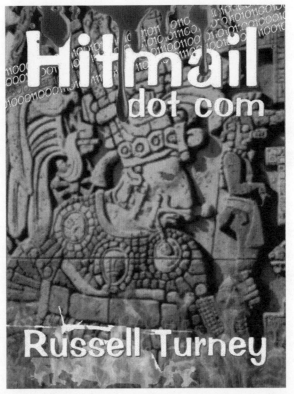

A sinister force is taking control of the world's teenagers. Maddi Wallace is the only person standing in the way of total chaos.

Paranormal/Thriller 136,000 words
Available soon in eBook and paperback from …
Amazon and Barnes & Noble

Hitmail dot com

Chapter One

June 1980.
Tennant, CA 96058. Population 74.

"Mad-i-son." The voice carried a dark malice, the sound somewhere between the hissing of a punctured tire and fingernails dragging across a blackboard. The sibilant word coiled around the young girl, snatching her from a troubled sleep. Madison jerked awake in the strange room of her uncle's farmhouse, clutching her teddybear tight to her chest.

"Mad-i-son." The voice taunted again, called to her, dared her to resist. "Hisssss. Come play with me, Mad-i-son." A cloying stench filled her nostrils, making her gag. Her stomach spasmed. The oily foulness of the smell, a cross between swamp gas and rotting flesh, an odour she hoped she might forget after her cousin took her to see a dead cow in a nearby sinkhole.

"No, go away." Madison's voice sounded louder and stronger than she felt. Tears ran down quivering cheeks and joined the blood from her bitten lip.

"**Ten k'a't a-pixan tz'e hun.**" The words, akin to broken glass being crushed under a marble rolling pin, tore at her young mind, urging her to comply. They were foreign and cruel, yet, somehow she knew what they meant.

I want your soul, little one.

But Madison's soul was older and stronger than the tender young body it inhabited, tougher than the malevolent visitor had supposed. Madison let out an ear splitting scream that vibrated the windows and loosened dust from overhead joists. The apparition hissed and withdrew a few feet.

"**Ten k'a't a-pixan tz'e hun**," the presence repeated. Rising fury tinged the words. A thick, vaporous mist slipped through the floor cracks and climbed like a vine up the wall and over the ceiling. Long wraithlike fingers reached down toward Madison as sinister glowing red eyes materialized in the ghostly fog.

"Go away. Leave me alone. I want Papa." Madison's screams rattled the roof tiles and reached every corner of the old stone walled house. "Papa. I want Papa. Make the nasty man go away. Papa. Where are you? Papaaaa."

The spectral figured snarled. The bony fingers retreated from Madison's high-pitched screams and the thumping of people moving in the house, footsteps running toward her room.

"Papa? Are you there? Papa? Make the mean man go away." The worn teddybear was at risk of being torn apart by her frantic, shaking hands. "Papaaaa. Papaaaa."

One final angry hiss resonated from the figure, before the mist sucked back into the floor cracks and vanished as the door crashed open.

Madison's father bellowed words of warning, repeating Madison's screams. "Go away, you nasty, smelly man. I don't like you. Madison doesn't like you. Papa doesn't like you. No one likes you. GO AWAY." He stood there with his hands set firmly on his hips. He frowned. Nothing like this had happened before. Nothing that had his baby crying and shaking with terror in her bed.

He crossed the room in three long paces and threw big strong arms around his trembling daughter.

Madison sniffled. "Is the nasty man gone, Papa? Can I look now?"

Papa glanced around the stark room. "Yes, Madison. He's gone, and he's not coming back. Papa loves you, Madison."

"I don't want to be called Madison anymore, Papa. Call me Maddi."

Papa took a breath and frowned again. "Papa loves you, Maddi. We all love you."

"I don't want to stay here."

"This room? You can sleep with Momma and I, just for tonight." He stroked her long, golden blonde hair, the touch soothing, calming.

"No. Not in this house. Ever again." Her trembling abated somewhat. "For tonight, I'll stay with you and Momma, Papa. Thank you." Her arms clamped tight around his neck.

***

"Aubrey, you let that girl wrap you round her little finger. Telling her we won't stay here. We have three more days holiday."

"Marcie, be reasonable. She's never behaved like this before." He sighed. Marcie never took Madison's side. "Lets just see what things are like in the morning."

"Humph, it's probably that friend of your nephews, Troy. That boy has been telling scary stories about the house."

"Says who?"

"Does it matter? I told you those boys were trouble together."

"What's Troy been saying?" Aubrey didn't believe it would make any difference, but he knew Marcie wanted to vent.

"He's been telling stories of ghostly apparitions, Indian burial grounds and an ancient evil in the area. That's all this is, a nightmare."

"Why do you always deny Madison's unusual stories. I've spoken with your mother often enough to -- ." Marcie cut him off short.

"That old crank is crazy. Thinks she's a sorceress, a psychic." Marcie swung around, her face flushed. "She's senile is what she is."

"And your grand-mother? Was she senile too?"

Marcie glared at him then turned and stormed out the room.

"She'll probably forget all about it anyway," he called after her. "Kid's usually do," he mumbled to himself.

***

December 2011

"I can't do this on my own." The wretched voice rebounded off cold stone walls. A sliver of light filtered through two tiny windows set into the wall just above ground level. "I need help. Pleeeease." Tears ran down pale, sunken cheeks.

Somewhere near a heavy door swung open, banging against more stone. *He's coming. NO.* "I'm sorry. I didn't mean it. Don't hurt me anymore. I'm working as hard as I can." The skeletal figure crawled under the desk, the only furniture in the room beside a chair and mattress. And the ever watching, ever humming computer. A rustic curtain in the corner led to a serviceable but unpleasant latrine and basin.

He craned his head, listening to the odd banging. The master never made a sound. Yet there was a noise this time, something being dragged. He squirmed his way as far back into the corner under the desk as he could go. Sore eyes that felt dry and gritty watched through shaking fingers as the door creaked open. He felt the tightness in his throat as his captor entered the room, a dark malevolent presence that turned his gut. His stomach heaved, as it did whenever the master came. The rank smell of His presence clung like a sooty grease. The taste of it lingered in his throat for days.

"Eye harve eh pre sent fur you." The voice seemed to speak to him from different parts of the room, each syllable from a new location.

The effect disoriented him, sent his head spinning. He gasped as four dark robes glided into the room, carrying a bundle between them. He tried to see their faces, their feet. He shuddered in terror as he realized he could see right through them. They had no feet, instead floating a few inches above the packed earth floor.

They placed the parcel on the ground and withdrew, in time for two more of these wraiths to enter with another table and chair. And another computer. The bundle moaned as the door swung closed, a heavy bolt crashing into a steel socket. *Trapped again.* Silence returned. Shivering, he crawled out from under his dubious cover and prodded the bundle, turning it over.

Janice. No. Not Janice. "Leave her alone. She hasn't done anything."

"You ask ed fur help. You dare nay say me?"

The prisoner dropped to the ground, using Janice's bound form as cover.

A twisted hand that appeared to be no more than mist materialized and lifted the prisoner off the ground by his neck, pinning him to the wall. His legs kicked, trying to find purchase.

"You weell werk. I com marnd et." The hand released him to drop in a heap on the floor. It hovered over Janice's now struggling form. "Ore she dies. Eye weell extract er soul and leeve er empty, to rot frome thee enside."

The prisoner slumped forward. With effort he raised his head and nodded. "By your will, master."

Available soon in eBook and paperback from ...
Amazon and Barnes & Noble

Russell Turney
Tough Justice – Seeds of Doom

**A compromised justice system,
a brutal drug running bike gang,
and new love collide**

Romantic/Thriller 127,000 words
Available in eBook and paperback from …
Amazon and Barnes & Noble

Robynn Sheahan
Storm of Arraron

**A forbidden birth. A remarkable young woman.
A marauding alien society. The battle begins.**

YA Science-Fiction/Fantasy 86,000 words
Available in eBook and paperback from …
Amazon and Barnes & Noble

Cynthia Rogan
Symphony of Dreams

Most of us ache for the opportunity to shine at the gift we're born with. Symphony Weber wants to give hers back.

Woman's Fiction/Suspense 106,000 words
Available in eBook and paperback from …
<u>Amazon</u> and Barnes & Noble